THE MIIONARIES

Other titles by Robin Jenkins available from Polygon:

Dust on the Paw
Love is a Fervent Fire
Lunderston Tales
Matthew and Sheila
The Missionaries
Some Kind of Grace
The Thistle and the Grail
A Very Scotch Affair
Willie Hogg

Robin Jenkins

THE MISSIONARIES

Polygon

This edition published in Great Britain in 2005 by Polygon
an imprint of Birlinn Ltd

West Newington House
10 Newington Road
Edinburgh
EH9 1QS

9 8 7 6 5 4 3 2 1

www.birlinn.co.uk

ISBN 10: 1 904598 59 5
ISBN 13: 978 1 904598 59 6

British Library Cataloguing-in-Publication Data
A catalogue record for this book is available
on request from the British Library

The publishers acknowledge subsidy from the

Scottish
Arts Council

towards the publication of this volume

Facsimile origination by Brinnoven, Livingston
Printed and bound in Denmark by Nørhaven Paperback A/S

There is no such island as Sollas, in Scotland or anywhere else; there were therefore no such evictions as are described in this story, and the characters are likewise imaginary; but there was, and perhaps still is, a Christian faith.

R. J.

One

BEFORE going down to face his uncle at the breakfast table, Andrew sought confirmation and, indeed, re-dedication, in his bedroom mirror. Unafraid of conceit, he gazed for a long minute at the tall, pale, ascetically handsome twentieth-century Jason in the black University blazer with its gold badge and within its buttonhole the small blue Argo. He searched for sincerity, and found it; he searched too for intimations of martyrdom, and found these also. As he laid his hand delicately on the gold-leaved New Testament on his dressing-table, given him a year ago on his twenty-first birthday, he remembered his well-loved minister father's warning against contaminating religion with mythology. What his father had murmured, others, fellow students, and even professors, had shouted with contemporary sarcasm. Few saw that the sunlit mysterious quest for the Golden Fleece was complementary to Christ's sombre inevitable journey towards Calvary; together, they were the inspiration needed for an age too smug for wonder, too mercenary for sacrifice, and too ethical for glory.

Downstairs, for instance, his uncle, the Sheriff, was waiting to destroy: neither like a many-headed dragon of myth, nor a Pharisee of history, but like the cool incorruptible guardian of modern sterile values. He would be angry, but no flames would gush from his mouth, no sanctimonious poison; he would coldly express opinions held by every dignitary in Church, State, and Law, and acquiesced in by the drugged millions: barren half-truths, representing the desert of the vast ever-increasing authoritarian mind. In such a situation, to abandon one's oasis would be not merely cowardice, it would be blasphemy; and if ever there was a green and fertile attitude to a human problem, his on these evictions from the Isle of Sollas was certainly one. Here the very soul of man was being desecrated, in the name of progress, humanitarianism, and the sanctity of ownership.

Composed, handkerchief neat in breast pocket, head high and sleek with brilliantine smelling of pine-woods, Andrew turned from the glass and walked downstairs.

Outside the dining-room he was accosted by Mrs. Crail, his uncle's slim, white-haired housekeeper, in appearance as dignified as an archbishop's wife. She gave him a gamin's wink.

"He's reading it now," she whispered.

Andrew smiled.

"And he doesn't look a bit pleased."

"I anticipated that, Mrs. Crail."

She laid her hand on his sleeve, and murmured what she knew was diabolical advice.

"Row wi' the tide, lad."

It was not the first time she had counselled him in marine terms: her people were fisher-folk from the East Coast. Indeed, on that ground she had claimed membership of the society he had founded at the University, called "The Argonauts". She was, in spite of her sixty-odd hard years, an incorrigible tease. There were of course no women in "The Argonauts".

"What if the tide is sweeping us to perdition, Mrs. Crail?" he asked, and without waiting for an answer entered the dining-room.

His uncle was hidden behind his newspaper.

"Good-morning, sir," said Andrew.

For a moment the bleak smile appeared, turning the table into a bench where legal justice, that barest of diets, was spread, and Andrew into a prisoner in the dock waiting for sentence.

But a prisoner whose crime is compassion courageously displayed, and universal truth adamantly upheld, ought not to cringe and whine for mercy; he ought rather to whistle in harmony with the blackbird in the lilac bush outside the window, and eat as if his plate was a dulcimer.

There was a minute or two's silence. Then the Sheriff, still hidden, began to read aloud.

" 'Authoritarianism is like a petrifaction: we say the words pity, honour, love, justice, truth, Christ; and they fall to the ground like stones.' "

In the silence that followed only the blackbird was merry. Yet Andrew smiled, and waited for the next quotation: just so a martyr at the stake might listen to the official account of his heresies.

" 'We must have permission for everything,' " went on the Sheriff. " 'For the privilege of not being trained to kill our fellow human beings; for the right to leave the country or change our coal merchant; and in the case of these poor people on Sollas for the right to renounce the benefits of our ulcerated civilisation.' "

Andrew's smile grew firmer.

" 'We who are blind ought not to presume to tell any man the road he should take.' "

Andrew could not help being impressed by that wisdom; that it was his own was incidental.

"These people on Sollas are scorned because it is said their religious outlook has not changed with the times. But have not the times rushed away from religion altogether?"

"Nobody can deny that," claimed Andrew reasonably.

" 'Society is built upon the sanctity, not of the human soul, as is everywhere proclaimed, but of property. The humble clerk, to safeguard his own few paltry pounds in the bank, will defend with his life the millionaire's millions.' "

"In fairness I must be allowed to point out," said Andrew, "that that is not a political opinion. None of them really is political. They are on a higher plane."

The Sheriff lowered his paper at last. He was smiling that smile which grounded experience has for winged youth, the

Sphinx's grimace that, somehow shedding responsibility, accepted the inevitability of prisons, poverty, disease, war, and expedient neglect of God. To protest against it too passionately was, Andrew knew, to wear it too soon. Far better to oppose it with that other smile, compassionate, faithful, creative, and expectant. But how on a human face, however eligible, even to practise such a smile, in the presence of any other human face?

"I had made up my mind, Andrew," said his uncle, "to say nothing about your wrong-headedness in this particular matter. Iconoclasm, I suppose, is a childish vanity we must outgrow."

"I am glad, sir," said Andrew, "you admit it is idols I am trying to break."

"There is no need for impudence, Andrew. This rubbish," and he indicated the newspaper, "forces me to speak. You know that I am personally involved in the Sollas business. Where is the difference then between your attitude and shabby disloyalty?"

"I never mentioned you, sir."

"Perhaps not. Please look."

Andrew took the newspaper. There were two headings: "University Debate." "Sheriff's Nephew's Speech." There was, however, no photograph, though one had been taken; and the whole report was tucked away in an obscure corner, alongside the racing programmes.

He handed it back.

"I am sorry you are implicated, sir," he said. "They promised they would not mention you. But I should have known that in the interests of sensation such a trifle as honour can hardly be heeded."

"In the interests of vanity, too, it appears."

"Vanity, sir?"

"Did you supply them with a copy of your speech?"

"Yes, but——"

"I suppose you're going to tell me it was your duty to have its wisdom disseminated as widely as possible?"

"Why not, sir?"

"Let me congratulate you, Andrew, on your eloquence; with a slight adjustment it should take you far."

"What adjustment, sir?"

"Just stand on your feet instead of your head."

Andrew refused to comment on such a puerility.

"It is a characteristic of youth," said the Sheriff, smiling, "to see things clearly, and co-ordinate them obtusely."

"Apparently not all youth, sir. You will have noticed that the motion against which I spoke was nevertheless carried?"

"Yes. I must confess it surprised me a little."

"It should not. There were women present and they voted. As a sex they lack imagination and magnanimity."

"All of them?"

"There are very few exceptions."

"Perhaps they think they possess practical good sense?"

"They do think so, but it is a fallacy that needs exploding."

"Do you propose to explode it?"

"I shall try."

"It may prove to be a labour of some difficulty. Even Hercules was not asked to undertake it. But arduous though it may be, it assuredly will command no handsome salary."

Andrew shook his head at that typical cynicism.

"Nor will it appear in your very sensible mother's eyes as a suitable profession; or your father's either. I had a letter from your mother this very morning, Andrew. She urges me to force you to a decision. Now that you have passed your degree examination, and very well, too, it is certainly time for you to decide. Is it to be kirk or court-house?"

"What would you advise, sir? You called me wrong-headed. Would such a quality hinder me more as a clergyman like my father, or as a lawyer like yourself?"

"I also called you impudent, Andrew. Whatever you choose,

make the choice humbly. Consider how you may be useful to the community, not how you may show yourself superior to it. If there is anything more revolting than academic pity, it is surely to jeer at humanity because it is not perfect according to your own definition of perfection. There is room for improvement, of course; but it is better to practise on oneself. In this affair of Sollas, you prefer that those unhappy and misguided people should be encouraged to oppose the law, in vindication of some adolescent theory you have about the rights of individuals. The decision has gone against them in a properly constituted court of law: you advise them to resist. It has been proved that they are suffering already from malnutrition: you urge them to go on being hungry and ill. You are able, with a full belly, to play at catching moonbeams and popping them into your mouth. Very well: it is a game you like, comparable to blowing pretty bubbles; but do not, please, pretend it is a crusade against the forces of evil. These have to be fought, no doubt, but with weapons you have as yet no conception of. I refer to patience, toleration, endurance, and the stoical concealment of much disappointment. Good morning, Andrew."

The Sheriff smiled, most disenchantingly, and in his uniform of dark jacket and striped trousers went off into the hall, where he picked up his black priest-like hat, umbrella, and portfolio. Then out into the sunshine he walked with brisk short steps, past the bush where the blackbird sang, and so along suburban avenues to the city streets where, in his court-house, he would deal out an aggregate of seven years' imprisonment.

In the dining-room Andrew, downcast, was joined by Mrs. Crail, cheerful.

"I wouldn't take it so ill, Andrew," she said, patting his shoulder. "You'll grow up."

"Unfortunately," he replied with bitterness, "the process seems to be a growing down. Our ideals set out as hawks, become sparrows, then butterflies, and finally worms."

Humming, she began to collect the dishes.

"Worms are more useful," she suggested.

"Especially if they are in human form."

"I never was at the university myself," she said, "and so I'm ignorant."

"That does not follow."

"To tell you the truth, laddie," she said with a laugh, "I never thought it did. But really I canna for the life of me see what all the stushie's about. If these folk want to stay on their wee island in the middle of the ocean, and die of starvation or monotony, let them."

"Exactly. Freedom must be absolute."

"That doesn't mean everybody's free to rob and murder?"

"Of course not."

"It sounded like it. But though I'm in favour of letting them stay on their island, I'd take their children from them."

"By what authority?"

"Don't shout, Andrew. I may be thick in the head, but I'm not deaf."

"I'm sorry. You seem to forget, Mrs. Crail, like everybody else, that there is no need for anybody on Sollas to go hungry. There *is* good land on the island."

"Aye, but I thought the owner farmed it."

"Owner? How did he become the owner?"

"In the same way you became the owner of this braw blazer: by putting down the money."

"I doubt if he's dug one peat in his life."

"Likely not, seeing he's rich enough to get others to dig them for him, though I'm thinking it'll be coal he'll use. But to be fair to the man, hasn't he offered them places elsewhere, better places?"

"Would you, Mrs. Crail, if hounded from your ancestral home, be satisfied if you were offered any other, however better?"

"Gosh, that I would, Andrew. But didn't I read that they're more or less incomers themselves?"

"Their ancestors lived on Sollas for hundreds of years."

"Oh well, I've got no head for arguments. They say he's a millionaire."

"Certainly he has been renovating Sollas House, at a fabulous cost."

"What's his name again?"

"Vontin. Henry Vontin."

"Sounds foreign to me. But I saw his daughter's picture in the paper the other day. A beauty, I must admit. I meant to cut it out and keep it for you."

"Why for me?"

"She looked spoiled, mind you; but then if my father had been a millionaire I'd have expected him to spoil me. Don't you vex yourself about these things, Andrew. Keep prospering at your studies as you've been doing, and you'll end up as a millionaire yourself some day."

"God forbid."

"Well then," she said, laughing, "you'll be a famous lawyer, far more successful than your uncle even. He's a Sheriff, and a head one, but you'll rise to the High Court, mark my words, with the black cap on your head."

"But, Mrs. Crail," he cried in horror," a judge only wears a black cap when he is about to pronounce sentence of death."

"I know that."

"And I am utterly, and irrevocably, opposed to capital punishment."

"I know that, too."

For some reason this simple-minded illogicality of his uncle's housekeeper was able, far more effectively than his uncle's mordant shrewdness, to shake Andrew's confidence; not indeed in the rightness of his beliefs, but in his prudence in voicing them so uncompromisingly. It was possible he would be defeated in the end, and forced to retreat to advancement: the way must not needlessly be barred. For instance, he had often dreamt of becoming a judge, whose utterances would be as potent in their pity as in their wisdom, humanising the administration of justice and so society itself, not during his own lifetime only but for centuries after; black caps interposed. Similarly, he often saw himself a minister of the Gospel, like his father; but whereas his father was content with beautiful roses in the manse garden and three dozen snoozers in the kirk on Sunday, he, Andrew, would speak from the most influential pulpit in the country, with the world as his congregation. But there was no doubt that the high road towards that honourable ambition lay far from the obscure path of lonely meditation, of frugality like a Tibetan lama's, of renunciation, and of inexpedient love of God. The truths he now boldly uttered might return, thick as bees, to sting him with ridicule and mortification, and so render him useless to the causes in whose interests they had been spoken. The world was imperfect. It might well be that his aim was unattainable: that was, of course, success without surrender. With the five fingers of one hand spread out, and the forefinger of the other ready to touch each in turn as the name of some predecessor occurred to him, one who had succeeded without surrendering, he had found himself unable to proceed beyond the thumb. There was no such predecessor. Illustrious names did occur, but each had to be rejected owing to some flaw. Great power of any kind, even spiritual power, corrupted. Had not Christ Himself, the fount of compassion and love, threatened sinners with the fires of hell. Only in obscurity could the soul remain pure; but even there might not the regret for wasted talents cast a stain?

Mrs. Crail was over looking out of the window. She had a silver salt-cellar in her hand. It appeared she had been chattering all the time, but he had not heard.

He addressed her earnestly: "Would you say, Mrs. Crail, that I ask too much of humanity?"

She stood chuckling, with the salt-cellar dancing in her hand, as if she was minded to toss some of its contents over her shoulder, or even sprinkle them upon some tail too arrogant in its friskings.

"What matters, Andrew," she said, "is what you ask of yourself."

He had not expected that move, and so his strategy was upset.

"Listen to that blackie singing," she said.

He listened, but this time the bird was a rival, not an ally.

"I like fine to hear it," she went on, "just as I like fine to hear you singing out your grand notions and ruffling your uncle till he's like a cat under the tree, not able to come up and claw you off your topmost branch."

He smiled: the simile was just.

"But—you want the truth, Andrew, as I see it?"

"Always, Mrs. Crail, always." But he waited in dismay.

"Whiles I think your song gives you as much pleasure and means as little as the blackie's."

"I don't understand," he muttered, but he did, and knew that she knew he did.

"I've heard you singing away for weeks about these folk being shifted from their island, and I've thought, Andrew, it was for the joy of hearing your own brain and tongue in motion, rather than out of any love for the folk themselves. How could it be otherwise, laddie? You're only twenty-two after all. You've never set eyes on this island, far less its folk, and you're not likely to. You're in love with your own cleverness; aye, and with your own nobleness of heart; but that's a different thing altogether, from being in love with strange folk. I shouldn't be saying this to you, Andrew: it should be your own mother's privilege, like the telling you there's no Santa Claus. But you asked me, and God forgive me, lad— I've been saving it up for you for the past year or twa."

She approached him in a hurry, as if the salt-cellar held salts for smelling.

"You don't mind an old woman blurting out the truth once in a while, do you?" she cried.

"I certainly do not," he stammered, "admit it to be the truth."

"You will," she said cheerfully, "even if you have to wait till you're perched up on the high bench with the black cap on your head. But I'll have to ask you to get up, for this is the morning Mrs. Birling comes to clean out this room, and she's like yourself, Andrew, furious with dusters."

He rose, and she faced up to him as if, white hair and all, she was going to seize him and waltz him round the room, to the blackbird's music.

"Cheer up, Andrew," she cried. "You've got the whole world ahead of you. Whatever you do make sure you can laugh at it. You'll do well, Andrew, and there's nobody will be better pleased than me."

"Thank you, Mrs. Crail," he said, smiling; but as he left the room he wondered at this uncontrollable levity of women, still active in her although she was sixty-five years of age and had lived through two world-shattering wars, losing her husband in one and her only son in the other. It was surely the weakness symbolised by the allegory of Eden, and illustrated last night in the Union debate, when the female vote had carried the motion approving the Court of Session's decision on Sollas, although his own speech in opposition had been praised by some of them as the best they had ever heard in that debating hall.

Two

As HE was going upstairs to the bathroom the telephone rang. Always curious to know who was at the other end, he always concealed that curiosity, like a shame; but he lingered at the bathroom door just in case the call might be for him. It was. Soon Mrs. Crail was shouting up.

He hurried down with dignity.

"It's a female's voice," she said, her interest sharpened by suspicion. "I canna say I've ever heard it before."

Perhaps, he thought, someone with deceitful congratulations on the speech she had helped to dishonour.

"She's certainly not one of your student friends," added Mrs. Crail.

"Did she say so?"

"There was no need. She's got a voice that never was dumbfoundered with Latin and such-like. I doubt if she wears specs."

But by this time he was rubbing his hands over the telephone silent on the table; then, with almost savage negligence, he snatched it up.

"Andrew Doig speaking," he said, crisply.

There came what might have been harmonious atmospherics, but which really was feminine laughter. He frowned.

"Good-morning, Mr. Doig," said a voice which more than justified Mrs. Crail's warning. It had more assurance than the blackbird's, and was just as melodious. "I must beg your pardon for ringing you up like this."

"Who is speaking, please?"

"My name's Marguerite Vontin."

"Indeed." Andrew smiled, and touched the Argo in his buttonhole. Now he understood. Here was a feeble ruse to try and deceive so experienced a campaigner in undergraduate warfare as he. Had he not during the last Rectorial election been kidnapped from the Union steps at half-past ten at night, taken by car into the hills, and there abandoned, in his stockinged feet, with his trousers saved only by a passionate harangue such as Demosthenes could not have bettered? Without doubt this was an end-of-term plot. In this matter of Sollas he had wounded many consciences, here then was the furtive revenge. They had hired some actress to lure him into some humiliating folly.

"Marguerite Vontin, did you say?"

"Yes, that's right."

"The daughter, I suppose, of Mr. Henry Vontin, who owns Sollas Island?"

"Yes." Then she waited, as if to receive instructions from her hirers by her side. "The sinister and crafty octopus with his tentacles gripping dozens of enterprises. The jaded plutocrat who hopes to find refreshment and solace under the simple skies of a Hesperidean isle."

"You have been reading my speech, I see."

"Yes, but I also heard it. I was in the gallery last night."

"Were you indeed?" Elbow on table, Andrew was now at his ease: woman's deceit, claws, or malice, were not formidable to a man prepared. "Now then, how much are they paying you for this?"

There was a pause, and then more harmonious atmospherics.

"You think this is some kind of hoax?"

"Young lady, I am not green."

"I suppose you have been pretty often hoaxed before?"

"Attempts have been made. This, I may say, is the most shabby. Other people's unhappiness is being exploited."

"That is a favourite word of yours, isn't it?"

"My favourite word is truth."

"Really? Why then don't you recognise it when you hear it?" Her voice became especially soft, coy, persuasive. "Mr. Doig, I *am* Marguerite Vontin."

"And I Cesare Borgia."

That was a masterstroke. She uttered a sound as if she'd rattled her teeth against the telephone.

"Yes," he hissed, "women who deceive me, I poison."

She laughed, as if she'd decided he was joking. When she next spoke it was to reveal surprising resource.

"If you'd said you were Jason," she said, "I might have believed you. Jason: captain of the Argo, seeker of the Golden Fleece. Weren't they calling you that last night?"

They had been: "Jason" Doig was so commonly used a nickname that many freshers, and even absent-minded or malicious professors, knew him by it.

"In that case," he retorted, "I would not have far to look for my Medea."

"Your Medea?"

"You remember her rôle?"

"Oh yes. But Mr. Doig, what I rang you up for was just to suggest that you come and have coffee with me here, and talk about Sollas."

"Where is here?" He asked, but he knew: here was some basement dungeon full of spiders.

"The Central Hotel."

He shook his head: they were surely overplaying their hand. In that hotel lodged film stars, crooners, Cabinet Ministers, and millionaires' daughters.

"Don't you realise," he asked, "all I have to do now is to telephone the hotel and so uncover your imposture?"

"Will you do that, please?"

His smile faltered: here was subtlety and resource indeed. Surely the manager of such a hotel could not be in the plot.

"Will you?" she coaxed.

"Very well."

"Shall I give you the number or would you prefer to find it for yourself?"

"I'll find it for myself, thank you."

He did, after a minute's brooding over the replaced telephone. When he asked for the manager, in his best sheriff's-nephew voice, he was at once put through to that functionary.

"Tell me," said Andrew coldly, "is Miss Marguerite Vontin a guest in the hotel?"

"That is so, sir. Do you wish to speak to Miss Vontin, sir? Whom shall I say?"

Andrew told him, and waited: so might the original Jason, entering an unknown harbour with all signs unpropitious, have gazed at the tutelary mast.

That voice again, sweet now with enticement, and yet meek in triumph. He could not shut his eyes to sudden vistas of wealth and power and opportunity.

"Convinced?" she asked.

"I owe you an apology, Miss Vontin." What were these shapes slinking like leopards through his mind? They looked like eligibilities. Influence, he knew, was a catapult that could shoot even mediocrity into the empyrean. Was it not his mother's constant advice to cultivate the acquaintance of worth-while people? These were treacherous considerations, but they were not to be banished by clutching at the Argo, or even by remembering the crofters on Sollas under sentence of expulsion.

"I'm on my way to Sollas," she said, gently, "to join my father."

Her father, the octopus. Would he be crawling among rocks on the sea-bed? No, he would be seated in puissance in Sollas House.

"Were you serious about what you said last night?" she

asked. "Orators often exaggerate, don't they. Especially student orators."

He should have grandiloquently denied that insinuation, but how could he, when a fierce dog had got in amongst his principles, turned to sheep and lambs? He had known of this weakness of course, but had thought his defences against it far more effective.

"I was serious enough," he muttered.

"What about that coffee?" she asked, brightly.

"Thank you."

"Do you mean you'll come?"

"Of course."

"Shall I expect you then at eleven?"

"Very good."

She paused. "Mr. Doig."

"Yes?"

"Come like Jason." Then she hung up, without explanation, and he was left with the telephone in his hand like some sinister black trophy.

The blackbird sang. Mrs. Birling in the dining-room now turned on the vacuum cleaner, which sounded like the breathing of some monster of myth.

Come like Jason, she had said: Jason, the intrepid seeker after the Golden Fleece, the ward of the Gods in the golden age, the witch's victim. Come like Jason: not like Andrew Doig, post-pubescent student of moral philosophy, equivocator, compromiser, and potential toady.

Come like Jason!

On the bus going into town Andrew patched up his armour of impenetrable misogyny and brittle idealism. Miss Vontin would be beautiful outwardly. History showed a connection between such supreme beauty and female turpitude. He conjured up several instances: Helen the adulteress, cause of

Troy's ruin; Delilah, betrayer of the strong man of God; Lucrece Borgia, lecheress and poisoner; and worst of all, Medea of legend, witch and murderess. Of course Marguerite Vontin was not so sensationally wicked as those. Today evil had learned to be discreet; Mammon was respectable. She, who had assisted her father to drive out the harmless islanders, had not used whips or dogs or guns: her weapons had been legal documents and kindness. So craftily had she and her father contrived the expulsion, they had won a national reputation as benefactors, while the stubborn islanders were condemned as squatters, ingrates, bigots, aborigines, reactionaries, and sloths. In the eyes of a world which worshipped wealth and power, Miss Vontin was revered as a princess scattering largesse to peasants too superstitious and doltish to pick it up, far less thank her for it. Only the immune, who were very few in number, saw her as the representative of that brilliant ultimate sorcery which was transforming the souls of men into automata. Truly, he required the courage and the single-mindedness of Jason to go into her presence and remain unbewitched.

With a rolled-up newspaper in his hand like a sword, he approached the entrance of the vast hotel, and passed the commissionaire on whose blue and golden chest medals rattled like scales. He glanced towards Andrew, but the latter wore not only his University blazer and tie but also his sheriff's-nephew sneer. Those were better even than a cloak of invisibility, for they brought him a salute from the dragon.

In the great hall, hesitating on the carpet which was the colour of dried blood, he saw a homunculus in a scarlet suit with a hundred buttons, and in spite of tramcars visible through the glass doors he felt once again that strangeness which, more than egotism, had caused him to form "The Argonauts". Often, as now, to his astonishment, the scummy veil of custom blew away, and behind it he saw life as simple and yet as sinisterly expectant as in mythological times. This page, for instance, with child's body and wiseacre's face, was in the employment of some baleful king; the dragon guarded the transparent gates; outside roared and lumbered great stinking beasts of metal; and downstairs was running, with jewelled fingers dancing on the banister, the daughter of that king, with hair as black as Pluto's stallions.

As she held out her hand to him, laughing, he noticed how the page in the scarlet suit seemed to be swelling with subservience while he himself was dwindling into an irresistible diffidence.

She *was* beautiful: her eyes, especially, were so dark, intense and vivacious that they seemed to him to have, not a squint, but a kind of bewitching obliquity. She was dressed in a mustard-coloured costume, with a white blouse; and smelled like Ceres.

He noticed that the clerk at the desk, the page-boy, the commissionaire, and a passing guest, were all gazing at him with a respect that he had not enjoyed since his christening.

Chatting pleasantly about the weather, she conducted him upstairs to a private lounge where, under a fresco of fat nude pink nymphs, she sat him down beside her, to wait for the coffee to be brought and for him to be released from his spell of belittlement. As he sat simpering he felt no larger than a nymph's toe.

She began to make faces and do peculiar things with her arms and hands.

"Octopus," she explained, "female."

He remained small and solemn.

"You don't still think I'm an imposter, do you?" she cried.

He shook his head.

"I hope I'm not causing you to play truant?"

"No."

The coffee arrived. She poured it out. It looked like ordinary coffee, but somehow his first sip restored him to normal size. He noticed that she wore no engagement ring.

She might be a month or two older than he, no more. She had, too, what he secretly approved in women, a small elegant bosom.

Anyone looking in at them, he thought, might have taken them for a honeymooning couple; yet the gulf between them was wider and deeper than love turned sour. He represented idealism, however inadequately; she materialism, so magnificently as to make it appear the far more attractive and successful doctrine. He was grave, she frivolous. She could not keep from laughing; indeed, his gravity fed her laughter.

He smoked the first of his three cigarettes per day.

"Well, Miss Vontin," he said, "just what did you want to speak to me about? If you heard me last night, you know my opinions."

"Were they really your opinions?" she asked. "I mean, you read books, I suppose, and pass examinations by cleverly writing down other men's opinions."

He remembered scornfully a comment that a lecturer had scribbled in the margin of his essay on Plato: "Poor Plato!" And under it, as a witty afterthought: "Or is it poor Mr. Doig?"

"I don't claim originality for anything I said," he replied. "Human beings know what to think. What they do not know is how to master their selfishness."

"I see. Do you?"

"I try."

"With any success?"

"I cannot be the judge of that."

She began to shake her head as she laughed. It was an amiable laughter, as if she found him likeable as well as amusing.

"You know," she said, "I'm usually good at it, but I just can't in your case."

He waited. She kept laughing at him.

"No, I can't."

"You can't what, Miss Vontin?"

"Make up my mind whether you're just another one."

"Another what?"

She whispered the word, bringing her head nearer to his, with lover-like caution. "Humbug."

He said nothing.

"You've no idea how many we've come into contact with."

"I suppose you mean in connection with these evictions?"

"We call them transplantings."

"Which is itself surely," he said, "an excellent example of humbug."

She no longer laughed. "No, it isn't," she said. "If plants aren't doing well because the soil doesn't suit them, surely it's better to place them in suitable soil than to let them wither?"

"Human beings aren't cabbages," he said.

She looked at him with a shrewdness refined rather than subtle.

"I hope you don't mind my saying it, Mr. Doig," she said, "but you don't give me the impression of one who dotes on his fellow man."

It was hardly brilliant of her to see so huge and permanent a snag. Idealists for thousands of years had been stumbling over it and breaking their ideals: how to reconcile their sky-ward hopes of man with their passionate denunciations of his grubby pettiness, blindness, and greed. Love, the reconciler, was rare; it could not easily be counterfeited.

"Cabbages, after all," she suggested, "are pleasanter than octopuses."

"I try, Miss Vontin," he said, "to see the truth of every situation, and act accordingly. I am not interested in politics. It is the morality of rich and poor, or privileged and deprived, of surfeited and hungry, that concerns me." As he uttered the words, they sounded feeble, false, and even pompous, com-pared to the assured silence of the jewel in her ring and the pearls of her necklace; yet they were the bravest and sincerest growth from his heart, that compost of human frailties. "Our civilisation is based upon an interpretation of Christianity that allows us all to indulge our selfish instincts, under the Cross. Consequently there is nothing in nature now so difficult to detect in its natural surroundings as a humbug."

She gazed at him as at flounder in sand or stoat in snow.

"Authority is not based on love," he said, "but those who wield it speak as though it were; so love is debased."

She seemed impressed.

"You will admit, though," she murmured, "*you* could be a humbug, too."

"Of course I admit it; but not in the matter of Sollas. If it gives you any satisfaction, I can tell you that most people, including my own mother, think I am one. She nurses the thought as indulgently as she once nursed me. She thinks it is a necessary phase. Like all mothers, she hopes that her son will become one of the important ones of the earth. That is a maternal treachery not altogether pardonable."

Miss Vontin now gaped a little.

"I doubt if Christ's mother rejoiced to see Him crucified," he said.

She let out her breath. "I'm sorry," she murmured.

"For what?"

"For suggesting you're a humbug. Whatever you are, you're not just that. All the same, I'm afraid I agree with your mother. People are mostly cabbages, and octopuses. It's silly to break your heart over them, if that's what you're doing. Cabbages that rot smell. Sollas is a lovely island. I doubt if there's one lovelier under heaven. Why should our enjoyment of it be ruined by the sight and sound of decay that's avoidable?"

"But these cabbages on Sollas, Miss Vontin, worship God."

"Yes." She spoke only that one word, charged with disgust, amazement, anxiety, annoyance, and awe.

From her fastidious hand shaking ash into the silver tray he glanced away to the great boulder on Sollas shore, called the Sanctuary Stone, because hundreds of years ago a saint had given thanks to God beside it for his salvation from shipwreck. It had become holy and potent. During the slaughterous and cruel history of those western isles Sollas, with its stone, had remained a sanctuary. Kings and chiefs had sheltered there from enemies. The saint had often been seen. Now, however, the stone had long ago lost its virtue. Today the handful of simple folk who still had faith in it were being forced to recognise that a legal document had superseded the wish of a saint and the favour of God.

With these thoughts in his mind, it seemed to him that all the artifices which had gone to make his companion's expensive and fashionable beauty, suddenly coalesced into a mask. If he, or she, could take it off, what would be revealed behind it.

"Whatever you may say, Mr. Doig," she said, haughtily, "the fact remains that the island belongs to my father, who surely has the right to use it as he wishes. That isn't a new doctrine. It's as old as the hills. It's never been repudiated; never."

"Death repudiates it daily," he replied. "It's more than a truism that no rich man can take his possessions with him."

She was about to show impatience, but changed it to resignation.

"I keep forgetting," she said, "that you're going to be a minister."

"Only if I consider myself worthy enough."

"And if not?"

"I shall become a lawyer. I shall aspire to the black cap."

She shivered, and laughed. "You say the oddest things." Then she decided on a truce. "More coffee?"

"Thank you."

As they drank and smoked and smiled they were again the honeymooning couple.

"How would you like to go to Sollas?" she asked suddenly. "I mean, as our guest. My father would very much enjoy having you."

He sat, agitated, listening to voices. Among them was his mother's, crying to him not to be foolish and let slip this god-send of an opportunity. No matter what the circumstances were in which one became the guest of a rich man and his daughter in their mansion on their delectable island, one must certainly prosper from the experience.

"I'd enjoy it too, of course," she added, smiling.

"It's very kind of you."

"I'd really like you to come."

"Certainly," he murmured, "after all these words and thoughts about Sollas I'd very much like to see it, and stand by the Sanctuary Stone."

"Would you expect a miracle?" she asked. "All you'd hear would be the roaring of the Atlantic breakers, and the singing of skylarks. Little blue butterflies would fly about you as thick as snowflakes. The whole machair would breath fragrance at you. A gull might scream, an oyster-catcher; a curlew might call. It would amount to a miracle."

Her enthusiasm, though quiet, was evidently deep; and her fondness too.

"If there's anything more pleasant than galloping over the machair and the sands of the Big Strand—five miles of them —I don't know what it is. Do you ride?"

"I used to ride ponies at the seaside," he said, "with my mother to hold me on."

She was so delighted with that stroke of humour that she even patted his hand.

"And now you're riding the whirlwind," she cried, "with nobody to hold you on. Oh, you must come, Andrew. Do you mind if I call you Andrew?"

"Not at all."

"And you must call me Marguerite. I'll not press for an answer now if you'll promise to write and let me know."

"I promise."

"Good."

Then they began to talk with guarded urbanity, like strangers at a funeral.

Three

THE SOLLAS affair, as it was generally known, was on the surface very simple. Sollas was one of the beautiful archipelagos off the west coast. At one time it had been populated by about a hundred families, but during the clearances of the past century it had been emptied except for the servants of the noble owner. Sollas House was a magnificent mansion. About a year ago a group of narrow sectarians, consisting of half a dozen families, had suddenly left their homes on an adjacent barren island and invaded Sollas. With resource and fortitude they had built up the old houses, cultivated the former fields, and restored the ancient priory. Their patriarch was an old man with visions; he claimed God had commanded the migration, and would protect it.

At first it had been looked on as a sort of pathetic joke. Newspapers had sent photographers and reporters who had helped to build up a picture of amiable sincere half-wits, ragged Canutes, who thought with spades and faith to keep back the tide of materialism. Indeed, for a little while, they had become national pets. Their experiment, though wrong-headed, archaic, and illegal, had nevertheless in it some of that uncompromising staunchness in religious affairs which was so proud a feature of the nation's history. It would inevitably fail, in the circumstances of the day, and no harm would have been done.

Unfortunately, though it did fail so far as the health and welfare of the invaders were concerned, they continued to resist the persuasions, and even the threats, of authority. The new owner of the island had at last taken legal action. Since he had already offered to settle the people upon land which he also owned on the mainland, and to furnish them there with better cottages than they had ever lived in before, few of their countrymen could honestly sympathise with them. Even fellow-Christians as devout as they saw no virtue in this foolish martyrdom. Holiness, they said, existed wherever God was genuinely worshipped : stones and relics, however blessed in the past, were hardly efficacious now. The Government too, acting with paternal caution and tenderness, could not accept this excuse of ancestral piety. So the case had been decided in court. It was hoped expulsion would not be necessary. The Society whose patriotic function it was to help to preserve traditional ways of life had sent emissaries to offer assistance and comfort, but also to exhort obedience to the law.

Meanwhile Mr. Vontin had been spending thousands of pounds on renovating Sollas House and restoring its celebrated garden.

The law had to press on with its unhappy mission. Out of dozens of volunteers six policemen were chosen to accompany the Sheriff and his two clerks when he went to enforce the eviction orders. Besides being uniformed and truncheoned officials, these were, of course, human beings, some of them married with children, some church-goers, and all of them with their own peculiar hopes and opinions.

On a morning a week or so before they were to set out for the island they were summoned to the Superintendent's office. Erect, attentive, respectful, and zealous, they stood in front of his desk and listened to his quiet words of counsel. Speer, the sergeant who would be in charge, was also present.

"I know you're all men I can trust," said the superintendent. "Now this is not a pleasant business. I don't have to tell you that. It's not for you, or for me, to argue the rights and wrongs of it. Our duty is just to see that the court's decision is carried out, as humanely as possible. I know there are policemen nearer than here, but it was considered better that it should be done by strangers: it helps to save bad feeling. I don't think there will be any trouble. But even if there is, it's up to you to keep calm and do only what's just. I expect there will be some newspaper people there. So there will be a certain amount of publicity. Now our country's got a well-deserved reputation for decency. It's up to us to maintain it."

He paused to glance at the pencil in his hand, and then to look up with more sternness. His gaze fell on the youngest policeman, who was also the beefiest, and had the nickname "Bull".

"I know what you're thinking," he said. "You'll have read in the papers that they've got guns."

"Surely, sir," said grey-haired Rollo, who had had a better education than the superintendent himself, "theirs is a religion of love. It wouldn't allow them to use guns on us."

The superintendent never trusted Rollo's irony.

"You'd think so, Rollo," he said. "But you can never depend on folk who claim to be inspired by visions and voices."

"They might hear a voice," agreed Rollo, "giving them permission. There's been a lot of shooting and killing approved by religion."

This gibe was intended for Creepe, big, powerful, and in Rollo's view obtusely religious. Creepe was not stung by it; he grinned and looked proud.

"The Lord has enemies," he said. "Sometimes He asks us to rid Him of them."

"Isn't there a chance, Creepe," asked Rollo, "that He might regard us as His enemies?"

"Not in this matter of the island," said Creepe, with fanatical assurance. "These people are fools."

"They are that, Creepe," agreed the superintendent. "I suppose there's hardly an important minister of the Church who will support them in the attitude they're taking up. Surely by this time we've learned the difference between true religion and superstition?"

Grooner, the worrier, intervened, with his usual canny pertinence.

"The Sheriff will know about their guns?" he asked.

The superintendent nodded. "He knows."

Grooner was relieved, but his long, grey, anxious face could scarcely show it.

"Whatever happens," said the superintendent, "we'll be prepared for it. Sergeant Speer has his orders. You have two duties: one is to see that the law is carried out, and the other is to protect the Sheriff. Those must be done, whatever the cost. You understand?"

"Yes, sir," each said.

"But I don't think the cost will be heavy," he said, with a smile. "All right, men, that'll do for now. Sergeant, I'd like you to wait."

Back in the common-room Bull began to strip off his tunic and shirt to give himself one of his frequent apparently superfluous washes. Naked to the waist he grinned round at his mates.

"What's all the fuss about?" he cried. "They're being bloody nuisances, aren't they? Well, out with them, arse-first."

He laughed as he saw disgust on some of their faces, on Grooner's, on Dand's, and on Rickie's, all family men. There was none on Rollo's or Creepe's.

"If it was my own mother," said Bull, "and she was making a bloody old fool of herself I'd have her out by the hair. In the old days they knew how to do it: set fire to their hovels and drive them out squealing like rats."

They watched him as, laughing fiercely, he turned and

began to wash himself. Though the youngest in years, he was, in his instinctive and reverent acceptance of the inevitability of violence and pain, older than the pyramids. He often boasted his was a vocation, like a priest's, not just a job with good pay and early pension. His colleagues disliked but also feared and flattered him. Just as good gardeners are said to have green fingers, so from Bull's huge dedicated paws sprouted success in his trade of coercion. His superiors, reluctant to squash a beetle under their polished shoes, praised him. He was sure of promotion.

As he dried himself his torso, glimpsed behind the towel, looked like a fat woman's, pale, hairless, and breasted. Yet his virility was, after duty, his loudest brag. His eyes, small in his large red face, were very blue, and had in them often an incomprehension akin to innocence. His teeth were very white; indeed, his cleanliness was as notorious as his lust. When he came in from handling any law-breaker he would wash himself like a collier.

Grooner was Bull's mate on patrol; it was an odious honour he accepted to propitiate authority. He suffered from a finical stomach, which might well force him to resign before his pension was due; it was partly the reason for his haggard face. On Sollas meals would probably be delayed or eaten hurriedly, and the diet necessary to keep his guts quiet might not be available. Nevertheless he had volunteered, against his wife's wish.

"My grudge against these folk," he said, for at least the sixth time, "is that they're making their kids suffer."

"Is that you at it again, Grooner," jeered Bull, "being sorry for kids?"

"Surely, Bull. Kids have got to live in the world we make for them."

"What's wrong with the world?" roared Bull. "I like the world. It suits me. Do you think I'm an imbecile or something, Grooner, because the world suits me?"

"Of course I don't, Bull."

Bull came closer. "What I don't get about you, Grooner, is why you begot the wee bastards just to be sorry for them. Now I'm going to have a dozen kids, but I'm damned if I'm going to be sorry for them. That's consistent, Grooner. Isn't that consistent, Rollo?"

The others looked at Rollo curiously. No one, certainly not Bull, was friendly with the tall handsome grey-haired man, so monastic in his dark uniform. He wished no friends. Years ago promotion had been offered him often but he had always refused. No one knew why; it was certainly not because he was humble. He was so mysterious that some of them, the most simple-minded, sometimes wondered if he was some kind of spy set in their very midst to report upon them all, even upon the superintendent himself. Such spies existed elsewhere; why not here too?

"Isn't it consistent," repeated Bull, "to say you like the world and then to bring kids into it?"

"It's been said, Bull," murmured Rollo, "that this era in which we live, and of which you are a proud representative, is the cruellest in history."

Grooner smiled in sad satisfaction at that support. At the same time, redeeming the cruel era, came a picture of his two children, Jean aged ten reading to Bob aged three.

Bull was slapping his fat thighs in appreciation of Rollo's compliment.

"Cruel if you like, Rollo," he cried. "This is the time I live in. I can't deny it, and I don't want to deny it. But what about yourself, Rollo? What about yourself, eh? Why did you volunteer? Tell me that. Grooner, Dand, and Rickie here, though their hearts are bleeding for the kids yonder, volunteered because of the bonus and the chance of promotion. I volunteered because it makes me sick to read of folk like them refusing to do what they've been told to do. Creepe here," and he turned upon the big grinning black-moustached man, "is going, I take it, because he thinks those folk have insulted his religion."

Creepe grinned and nodded, as if in indulgence to a half-truth.

"But as for you, Rollo," went on Bull, "I just don't know. What's your reason?"

"Is it just for the fun, Rollo?" asked Grooner.

"Fun, Grooner? Will there be any fun in shoving out those self-anointed saints?"

"For you, Rollo, there might be. For you there's fun in everything."

"Do you think so, Grooner?"

"You talk as though it was the case, Rollo. If I've been misunderstanding you, I'm sorry."

Rollo smiled and turned to Bull.

"So you want to know, Bull?"

"I would, Rollo."

"Then I'll tell you." He paused, while they waited. "I want to fish."

"Fish!" howled Bull, astonished and delighted.

"Why not? The lochs on Sollas are teeming with salmon and sea-trout. You know I'm an enthusiastic angler. I can't say how long we'll be there, but I should fancy there'll be time for an hour or two's fishing."

They were puzzled.

"Do you mean that, Rollo?" asked Grooner.

"Certainly. Why shouldn't I?"

"Well, it's not a holiday, is it?"

"Did you not say yourself, Grooner, that for me everything and everywhere was a holiday? I take it, you expect to have a few hours' off-duty on the island. I mean, we'll have to sleep."

"I suppose so."

"How do you propose to spend any leisure time?"

"I haven't given it a thought, Rollo. Play cards, I suppose, read, go for a stroll."

"Then why not fish? Is there a more discreet sport?"

"Sure," cried Bull, "I could name you one, and the graith for it's a damned sight easier carried than your rod and net, Rollo."

As Bull roared at his own bawdy humour, Creepe scowled. It wasn't Bull's indecency that offended him; the sect to which Creepe belonged had the world's sins courageously catalogued, for proper castigation. It was Bull's boastfulness. Creepe was the stronger of the two men, and the more virile; therefore, when confronted by these boasts of Bull's, he always felt, obscurely and suffocatingly, that his own pious and monogamous brawn was being wasted. Had he lived in the days of Abraham, in body as he did in mind, he would have had a dozen wives and a hundred children. As it was, in this cruellest era, he not only had no children, but had a wife to whom piety represented long bouts of denying his flesh.

The others, however, were still interested in Rollo.

"What about Speer?" asked Dand, who in his modester way was as dutiful as Bull. "He'll object. You know how pernicketty he is."

"There are authorities above Speer."

"You mean the superintendent?"

"Higher."

"Not the Chief himself?"

"Still higher, Dand."

"Who's higher than the Chief?"

"The Sheriff."

Even Creepe joined in the astonishment at that cool answer.

"You'd never have the nerve to approach him," said Grooner.

"Why not? Is he a god?"

"They say he thinks he is," said Rickie. "I was told by a lawyer once that the Sheriff thinks he should have been a High Court judge."

"Whatever he is," said Dand, "he'll not be pleased if Rollo

here goes knocking to his door, like a schoolboy to the head-master, and asks leave to take his fishing-rod with him."

"It is not obligatory to please the Sheriff," said Rollo. "However, there are intermediaries who can be sounded. As a matter of fact, I am going there now."

"You're on duty in half an hour," said Dand.

"Half an hour will be long enough, Dand."

They watched him put on his helmet, making sure it was at the correct angle. This vanity surprised them, for he seemed to have so many other qualities which he neglected. Had he wished he could have been a superintendent himself.

"He's a strange one," said Grooner, when he had gone.

"I can't make him out at all," said Dand.

Rickie nodded; even Bull was in agreement. Rollo was a mystery.

Creepe shook his head, repudiating this culpable ignorance.

"Is he not Satan?" he asked, simply.

They were embarrassed. For any man to reveal such beliefs was distressing, but for Creepe, so massive and belligerent, it was agonising. Laughter was dangerous; even smiling was a risk. As for contradiction, it was useless.

"Satan takes many shapes," said Creepe, "and walks the earth."

"Do you think we'll find him on Sollas?" asked Grooner, apparently serious.

"He will be there," replied Creepe, proudly; it was as if he had arranged it.

Not even Bull could find a rejoinder to that.

Four

Rollo did not really want to fish on the island: to study the antics of the human beings there in their vast pool of sea-enchanted air would be more fascinating. Even if, through some pompous idiosyncrasy of the official mind, his request was received, considered, deprecated, and conditionally granted, he would still not take his rod with him. All his pleasure was in this humble asking, this slipping of a tiny itching burr down the neck of authority. First he would approach the clerks who were to accompany the Sheriff, and with simplicity, indeed with the earnest stupidity expected of an unpromoted policeman, would explain his problem. He would be a spy within the citadel, only his discoveries were for himself; and they would be used, within his own mind, to bring nearer that ultimate capitulation of humanity. For so far, despite Bull and Creepe and the time-servers like Grooner, despite authority so often itched into infantile exasperations, and despite cruelty, he still was able to see reasons why mankind had not yet given in to despair. With patience those reasons could be found to be invalid.

He lingered by the ramparts and surveyed the city. A bee buzzed past him though no flowers grew up there; it must have floated up from the gardens below. He yawned, to obscure his instinctive and treacherous pride as he gazed about him at his native land. Much of its history had originated on that high rock where he now stood. Fifty yards away was the flagstone where three hundred years ago a bishop had died because through his grey beard's perturbation he had kept crying to his assassins that the way to God was his way, and

34

not theirs. Now there was no way in dispute. Perhaps at that moment the visionaries of Sollas were on their knees beside their holy stone, praying to God to intercede. If such intercession were possible, wondered Rollo, what form would it take?

A bird flew below. Reaching over, he tried to drop a spittle upon it. He failed but the gesture itself succeeded. Thus God in His high heaven responded to men's prayers.   .

He knew where the clerks were to be found. Once, whilst a witness in a case of rape, he had had a cup of tea from Mr. Nigg and Mr. Quorr, with the former, an agitated dapper finch of a man, acting as host. Nigg, it seemed, was married to an eagle, and all the tasks about that unnatural nest were allotted to him. No man was more loyal to authority: at all unorthodoxies, in religion, politics, and morals, he pecked as a bird might at a worm of a kind it had not seen before. This inquiry about a fishing-rod would send him into a great chirp and flutter; hands going like wings he would shake off all responsibility; head to one side, with small eyes unblinking, he would listen in horror to his big colleague's loud amusement.

Quorr was a great shaggy stallion of a man, who loved horses so much he said openly he wished he had been born one; as it was, only his teeth qualified. Those teeth were used to crunch peppermints all day long, either to drown the smell of whisky off his breath, or soothe his stomach, or both. He was as unlikely in that office as a racehorse in the shafts of a tinker's cart.

Only Nigg was in when Rollo knocked and entered.

"Good afternoon, constable," he said, and waited with his pen as agitated as an arrested ant.

"Is Mr. Quorr about?" asked Rollo.

"He'll be here in a minute, I should say. Can I help?"

"Perhaps you can, Mr. Nigg."

Rollo stood, helmet in hand, so obviously knowing his place

that Nigg was touched. The small clerk swivelled round in his chair and took off his spectacles. He looked keenly competent to advise the taking of an extra pair of socks in one's kitbag.

As Rollo explained Nigg kept smiling politely, while horror gathered in his eyes. He blessed his soul two or three times. Before, however, he could express that soul in came Quorr, burly, almost white-haired, with baggy candid eyes and crunching jaws.

"Hello, Rollo," he said, and then noticed his colleague's horror-stricken face. "What's going on?"

"This constable," said Nigg, "is one of those going with us to Sollas."

"Congratulations," said Quorr, with a grin.

"He is here," went on Nigg, "with the most absurd request you could imagine."

"Does he want overtime rates?"

"Far worse than that!" cried Nigg.

Rollo explained.

Quorr was amused. "What about your pail and spade while you're at it?"

"Just so," said Nigg, with a sharp nod. "I shall be frank with you, constable. Your request seems to me quite callous."

"Why?"

"What we are going to do is, I believe, necessary and just; but it is not pleasant, and may cause unhappiness. We must surely not appear to gloat. At the same time we must also not appear indifferent."

"A man fishing," said Rollo, "can be a man sorrowing."

"Especially if he's catching nothing," chuckled Quorr.

Nigg grew bold and menacing.

"There is another aspect altogether," he said. "What about the fish themselves? They have feelings, too. Perhaps you did not know that? Perhaps you prefer not to know it? Tell me, Mr. Rollo, would you be so keen on fishing if, when you dragged the poor creature out of its native element, with the hook through its mouth or its eye, it screamed?" He almost screamed himself at that climax, and looked ready to dart like an incensed minnow at Rollo.

"If fish screamed," said Rollo, "I might be a worm that fish ate."

Nigg was puzzled, but Quorr patted his back and cried: "That's right, Niggie. With your screaming fish you've altered all creation. Anyhow, couldn't our mission itself be seen as a spot of fishing? The Sheriff's the hook, Rollo and his mates the rod, the State the angler, and of course the squatters are the fish. You and I, Niggie, will be there to see that the hook's fine and sharp and well attached."

"A most ridiculous analogy," said Nigg, and turned to get on with his work.

Quorr leant back in his chair and winked at Rollo.

"If you think you've struck on something original, constable," he said, "let me tell you you're just not in it compared with Mr. Nigg here."

Nigg turned. "I hope, Robert," he said, "you're not going to betray a confidence?"

"What's confidential about it, Hector? You'll be doing it in daylight, won't you? It's nothing to be ashamed of. On the contrary. In any case, hasn't the Sheriff given his approval?"

"I did not quite say that."

"But he didn't positively object?"

"No."

"I don't see how he possibly could have objected. Besides, really it's none of his business. You see, Rollo, Mr. Nigg's been commissioned by Mrs. Nigg to gather some sea-shells for her on Sollas. It's to make her a necklace. It seems on the sands there are certain rather rare and beautiful shells. If pierced—seemingly it takes an expert to do this without shattering them—they make exquisite necklaces."

"Won't they smell always of the sea?" asked Rollo, as if sincerely concerned.

"Well, isn't that a grand smell?" asked Quorr.

Nigg bent over his desk. When Mirren had first issued the order he had been incredulous, despite his long experience of inconvenient and inconsiderate errands; when convinced, he had with affection and dignity declined, pointing out not only how solemn was the mission to the island but also how subordinate his rôle in it would be. She had taken his refusal and shattered it to smaller fragments than those elusive seashells. Producing a tiny silver thimble she had told him it would be his measuring vessel; if a shell slid in and out easily it would do for size; but the smallest imperfection would of course disqualify it. She had read of those shells of Sollas: not only were they beautiful, with their mother-of-pearl iridescence spotted red like blood, but they were also reputed to be lucky. He had not been sufficiently composed at the time to refute that superstition by pointing out that obviously no luck had been brought to the people now under sentence of eviction. That argument occurred to him later in the bathroom, but when he proffered it she flung it scornfully aside as the result of premeditated disobligingness: he had brooded for hours to hatch a way to spite her.

"Do you know what I would like to do yonder?" Quorr was saying. "I'd like to borrow a horse, a fast horse, and go for a gallop across the machairs. They're flat as aerodromes and stretch for miles; beautiful green turf, too, at this time of the year scented with millions of wild flowers. I might get the chance, too, with a little luck and a lot of push. This Mr. Vontin who owns the place, I understand he won't have a motor car on the island; he prefers horses. If it's true, then I don't give a damn what anybody says, the man who's fond of horses is in the right of it. Mind you, to be fair, these poor blighters have their own ponies; small, strong, sensible beasts they are, too, from all accounts. I've heard they'd rather their children went hungry than their ponies. Now that would be a hard choice, a man's kids or his horses; but I know what I'd choose."

"Your children surely?" said Nigg.

"No, by God I wouldn't. Horses are becoming extinct in this mad world, whereas human beings are increasing so fast they'll soon have to fall back on cannibalism."

"I admire horses, too," said Nigg, "but surely human beings are more important?"

"Not to me. A thoroughbred horse, swift as the wind, gleaming like a chestnut, with mane flying; or that brat from the slums, Nigg, who tore all the roses off your prize bush? Be honest now. Which would you rather keep in the world?"

"Destroying the roses was an act of hideous vandalism," admitted Nigg, "and I have said I admire horses; but all the same I must repeat that a human being, possessing a soul, however depraved, is more precious than any horse. Does not the law itself support me? If I shoot the beautiful horse, I am jailed; but if I shoot the urchin who despoils my roses, I am hanged."

"Have you any children, Mr. Nigg?" asked Rollo, knowing he had none.

"No." Nigg was unaccountably cast down; it was as if he was ashamed of that lack. "No." He returned to his clerking. "No," he said again.

Quorr winked at Rollo; there was sympathy in it, as well as humour.

"So we're all going to enjoy ourselves on Sollas," he said. "Nigg gathering his shells, you Rollo fishing, and me galloping like Cortes."

"What of the Sheriff?" asked Rollo, meekly. "How will he spend his leisure?"

"I don't know. He's writing a book; his autobiography, I think it is. I suppose he might take notes for it. After all, from that point of view, this case on Sollas is interesting. He mentioned that Sollas House has a fine library."

"I believe it's a fine house altogether. I've read that the paintings themselves are worth about a hundred thousand pounds."

"Between you and me," said Quorr, "you've hit the nail on the head. This man Vontin wants the island for himself. It makes sense to me. When he bought it it was empty, so he started to build himself a sanctuary there, a place to retreat to. Then he found himself invaded by a shower of crackpots with views that subsided with Noah's flood. So he tried to bribe them to go quietly. They refused. So he's turned the bloodhounds on them at last. We're the bloodhounds. Now I've no objection to religion if it's intelligently displayed, but I've got no time for mumbo-jumbo about sacred stones and shipwrecked holy men and messages from God. Besides, any man that loves horses can be trusted."

"Really," asked Nigg, "is that a sound criterion?"

"For me it is."

"They are fine animals," agreed Rollo, "patient, loyal, and uncomplaining."

"And beautiful," added Quorr, banging his fist on the desk.

A few minutes later Rollo took his leave. Again he lingered by the ramparts, this time musing on this strange variety of human nature sampled by him within an hour: Bull, connoisseur of lust, priest of duty; Grooner, pitier of children, volunteer for Sollas, where children lived; Creepe, for whom only a sadistic God made sense; Nigg, protector of fish, gatherer of shells, yearner for paternity; and Quorr, ugly himself, insisting on the beauty of horses.

While he was wiping his elbows, ready to set off to report for duty, he heard footsteps on the causeys behind him. Turning, he saw the Sheriff and immediately saluted. But his salute was not for the black-hatted, severe-faced, little legal master, although the latter acknowledged it; it was for something nameless, of which he, and the Sheriff, and Bull, and Creepe, and Nigg, and Quorr, and the folk on Sollas, were all involuntary doomed parts.

Five

THE SHERIFF's superiors had suggested that the journey to the northern pier be made by private car, rather than by public railway: thus would provocation be minimised, and in any case did not discreetness help to nullify that little element of injustice inevitably present where individuals had to be sacrificed so that the whole community might be preserved? The Sheriff demurred: it seemed to him, he said, wiser that the community should be made to appreciate the cost of its preservation. But his chief objection to the long hilly journey by car was that, since boyhood, that mode of travel had caused a nausea in him, which pills could not quell. Even a short run was a risk, so that he frequently walked rather than take a bus. It was no doubt ludicrous, and certainly it was inconvenient, in a mechanical age, that he should suffer from such an allergy; but though the law might be inviolable and immortal, its servants were creatures of flesh. He offered an illustration. A friend of his, a High Court judge, now deceased, had confessed to him having once sat through a diet of cases with a boil on his hip. He had envied the wretches in the dock, able to squirm as freely as they pleased on their hard bench; and he had never been able to convince himself afterwards that the sentences which he had meted out had not been lengthened by that very envy, so illogical, unjust, and unpardonable, but also so human.

The train left the capital soon after dawn. No demonstrators were about. The posse of police secreted in the station was not called upon to appear. No force of any kind was needed to subdue or silence the one person in the station who disapproved. This was a tall cadaverous man in a bowler hat and long black coat, who, without uttering a word, walked up and down carrying a sandwich board, which proclaimed on one side: PUT NOT YOUR TRUST IN MAN, and on the other the same faded exhortation. He was a kenspeckle sight in the city streets, promenading the gutters in rain, snow, or sun. If a royal personage visited the city he would be there, vexing the multitude. If an important football match was to be played, he would be outside the gates, imperturbable in face of the ribaldry directed at him by the devotees of that other cult. At election times he would appear outside one polling station after another, to the embarrassment of all candidates. No one knew who financed him. No one knew where he lived. No one knew his name. He had been on the scene for over thirty years, and many thought the authorities remiss in not having had him shut up in an institution for the senile. His lunacy did not consist in parading that advice, but rather in not being aware that it wasn't required; everybody knew regretfully that trust, whether between men or nations, was too dangerous to be depended upon alone, without strong safeguards.

Andrew Doig, however, did not accept that failure of trust. As a consequence he could feel no pity for the foolish old man. On such a glorious, such an Argonaut's morning, with the sunrise so beautiful· as to recall an age of innocence, it seemed to him that this sneer at humanity was the blackest and the most despairing of all blasphemies. Though much evil existed, and though persecution, rape, murder, cruelty, torture, and hatred had been in time more numerous than the pebbles on Sollas's beaches, still it was not true to say trust had been obliterated. It had been terrified, starved, tormented, paralysed, and near to death very often, but it had not died.

This faculty of being able so early in the morning to engage in comprehensive moralising had been born in Andrew. He had first displayed it at the age of three. Then, one wet Sunday, before breakfast, he had stood in his cot and asked why God didn't strike people dead who wouldn't attend his father's church just because of the rain. The gift had worried his father, himself a canny awakener; but it had pleased his mother who saw it as a sign of grace, too nagging to be ignored like her husband's.

As soon as he had booked a seat, by placing his suitcase upon it, Andrew hurried out again on to the platform. He did not want to miss the arrival of the policemen. According to the cant of the time, they were not really policemen at all, they were the mystics of the State, the missionaries of Authority. He did not expect them to come panoplied or enhaloed, but certainly looked for some extraordinary emanation from them, detectable by so sensitive an apparatus as himself. If he did detect it, then of course he would at once admit he was in the wrong about the whole business. Trust, rather than being in danger of extinction, would be seen to be under the protection of government.

He saw Bull first, and saw, therefore, not just a policeman with a raw, red, grinning face, massive thighs, and splayed feet, but the betrayal of hope, the extinguisher of faith. For Bull was as young as himself.

Beside Bull strode Speer the sergeant, peering about with weaselly flexibility of neck as if to make sure each minion was exemplarily uniformed, boots shining, metal number on collar bright, face well shaven, truncheon out of sight, knapsack tidy, helmet strap properly adjusted. No doubt he had already inspected them and corrected faults. He was insatiable for perfection, but it was the perfection of nihilism. These were not mystics or missionaries; they were crude ordinary men acting under orders; they were doing their duty according to contract, for pay; and the sheepishness of two or three of them, even more than the arrogance of the beefy youth, proved that in them existed no fabulous love.

When the policemen had entered their compartment Speer half-lowered the blind. Was this, wondered Andrew, out of an obscure sense of mourning or shame, or was it simply the crassness of the ostrich? His attention was diverted by the arrival of Nigg, whom he knew by sight.

The little clerk was dressed as if for a funeral, save for one detail: this was a small red rose, which he held in his hand. It was from his own garden, and he had plucked it to put into his button-hole, as a charm. Only when entering the station had it occurred to him that the purpose of the flower might be misinterpreted, and he had snatched it out in time. Now advancing up the platform, past a great snorting loco- motive, he held the rose in his hand as if he was about to be confronted by some other monster, far more terrifying, which must be propitiated by an offering of beauty.

Andrew might have spoken to him had not the Sheriff been approaching. With the latter he had still to be reconciled.

They had fallen out over Andrew's invitation to Sollas. When he had mentioned it his uncle had been displeased by such flippancy; thereafter he had been astonishingly severe on the subject of Andrew's hypocrisy and luck. The luck espec- ially seemed to embitter him. Envy was not absent. He had, with exceeding irrelevance, expatiated on the great wealth and influence of Mr. Vontin. That Andrew, so early in his career, at the height as it were of his callowness, should have been taken up by such people, no matter for what reason, had shocked the Sheriff out of his usual pose of judicial imparti- ality. Other men, he had pointed out, men with greater ability and no infantile delusions, had had to struggle for years to achieve what small distinction the world was willing to allow them. It became obvious he was referring to him- self: for his father, Andrew's grandfather, had been a country minister too, with a stipend hardly able to keep butter on the manse table far less push a brilliant son into the company of rich and powerful people. Now here that very pushing had happened to Andrew, who so little deserved it. Perversity was a favourite trick of youthful mountebanks: successful men, like Henry Vontin, were more likely to be attracted by idealistic simpletons who pretended to assail them than by modest sensible realists who admired them and supported their work.

Andrew had been astounded, horrified, and interested. The legal automaton, the machine for the manufacturing of impartiality, had suddenly become human and shown itself to be consumed by envy, disappointment, and spite. It was like a peep behind the façade of civilisation. Though it was shocking, alarming, and ominous, it was also pathetic; and unhappily, out of respect and tact, Andrew had emphasised the pathos. He had shown himself sorry for his uncle so aggrieved. It had turned out to be the least profitable attitude. His uncle, freezing again into his customary character, had been insulted; icily he had ordered Andrew out of the room.

Within a week the term had ended and Andrew had gone home. No reconciliation had been made with his uncle. His mother, delighted with the invitation to Sollas, had written to her brother. The reply had been brief; her son, the Sheriff had said, was a typical product of his generation, prepared to use the diving-board of idealism for a plunge into the profits of materialism. What amazed Andrew most about that expression was that it might have been uttered by himself; indeed, he suspected his uncle had stolen it from him. But far more heinous than the plagiarism was the unscrupulous tactic of accusing Andrew of the sin of which he, Andrew, had accused a multitude of others. It was really back to pathos, for could there be a more pathetic example of "tu quoque" than this? He had thereupon written to his uncle, manfully apologising for the unpleasantness which had arisen between them, and hoping to be forgiven next time they met.

Here then on the platform was that next time. A porter carried the Sheriff's luggage; he carried his portfolio and raincoat himself. Though it was sunny, with beams of light slanting from the sooty windows in the vaulted roof, he wore his black hat, dark suit, and stiff white collar. He noticed Andrew but came on as though he did not know him. No smile like a sunbeam shone on his sombre face.

"Good morning, Uncle Peter," said Andrew, with his hand outstretched.

The Sheriff paused. He touched the offered hand very briefly.

"Good morning, Andrew," he replied. "So you have had the hardihood to come?"

"Yes, sir. I hope you don't mind."

"I do mind."

"What I am doing, sir, is for my own good."

"I am well aware of that, Andrew."

"I meant for my moral good, sir."

"Do yourself a favour, Andrew. Do not use that word again for at least a year."

"What word, sir?"

But the Sheriff had passed on without answering.

"It must have been 'moral'," murmured Andrew, smiling. "What did he mean? Is not man meaningless without morality?"

He was displeased and saddened. There is nothing so unsatisfying as a crumb of reconciliation when one is hungry for a full meal. To become reconciled with one man is to become reconciled with all men.

As he walked along to his own compartment he noticed the young beefy constable grinning out at him with peculiar and sinister amiability. No doubt it had been mentioned to him that Andrew was the Sheriff's nephew. Andrew did not smile back.

Seated in his corner, Andrew took from his pocket the envelope containing Marguerite Vontin's letter and snapshots. He did not at once look at them. He was not obtuse; he knew that, if his uncle's charge was justified, this envelope, smooth, mauve, and fragrant, represented the proof of his treaty with the powers of wealth and prestige. He recollected Marguerite's dark eyes with their intensity that gave them the look of squinting. Had her hair, also black, gleamed greenly, like a beetle? She had wriggled her long delicate fingers, pretending to be an octopus. Sollas House was no submarine cave, festooned with seaweed, but in his imagination she glided through its many rooms, with her beautiful face always smiling, and always a little baleful. Her father could not be imagined; he was as remote as a mythological king.

The train began to move. As if it was a signal for affability, the only other passenger in the compartment, a fat, smug-faced man, leant forward and touched Andrew's knee.

"I see," he whispered, with a wink, "we've got the police on board."

"Yes."

"Going to this island Sollas."

"Yes."

"To make them get out, or else." The fat man laughed in a kind of sorrow. "Mind you, I'm sorry for them. I suppose any decent man would be."

"For the police?"

"No, no. They can look after themselves. It'll be like a holiday for them. For the folk being put off, I meant. Do you know what I said to my wife? I said to her, Effie, it's a shame; they're like kids with a toy that doesn't belong to them. Of course they've got to give it up, but it's heartbreaking to see it all the same. Do you know what she replied? Women are smart, you know."

Not smart, thought Andrew, instinctively sly, like cats.

"She said the gentleman that owns the place has offered to give them a toy just as good, even better. Now that's true, and it's the crux of the matter."

"Can you call the love of an ancestral island, sanctified by a famous saint, a toy?" asked Andrew.

The fat man laughed. "Well, you know what I mean," he said. "It's all superstitious, really."

"To believe in the sanctity of a place?"

"No. Well yes, in a way. We don't believe any longer in that sort of thing, do we?"

"Is belief in God a fashion?"

"No. I see what you mean all right, and every man's entitled to his opinion. You aren't a Catholic, are you?"

"No."

The man looked relieved. "I was beginning to think you were, you know. You've to watch yourself arguing religion with a Catholic. You can offend him pretty easily. Mind you, I could understand these people on Sollas much better if they were Catholics. It's an odd thing in this day and age for Protestants to say their saint appears amongst them. That's just plain downright superstition, whatever anybody says. I can see from your blazer you're a University student, so you'll be better read than me; but you'll not convince me seeing saints isn't pathological nowadays."

He laughed so heartily at that remark that it gave Andrew an opportunity to take refuge in the letter and the photographs.

He looked at the photographs first. His companion glanced across with a silly yearning smile, which seemed to say: Aren't we all members of the one family? Why not let me too see these photographs of your sweetheart or wife or mother or even your father? No matter how plain or uninteresting they are, I'll praise them and take delight in them. The human face, in any shape, is a solace and refreshment to me.

Unheeded, he had to open his newspaper, where there were other photographs; but these were of distant people, who had no interpreter.

There was one of Sollas House. "Bigger than my kirk," his father had said, and then had tried to distinguish among the shrubbery some of the rare specimens he had read flourished there. His mother had just smiled.

There was one too showing a typical patched-up house. It was a small stone box with windows like mean little eyes; the tin roof by contrast with the rest looked new, but by no means safe or watertight. Andrew's mother had been unable to understand why people would prefer to live in such hovels than in the modern hygienic cottages prepared for them on the mainland.

The third and last photograph was of the Sanctuary Stone. It showed amid sand a large boulder with nothing exceptional in its appearance. Millions of such boulders were scattered about the beaches of the earth; there were no doubt more on the moon.

He read the letter. Dear Andrew, or is it Jason? I hesitate to display my poverty of language to one like yourself with such a superabundance. But the risk must be run. My father joins me in sending you a warm invitation to pay us a visit here, any time that's convenient to you. We know your purpose is a serious one—anthropology, is it?—but surely while you're here you'll be able to take part in the pleasures of Sollas too. There may be one or two people about, but my father says that if you're out to reform the world it's as well for you to know what you're up against. That's his way of saying he doesn't approve of my friends very much. I'm sure you'll be an exception. By the way, he's very interested in your Argonauts society, and hopes you'll bring him a badge of membership. He thinks he's entitled to one because it was him (should it be he?) who named our yacht *Argo* two years ago.

The steamer will take you to Mula. If you let me know when to expect you I'll be there to ferry you over to Sollas.

She had signed herself just Marguerite.

Meanwhile in the policemen's compartment Bull was looking at photographs, too; he had confiscated them from a drunk man and studied them as often as Creepe did his tracts. They were the most obscene he had ever had the luck to possess. Now in the train, with lochs and hills streaming by outside in a sunny tedium, he took them out with the innocent intention of passing a little time. Speer, now dozing, had not allowed them to unbutton their tunics or loosen their laces; he had agreed only to their placing their helmets in a neat row along the rack. Rollo was reading; his book was a history of the western isles, including Sollas. Grooner, Dand, and Rickie were yawning over newspapers. Creepe scowled over a tract.

With the impulse of one wishing to share a delight Bull nudged Rollo. "Look at that," he whispered, and held out for Rollo's inspection his own favourite.

Rollo's eyes slowly left the closely-printed pages of his book, in which there were also photographs, of Celtic crosses, ancient ruins, castles and kirks, and brochs. He gazed for half a minute while Bull's hand tired. But Bull was pleased; here was confirmation of his judgment, in a sphere where he liked to be considered expert. And it was not often he got the chance to impress Rollo.

"French," he whispered.

Stimulated by that still speechless admiration, he looked again himself, and was overawed again by those ecstatic convolutions of lust. He knew that the law regarded such poses and the photographing of them as wrong, and punished them with imprisonment; but in this case he thought the law mistaken. If he was ever sent to arrest this black-haired white-

skinned priestess of lust he would do it with the greatest reluctance. Sexual potency and versatility were to Bull two of
the most honourable and praiseworthy attributes of any man
or woman. He judged people by their possession or lack of
them. For instance, Grooner, despite his two children, was
deficient; his wife, Nell, on the other hand, was well-en-
dowed; and Bull sincerely lusted after her, so much so that
he had never noticed how much she hated and distrusted him.
As for Rollo, now entranced, nobody really knew what
dealings he had with women; some said none at all, others
whispered he was a secret and exorbitant lecher.

What possessed Bull then he couldn't have said. Usually
he kept clear of Creepe, whose religion banned sex except on
Sundays, with enjoyment omitted. He had once seen Creepe's
wife and his own pleasure had afterwards been diminished,
because every woman had been strangely transformed into
likenesses of yon tall thin sour scourge. That sorcery indeed
was still not quite overcome.

Perhaps, therefore, it was for revenge that he suddenly,
surprising himself as much as the others, leant past Rollo and
placed the photograph on the open page of Creepe's booklet.
Creepe at the moment slept. The others, except Speer, became
aware of tension. Grooner glanced across, saw the photograph, which he recognised though it was upside down, and
shook his head at Bull, signifying he shouldn't have done it
and should undo it at once while there was time.

It was too late. Creepe awoke with a little jump, sighed,
and resumed his reading of the many reasons for believing in
Christ's wrath. One of those reasons, the chief, lay illustrated
on his book. So confused was he, with sleep and satisfied
piety, he thought for an instant that the picture was intended
to be there, as a warning. Certainly if, as his sect believed,
the world was a vast Gomorrah, here was proof.

He glanced up, saw Bull, and understood. His fist covered
the photograph in a disgust so quiet and yet so powerful it

seemed to Bull there was something sexual in it. Bull did not move. Suddenly, Creepe leapt up and threw the photograph out of the window. Too late Bull tried to save it. He stuck his head out and saw it fluttering down amongst some flowers on the embankment. Two white butterflies fluttered there too, the one pursuing the other in dancing circles. In the grass would be insects in similar pursuit. The entire earth heaved with such activity; it had to, to keep life going.

When he brought his head in again he said to Creepe, peaceably: "There wasn't any need to do that, Creepe."

"Think yourself lucky," said Creepe, "that it wasn't you I flung out."

Speer was now awake. He was told what had happened.

"Listen, you two," he said, "don't you think this job we've got on our hands isn't hard enough without squabbling among ourselves?"

"He insulted me," said Creepe.

"Did I insult him, Rollo?" asked Bull.

"I'm no judge whether Creepe's insulted or not," replied Rollo.

"I'm the judge of that," said Creepe. "He insulted my religion."

Speer at that awkward word leant back. Religion was the cause of their going to this island. He wished it had never been invented; all it had ever done, so far as he could see, was to cause trouble. There was no harm in people going to church, but if they became religious they became nuisances.

"If my religion is insulted," persisted Creepe, "I shall punish whoever does it."

"You've got to ask yourself, Creepe," said Speer, "if it's fair to make a show of your religion during duty hours. We know your opinions, and we're prepared to respect them; but you've got in return to keep them private."

"Talk to him, sergeant," said Creepe, pointing to Bull. "Is he to be allowed to thrust his filth upon other people?"

"No," said Speer, impartially.

"What you call filth, Creepe," said Bull, "might not be filth."

"For God's sake," said Grooner, "change the subject."

They fell silent.

Six

IN THE bows of the steamer crossing to the larger island of Mula, whence a ferry communicated with Sollas, Andrew was accosted by Mr. Nigg who, holding on to his hat, appeared from behind the shelter of the captain's bridge, and stood for a few seconds facing the bright breezy west, in some kind of peculiar homage. He looked out of place with his white cuffs, his hard collar, his sleek Sunday overcoat, and his small clerical face. In front loomed Mula, "isle of high towering mountains and sparkling waters" as the song said; through its woods deer roamed in primeval innocence. Against his will Andrew had been transformed into Jason by a gull asleep on top of a flag-pole. Profound premonitions were stirring in him. They were at once stultified by the arrival of the small man in the ludicrous city hat.

"I hope you'll pardon this intrusion, Mr. Doig," said Nigg. "My name is Nigg, Hector Nigg. You, I know, are Sir Peter's nephew, Mr. Andrew Doig."

Andrew had to agree. According to Nigg's conventional view those were facts. In this mundane presence it would be foolish to say, quietly: "No, I am not Andrew Doig, and you are not Hector Nigg. I am Jason, and you are one of the withered old men who wish my quest to fail. Look, old man, this gull upon the pole has come to me with a warning from the gods. Yonder lies Mula, where an enchantress awaits me. Either I overcome her spells or she takes me to her palace and turns me into a wrinkled and desiccated conformist like yourself."

"Are you aware, Mr. Doig," said Nigg, "that the captain

has not so far welcomed Sir Peter on board his ship, and shows no sign of doing so?"

"He has his ship to navigate."

"No. That cannot be the reason. A seaman in a jersey has the helm. No, I'm afraid Sir Peter has been insulted."

"Perhaps the captain does not approve of your mission, Mr. Nigg?"

No seaman would, thought Andrew, and then realised how untrue that was. Had not Magellan, Columbus, Da Gama, and Jason himself, been ruthless? Circumnavigators of worlds inward or without must sail past innumerable scruples.

"It is not my mission, Mr. Doig," replied Nigg gently. "Nor is it your uncle's. It is the nation's. It is your own. Of course, I understand you disapprove; I read the report of your University speech."

"You disapproved of it?"

"Not altogether. I regretted of course the inconvenience caused to the Sheriff. But it is a good thing, or so it seems to me, that young men with ability should challenge every act of authority."

Andrew showed his surprise.

"Yes, indeed, Mr. Doig. It may surprise you to know that when I was as young as you I carried a banner through the city streets, protesting against the cruelty of vivisection. Metaphorically, I still carry that banner. It still seems to me immoral that we should inflict suffering on helpless creatures in order to avoid suffering ourselves."

"Hear, hear," said Andrew, who previously had never given a thought to vivisection.

"We are the lords of creation," went on Nigg, "but we give ourselves the title. I doubt if we have earned it yet. I suppose, however, it is an error to judge the race by oneself."

"It is," agreed Andrew, who considered himself far above the average.

"For instance," said Nigg, with a sick smile, "at this moment I am consumed by a needless and shameful fear."

"Of what?"

"Of the sea. Of drowning. I have had it ever since I can remember. I suppose psychologists would tell me my mother once held my head too long under in my bath when I was a baby." He chuckled sadly at his joke. "Or perhaps they would delve deeper than that and find for me an ancestry that dwelt exclusively in inland trees. At any rate, it is true I am a coward on the sea. Even on a steamer as large as this, I am not immune. In a small boat my face, so my wife tells me, turns a green colour new even to the sea."

"Every man has his secret fear," said Andrew, wondering what his own was.

Nigg did not inquire.

"I suppose," he said, gazing out at the sea, "that if I had had children I might have been able to conquer my fear. Time is the sea in which we all ultimately drown. Children are hands across that dark sea. That is an image I have. Perhaps it is muddled. But I'm afraid I have no right to be wearying you with my foolish chatter."

"No, no," said Andrew, interested in this queer little man whose wife discovered a new green in his face, and who saw children as hands across a dark sea. "Tell me, Mr. Nigg," he asked, "what is your personal opinion of this business on Sollas? You may speak in complete confidence."

"It is good of you, Mr. Doig, to want to know my opinion. I do not often get the chance to express it frankly. Am I right in saying that these people on Sollas base their claim to the island, or to their part of it, on the ground that God, who possesses the entire earth, gave them sanction?"

"Yes, you are."

"Well then, apart altogether from the authenticity of that claim, is it really true that God possesses the earth? It seems to me that mankind has always been too jealous for that. I have no doubt that, if He willed, God could possess it now, this very minute. He could, I am sure, cause this sea to empty, and those mountains to dissolve in dust. But He waits for us to give Him back His earth. He has illimitable patience. He needs it."

"I agree entirely," said Andrew.

Nigg changed the hand holding on to his hat.

"You see, then," he went on, "it is really no good their merely saying that God gave them the right; they must also prove it."

"But how are they to do that, Mr. Nigg, especially in an age of enfeebled faith, such as ours."

"I would say, particularly in such an age, though perhaps faith is not so enfeebled as you think."

"But, Mr. Nigg, they cannot produce God as a witness."

"No, like yourself I do not think they can; but that is because I could not produce Him myself. I do not know how. Faith is not enfeebled so much as lost. It can be found again. Perhaps these people have found it."

Doig bent to look into his small companion's watering eyes as into mysterious seas.

"What do you expect, Mr. Nigg?" he asked.

Nigg shook his head, sending moisture dancing down his cheeks.

"A chill in the head, I'm afraid, if I stay out in this wind much longer."

"No. You know I meant in Sollas. Do you expect a miracle?"

"Would it require a miracle to have God as a witness on your behalf? Perhaps it would. I understand you are for Sollas yourself?"

"Yes. I was invited by Miss Vontin."

"You'll be staying for a week or two?"

"I don't know. Please don't misunderstand me, Mr. Nigg. I want to see for myself. It is no holiday."

"I understand. You believe the expulsion is an act of injustice?"

"Yes."

"Not according to man's law, surely?"

"According to any law."

"I'm afraid I can't agree. These people are trespassers."

"In the law's eyes."

"The law is capable of wise vision, Mr. Doig. It sees very clearly the barrier that separates civilisation from anarchy. If you have a garden, do you object to intruders who steal your apples and destroy your flowers. I do, and I expect the law to protect me. Mr. Vontin's garden may be vast, but it is still his."

"Stolen from God, did you not say?"

"That is always understood, of course. But where God is silent, man's law must prevail, and according to it Sollas is the property of Mr. Vontin who may do with it as he pleases. Certainly he has the right to be protected against intruders."

"Even if they are sent by God?"

"That is for them to prove. So far they have not done so."

"Many martyrs were burnt at the stake without any sign to prove their sincerity."

"I think the burning flesh must have been such a sign, Mr. Doig. It would prove sincerity all right, but it is genuineness that has to be proved."

"But, Mr. Nigg, do you not realise that by implication you are rejecting as false almost every sufferer for God?"

"Am I?" whispered Nigg.

"I'm afraid so, if you're looking for a sign from God every time a martyr dies."

"Perhaps the sign need not be as sensational as you think. But I'm afraid I'll have to go below, otherwise I shall take a dreadful earache. My wife tells me I lay claim to every physical discomfort there is. My eyes water, my ears ache, my legs grow stiff, my stomach cramps, my throat grows husky.

But it would be surely blasphemous for me to suggest that all this suffering has a purpose in the eyes of God?"

Andrew was silent, not knowing any answer.

"Perhaps we may meet again, Mr. Doig, and have another little chat?"

"Surely."

"Goodbye then, in the meantime."

"Goodbye."

Using his free hand as support Nigg went off and soon disappeared down the stairs leading to the lounge. He walked cautiously, like a city clerk allergic to the motion of the sea. Yet, as Andrew now knew, he was as strange a creature as any that the original Jason ever met.

Seven

In THE late afternoon, with the sunlight mellow on sea and hills, the steamer rounded the last wooded headland and glided across Galleon Bay towards the little red-and-white pier. Here was its terminus and resting-place; tomorrow it would go back to the mainland and return again. This arrival, therefore, was daily and familiar; it was said that the captain could berth his boat with his eyes shut; certainly he always did it with them glancing up at his wife waving a white sheet from her garden on the hillside. This afternoon, unexpectedly, he sounded his siren, once, twice, three times, so that blasts and echoes chased each other round the bay, before escaping into the sunny hills to carry, it seemed, that harsh melancholy throughout the world.

Bull was one of those startled. He was also interested. Leaning over the rail he could see no small craft in the way.

"What's up?" he asked a seaman with rope coiled to throw on to the pier. "What's he sounding for?"

He was an elderly man, brown and brawny. He did not answer.

"Maybe he always sounds when he comes in," suggested Grooner.

"No," said Bull, "that was special. Do you know what I think? I think the captain hates our guts."

They glanced up at the bridge. The captain was superintending the creeping in and tying up of the steamer.

"He hates somebody's guts," agreed Dand.

"Maybe his own," said Grooner, with a sympathetic grin. "After all, he's to eat with the stink of the sea in his nose all the time."

"Don't you like the sea, Grooner?" asked Rollo.

"Not this time," replied Grooner, not quite knowing what he meant.

His mates thought he was referring to the greasy sausage roll he had eaten on board; it had turned him squeamish for a while. But now they were more interested in watching the scene on the pier.

Bull had eyes only for the one woman there. Two men in sailors' uniform who stood behind her seemed to be her attendants or bodyguard. Even at that distance, unable to smell her perfume, Bull knew she was not for him: his virility, though immense, was also modest; it knew its place. What she wore was ordinary enough, light-blue slacks, white jumper, and moccasins; and what she possessed, in the shape of a bust, was rather meagre for his taste. She was, however, one of the élite. Fashioned outwardly like other women, she was nevertheless as inaccessible for him as a mermaid at the bottom of the sea. When word reached him she was Miss Vontin, the daughter of the rich man who owned Sollas, he was not surprised. He burned then to do homage. If only one of those dark-faced islanders gathered on the hillside above the pier would attempt to molest her, even by the throwing of a lump of peat, he would be off this boat and over that wall, at the culprit's throat before anybody else could move. The white yacht in the bay was hers; it had seemed to Bull like a dream of boyhood come true, so white and splendid and swift it looked. She had come over from Sollas in it, to pick up a guest. There she was waving at that guest, whom Bull now saw to be the tall, fair-haired young fellow in the University blazer, the Sheriff's nephew.

Here was the kind of romance Bull preferred even to his own: his satisfaction was never keener than when he caught an intimate glimpse, in a chauffeur-driven limousine or in the lounge of a high-class hotel, of a handsome man and a beautiful woman linked by wealth and power and influence, as well as by sex. His own love-making, with waitress or typist or even chorus-girl, was always successful, for he was as conscientious in it as in his duty; but from it was inevitably absent that glamour peculiar to great wealth.

Somebody had noticed Bull's adoration. Coming down the gangway, Rollo, who was behind him, whispered: "Just think of it, Bull, to lie in a hollow among the sand dunes, with a million pounds?"

Bull recognised the tempter's voice; he did not answer.

"With larks serenading you, Bull?"

"Shut up, Rollo. I don't know what you're talking about."

"He's no older than you, Bull. But then, your uncle's not the Sheriff. Look at them, Bull; look at our masters."

Miss Vontin and Doig had come across to the Sheriff and the Procurator-Fiscal of Mula and the Islands, who had been on the pier to meet the steamer.

"The Sheriff's being put up at Sollas House," whispered Rollo. "There's no hotel there."

"What about us?" asked Grooner.

"Us, Grooner? I doubt if they'll take us into the big house. It may be some shed littered with cow-pissed straw."

His colleagues gazed across at their smiling and chatting superiors. Young Doig was prominent among them, with his fair head held high. The girl seemed to be holding on to his arm.

"What age was Judas?" asked Rollo.

They were mystified.

"He was young," Rollo told them. "Why should an old man betray? He's got nothing to win but death."

Speer, hovering in the space between his men and the Sheriff's company, came closer to the former to whisper to them to keep quiet.

Rollo paid no heed. "The young fellow, Doig," he said, "what's he doing here?"

"Having a holiday," said Grooner.

"Didn't you read his speech?"

"You read it to me, Rollo."

"Then why is he here? Didn't he make out that in his opinion the putting out of the folk from Sollas was a disgrace to civilisation?"

"These students at their debates say anything," said Dand. "It's just for practice in speaking."

"He's going to be a lawyer like his uncle," put in Rickie.

Again Speer drew close.

"Will you shut your mouths?" he whispered.

"It's Rollo, sergeant," said Bull.

"It's the lot of you. You're chatting here as if you were on holiday." He came still closer. "You don't seem to realise this is a dangerous situation. There's been trouble here."

They had noticed the gates were shut, with two local policemen guarding them. Other local policemen were placed discreetly about the pier. The islanders on the hillside now and again let out a shout. The other passengers were off the steamer and out of the pier.

"It's touch and go," whispered Speer, and with a wink of caution he walked apart again.

"I meant to tell you, Bull," said Rollo, "something I read about the salmon of Sollas."

"To hell with you and the salmon on Sollas," muttered Bull.

"You'll be interested in this, Bull. They say that if you eat their flesh, while you're on the island, you're forever purged of lust."

The others chuckled at Bull's scowling.

Then they had to look alert for Speer was upon them again, importantly.

"All right, men," he said. "We're moving."

"High time," said Dand. "The sooner we get this finished with the better."

"Are they still sticking it out, sergeant?" asked Rickie.

Speer nodded. "They're still there. Mr. Limmer, he's the Fiscal here, thinks they're waiting for us to arrive. Then they'll go singing hymns and feeling grand for Jesus; you know the kind of thing?"

"I know the kind of thing, sergeant," said Creepe, in reproof.

"Are we going in the yacht, sergeant?" asked Bull.

"No. The Sheriff is. Maybe his two clerks too."

"What are they here for?" asked Grooner. "They're not needed."

"They've to carry the Sheriff's hat and bag," said Dand.

"I suppose it wouldn't do," said Rickie, "for the Sheriff just to have flatfeet to talk to."

During these whisperings Speer was lining them up. He wasn't sure whether he should march them or let them stroll along: the first might seem provocative, the second would offend his own punctilious soul.

The Sheriff and his company went out of the gate, with the two seamen from the yacht carrying his and his nephew's luggage. Nigg and Quorr carried their own. The local policemen walked in front, nodding to acquaintances among the islanders, who lined the side of the street where the houses and hotels were; the other side was open to the bay.

The sun shone as brightly as ever. On the steps of hotels and from their gardens people watched. The hedges were of fuchsia, with their flowers like drops of blood. Two girls in bathing-costumes, with towels thrown across their shoulders, swayed across the road ahead of the procession. A little boy banged the bottom of his pail with his spade. A dog barked in the distance. Another boy, with six tiny crabs running across his hand and up his sleeve, glanced up at this other spectacle on the road.

A crowd kept following. Now and then it flung a cry of hostility. No one hurried. The Sheriff was seen to be smiling. Nigg kept changing his case from one hand to the other;

always with the free hand he held on his hat, for there was still a fresh breeze off the water. Miss Vontin kept close to Doig; she was well known by sight in this town, and some of the cries were against her.

They halted at a jetty, to which were moored a large motor launch and a dinghy. Into the smaller boat stepped Miss Vontin, refusing the assistance of the sailors, but accepting that of Andrew Doig. Next came Andrew himself, who sat down in the stern beside her. She smiled and chatted, but he looked glum. To the anxious Bull it seemed the romance was not prospering as it should. Then the Sheriff was helped aboard and sat down in the bows, where he waved to the Fiscal and the others left on the jetty. The sailors took their places, an oar each, and began to row out to the yacht.

Cries that were not of goodwill followed them.

Speer gave the word, and one by one the clerks and police-men climbed aboard the launch, out of whose cabin just then for the first time appeared a little brown-faced man with a twisted nose. His appearance roused the crowd to loud anger.

"He hired his boat," explained the local police inspector to Speer. "He would hire it to carry his own children to their execution."

"Greedy for the money?" asked Speer.

"That, and for hate too. Nobody likes him. He thrives on it."

"It's a nice boat." Speer looked at it; its name was *Morning Star*.

"The boat's fine. You won't sink; though, mind you, if prayers were answered, I wouldn't think much of your chances of ever reaching Sollas."

"Who would answer prayers like that?" asked Speer, grin-ning, but his glance up at the radiant sky was a little clouded.

The Fiscal approached. "I think you should go now, sergeant," he said.

"Very good, sir." Speer saluted and walked smartly down the jetty.

"Good luck," he heard behind him.

Luck was as superstitious as prayer, he thought, as he made to step off the green slippery jetty into the boat. A particularly aggressive shout caused him to turn his head for a moment, time enough for him to receive full in his mouth a round chuckie or pebble, as white as teeth and much harder. Spluttering blood and curses of dismay, he staggered and would have fallen if some of his mates hadn't seized him and pulled him on board.

The Fiscal rushed down the jetty, shouting to the boatman to push off. On the roadway a struggle was going on between the local policemen and some islanders.

"I hope they massacre his guts," said Bull, grinding his teeth and brandishing his fists, which yearned to take part in that massacring. He did not love Speer any more than his mates did, but for him that stone hadn't just split the sergeant's lips and broken his tooth and bruised the point of his tongue; it had outraged the law; it was defiance from those whose function was submission.

The others had first-aid kit out and were cleaning the sergeant's mouth with cotton-wool soaked in antiseptic. He lay back on a seat to prevent the blood from soiling his uniform; he could not speak, but he could make moaning noises of rage and self-solicitude.

Grooner wielded the cotton-wool. Dand and Rickie helped. Creepe and Rollo gazed back at the land, where fighting seemed to be going on. They saw a helmet fly up like a football and splash into the sea; their own heads tingled with apprehension for the head thus denuded.

"I suppose," murmured Rollo, glancing aside at Speer, "we can consider ourselves lucky. In the old days if we had come up here on such a mission as ours they'd have gutted us like herring."

"Is this just the beginning?" asked Creepe, in a gloating tone.

"I think you'd enjoy it, Creepe," said Rollo, "if you had to bang a few heads."

"Some heads need banging for their own good."

"Put the fear of God into them, is that it? You and Bull, Creepe, are really on the same side of the fence."

Then the boatman, as he had been instructed, brought them alongside the yacht. The stone had been meant for him; it was not the first one that had missed; therefore his mouth, as it smiled, felt and looked full of ease and sweetness.

The Sheriff had been watching the fracas through binoculars. Quiet with anger, he leant over the rail.

"What happened, Mr. Quorr?" he called down.

"Some fool threw a stone, sir. It struck the sergeant."

Here the boatman giggled. "It was meant for me," he said, speaking to his boat, to the sky, to the sea, to the fish in the sea, but not, it seemed, to any human being.

His passengers glanced oddly at him.

"Is he badly hurt?" asked the Sheriff.

Quorr leant across. "Is he?" he whispered to Grooner.

"Bad enough."

"If he was down to give a recital of songs tomorrow," murmured Rollo, "he wouldn't manage."

"No, I see that." Quorr quickly removed his grin. "But it won't be fatal, I take it?"

"Hardly," said Grooner.

Quorr reported to the Sheriff. "It seems quite a nasty crack, sir."

"Should he see a doctor while we're here? There are none on Sollas. Are any, stitches needed?"

Again Quorr consulted Grooner. "See for yourself," muttered the latter.

Quorr did. The sergeant lay like a man dead, his eyes closed. The wound did not seem to Quorr so bad as to justify such prostration; he had seen a boy get worse in a playground fight.

"What about it, sergeant?" he asked. "How do you feel? The Sheriff wants to know."

Speer made a brave effort and opened his eyes.

"I never did anybody any harm in my life," he mumbled, through blood.

"I couldn't say as much myself," said Quorr. "Are you feeling all right? Do you think you'd like to see a doctor? For what it's worth, my opinion is no stitches are needed. The lips and tongue heal quickly."

Seeing the Sheriff, Speer's hand crept to his brow in piteous salute. Beside the Sheriff stood Miss Vontin and the young man who was the Sheriff's nephew; near them was the captain of the yacht, who did not seem to Speer as solemn as the occasion deserved.

Courageously he estimated the damage with a tongue as tender as a snail's horn.

"Is it just the one tooth?" he asked.

"Just the one," said Quorr cheerfully.

"How do I look?"

"Like a hero."

Speer remembered revenge. He twisted round and stared landward. "I was sorry for them," he said. "Now they can rot in hell."

"How do you feel, sergeant?" called the Sheriff.

"It's still a bit painful, sir."

"Yes, I can appreciate that. Do you feel able to proceed to Sollas?"

Speer nodded.

"Very well. Mr. Quorr, do you and Mr. Nigg wish to come aboard here?"

"I'll stay here, sir; but Mr. Nigg would like to travel with you. He's nervous about small boats."

Nigg, hitherto obscure, was too honest and fearful to deny

his fear. He allowed himself and his case to be hauled aboard the yacht.

"I understand we'll be in at Sollas pier shortly before you," said the Sheriff. "We'll wait there, in any case."

"Very good, sir."

Then they pushed off from the yacht and swinging round made out of the bay round the headland for the sea.

Quorr found Rollo seated beside him.

"Well, Rollo," he asked, "was it an omen?"

"You mean, of resistance? I hardly think so. The stone was for the boatman. He is a traitor; we are merely the enemy."

"Look at him smile," whispered Quorr. "You'd think he was ferrying us to hell."

"Like Charon?"

Quorr glanced up at the tall woods above them. They seemed strange; so did the very rocks on the shore, and the surf breaking upon them. "There are centaurs in those woods," he thought; and he saw those divine creatures, myth's masterpieces, go galloping across the hills, with their hoof-beats like music. Catching sight of Speer with the cotton-wool at his mouth, he fancied that it had not been a stone thrown by an angry aborigine that had done it, but rather a blow from one of those flashing hoofs.

There might well be other such blows.

Eight

THE FIRST thing Andrew had noticed when he had gone down
the gangway and crossed to meet Marguerite was the name
Argo on the two seamen's caps; one of them had it on his
jersey, too. Then he noticed her eyes, which in no way
squinted, but looked at him straight and candidly; they were
a very dark blue, and glowed rather than sparkled. She
greeted him with a kind of humour in her friendliness. Her
hand was soft, cool, and very steady. She was smaller than
he had remembered, but quite as formidable; in that guarded
place, with hostility poisoning the sunshine, she, at the very
centre, seemed the calmest and the most immune.

He glanced above her head at the people watching from
the hillside. Now and then one of them would shout.

"I'm sorry for bringing you here at this time," he said.

"Why?"

It seemed strange she should ask why. He could only smile.

"My father and I aren't ashamed of what we're doing,"
she said. "If we had been we'd have gone away till it was
over. But if I hadn't been coming for you I'd have come for
the Sheriff in any case. You see, he's to stay with us while
he's on Sollas. It's the only arrangement possible."

He was about to say that surely impartiality would suffer,
but somehow the jeer, which would have embellished a
platform speech, here in her smiling presence, with Sollas less
than an hour's sailing away, seemed puerile. Therefore he
was silent. Often he had maintained that castigators of injustice ought never to be muzzled; their fate was to be
reviled as bores, pests, cranks, and even boors. Those names

71

he had been frequently called. Here he seemed to be afraid of some other name, though what it was he could not say; all the time her gaiety hinted at it. He began to realise that he shouldn't have come; he should have stayed at home and drilled his principles.

He introduced her to the Sheriff. She introduced him to the Fiscal. They chatted about the weather, and about the journey from the city. To Andrew's surprise the Sheriff, who had not spoken to him on the train or boat, was as affable to him as he was courteous to her. Though there was no wink, and no outward sign at all, he had a feeling that his uncle was offering a truce, for the honour and furtherance of the family. After all, the seeing of the squatters off the island was a little matter soon over; this friendship with the Vontins was important and must be cultivated.

As they walked from the pier to the jetty, with all the holiday-makers watching from their hotels, and the local people, men, women, and children, following like one conglomerate waiting creature, Andrew wondered what he ought to do before it became too late to do anything but succumb. His sympathies were with these resentful people, yet he felt angry with them, for it seemed to him it was he whom they were really hounding, into a dark small cave of the mind, where his ideals lay like broken and disenchanted toys. Marguerite, on the contrary, as she walked by his side, touching him, seemed in mind as well as in body to be surrounded by sunshine.

By the time they reached the jetty he knew what he ought to do, but knew also that he would not do it: that was, to stop, apologise, say he could go no farther, take his case, and walk away. Whether she would look after him in amusement, annoyance, or disappointment, should make no difference. He would keep on walking, past little Nigg, past the big beefy young policeman, and so on till he reached these natives of Mula, to whom he would say nothing. Tomorrow he would return to the mainland and spend the rest of his holidays at his studies. He would not allow his mother to mention Sollas to him. Never again would he allow his eloquence to blow him into dangerous seas. He would, like all the rest, stay in the safe shallows. Jason Doig would have retired.

As he sat beside Marguerite in the stern of the dinghy, he could see that other self walk so forlornly away, and never had he felt such exasperated sorrow for any human being; indeed, he had an intimation of what many others, including his uncle, must often have felt about him.

So far he had hardly spoken a dozen words to her. Now, as the boat was rowed across to the yacht, he turned and faced seawards, past her ear with its tiny periwinkle of gold.

"Why did you ask me to come?" he whispered.

By contrast her voice was as cool as the water dripping from the oars.

"You wanted to, didn't you?"

"Yes." He had to admit it. "Yes."

"Well, that's as good a reason as any, isn't it?"

"Yes."

There the conversation ceased.

They had just reached the yacht when the disturbance broke out on shore. Climbing quickly aboard, they gazed through binoculars. The captain came to join them, lean, brown-skinned, with hands dexterous and sensitive: not only was he in appearance a likelier Jason, but he could also navigate a ship. He was very wary of Marguerite. The ordinary seamen, Andrew had noticed, were also deferential towards her. They had handled her from boat to yacht as if she was fragile; yet it was plain they thought her as tough as steel.

The Sheriff was provoked into an outburst that for him was sentimentality.

"In no other country in the world," he said, "would an enterprise such as ours have been carried out with such an exaggerated sense of decency. We have almost compromised the law in our wish to avoid even the faintest suspicion of persecution. This is our thanks. It would seem that leniency has its dangers, too."

Marguerite only smiled. Andrew was silent. Then the launch with the bleeding sergeant came alongside.

From Mula out to Sollas was about ten miles. There was time for Andrew to be shown round the yacht; the Sheriff declined, apparently wishing it to be remembered he was not there as a guest; Nigg, too, was content with being shown where he could lie down and recover from the sight of that sudden jelly-fish on Speer's mouth.

The yacht was magnificent; it no more deserved its noble name, in Andrew's opinion, than did what today was called Christianity. The original Argonauts had not known or wanted luxury. During the inspection that alacrity of the crew, in vanishing from her path with swiftest deference, was again noticeable. Never having been on a rich man's yacht before, with the rich man's daughter, Andrew could not say whether this relationship between the sailors and Marguerite was customary. He thought not: surely a little warmth could be shown towards those in whose keeping your very life was? To compensate he himself smiled, but no one smiled back.

She and he sat on deck behind an awning, drinking tea; again the Sheriff had declined to join them; Nigg had not been asked. It was served by a steward in a white jacket. The cups, sky-blue, had paintings of the yacht in white upon them. The teapot was of silver, shaped like a boat, with the spout its bowsprit.

It seemed there were no other guests at Sollas House.

"You mentioned there might be," said Andrew.

"Yes, but we thought it might be better to have the place to ourselves in the meantime. Spring-cleaning's not the time for visitors. In any case, my father isn't very fond of company."

Behind her dark glasses she smiled, so that he had a vision of her father sulking in the depths of the great house. He had noticed her rather heartless joke about spring-cleaning: he supposed she had meant that the dust and cobwebs being swept out were the squatters.

"Besides," she added coolly, "he isn't very well."

He murmured the usual condolence.

She laughed. "Oh, he's not as bad as that. It's nothing physical. In fact, Andrew, I'm looking to you to get him better."

"Me?"

"Yes, you. It's this business of these wretched people which has upset him."

He tried hard to look both credulous and sympathetic.

"I expect you think that's ridiculous," she said, "and so it is. But it's true all the same."

"I don't think it's ridiculous," said Andrew. "I'm surprised, that's all."

"Of course, you haven't met Donald McInver."

McInver was the squatters' leader or patriarch, a white-bearded visionary.

"My father's never been able to make up his mind whether Donald's a fraud or not."

"You have, though?"

"Right from the beginning. An old fraud, a sly-witted bigot, an old fool who wants to put the clock back a thousand years."

She was even more formidable than he had thought.

"Your father," he said, his voice trembling a little, "doesn't agree?"

"He does, most of the time. But there are other times when he becomes worried. If I was as superstitious as they are, I'd believe they put spells on him. They seem to spend a good part of the time in praying, and what's that but trying to put spells on people? These moods come on him so suddenly. He'll be walking in the garden, and stretching out his hand to pluck a flower; before he's plucked it down comes this mood. It's not a smiling matter."

Andrew had not been aware he was smiling.

"I'm sorry," he murmured.

"It's not just an ordinary depression," she said. "We all suffer from those."

"Do you, Marguerite?"

"Yes, I do."

Though she stared at him daring him to disbelieve, he found it very hard to look convinced. Yet what was he accusing her of? Perennial happiness and confidence?

"Is your father's trouble not just a simple case of conscience?" he asked. "I suppose it was him who finally made the decision?"

"As a matter of fact," she said, "it was me. *He* made the decision to offer them homes in Ross. I suppose you know he's spent thousands on building houses there?"

"Yes, I read about it."

"And he's offering them work in afforestation on our estate there."

"Yes, I read about that, too."

"What's he got to be worried about then?" she asked. "Isn't he doing them good?"

"By his standards, yes."

"By any intelligent standards. There's nothing for them on Sollas but poverty."

"Happiness and grace can grow out of poverty," he said. "They were poor men in Galilee two thousand years ago."

Before she could reply, while the distaste was still on her face, they were interrupted by a sailor who saluted.

"Captain's compliments, Miss Vontin," he said, "but he wants to know if you've noticed the cloud that's above Sollas Isle?"

She was astonished. "Is he joking?"

"No, Miss Vontin. It's a queer cloud. We've all been watching it."

"All right." Laughing she rose and walked to the side. Andrew followed her.

It wasn't necessary to ask what cloud the captain had meant. It was the only one in the sky, except for those massed round the horizons. Right above Sollas, now less than two miles away, it hovered like a great bird with its wings outspread. Those wings, rimmed with dazzling brightness, were serrated at the edges; the head, with long sharp beak, was pointing to the earth. It was like a gigantic gannet diving.

The captain joined them.

"It's the best I've ever seen," he said. "I thought you'd like to see it."

"Yes, thank you," she said. She had taken off her dark glasses.

"Like a gannet," he said.

"Yes."

The three of them glanced from the immense bird suspended high in the air to the blue lively waters above which real gannets were flying; they saw at least three go plummeting down, with splashes. When they looked up again there it was, even larger; the breeze in their ears was like the wind of its descent.

"Uncanny," said the captain.

"Do you think so?" she asked. "When I was a child I was always seeing animals in the sky: elephants, kangaroos, giraffes. I'm sure you were too, Andrew?"

"I suppose so."

"Likely it's not over Sollas at all," she said. "It's really miles away."

"Likely enough," agreed the captain. "But from here it looks like it."

"There it goes," she said, with relief as well as triumph in her voice.

The neck was thinning to nothing, soon the head was separated from the body. The wings disintegrated, became wisps of cloud. In another minute there was no resemblance to anything.

"Strange," said the captain, and walked away, smiling.

Andrew looked back and saw the motor launch following them. He wondered if those in it had seen that wonderful bird. Then, apocalyptically, as if he had been until that moment blind, he became aware of the beauty of the scene around him: the blue sea, the plunging gannets, the little launch, the mountains of Mula, the pink cloud castles on the horizons, and Sollas coming close with its high red cliffs, its green hills, and its bays of tawny sand. It was like a glimpse of the earth unencumbered by conscience; purity and joy were in every sight and sound. That fantastic bird had been responsible; in that way, if in no other, it had been divine.

Beside him he became aware of Marguerite, clutching the rail with both hands. Her hair, blacker than night, moved in the breeze, and it made him remember that other beauty, alien, mysterious, and incommunicable, which lay at the bottom of the sea.

Nine

THE PIER on Sollas was in a little rocky bay. Not far back,
screened partly by spruce trees and evergreen shrubs which
grew in a sloping field of bright turf, stood the great house
built of stone as red as the rocks. Its garden stretched down
to the sea, for the rocks were covered with tangle, pink thrift,
and tall sea-daisies; and the sea itself at the edge was a pellucid
green through which shells on the sandy bottom glittered.

As the yacht glided in cautiously, there could be seen
approaching the pier from the house two men, one small,
walking with short steps, and the other much taller, pacing
with long, slow stride.

Marguerite began to wave, and Andrew saw it was the
smaller of the two men who waved back. It was a curiously
restricted gesture for all its enthusiasm, due, it seemed, to the
shortness of his arms. His companion did not wave; he was
obviously a subordinate. He was, Marguerite explained, the
grieve who managed the island and took care of the house
when its owners weren't at home. When the squatters had
moved in Cloud had been in hospital going through an
operation. Even God, she said, waited for opportunities.

She was first off. Racing to her father, she kissed him on
the cheek. Andrew, close behind, saw she was the taller of
the two; as for himself, when she called him forward to
introduce him, he felt embarrassed at his advantage in height,
which, added to the shortness of Mr. Vontin's fingers, made
the shaking of hands a little awkward, especially as all the
condescension was on the part of the smaller man. Nor did
it help Andrew to feel at ease, remembering how in his

University speech he had insulted this little man, now his host, by calling him an octopus with long tentacles.

Apart from his smallness, Mr. Vontin's appearance suited his part as despot of the island. His head was large in proportion to his body and bald save for some white hair at the sides. That baldness, strangely pale for one master of so sunny a domain, seemed to extend all over his face, which looked not so much well-shaven as never to have needed shaving at all; this, and his long fine nose, large pale-blue eyes, and full well-carved lips, gave him a resemblance to the Roman Emperors, pictures of whose busts had illustrated Andrew's Latin text-books.

He gave Andrew a smile which, though small in scope, seemed to be the maximum for strangers; the one the Sheriff got was smaller still; and Nigg, who at long last held his hat in his hand in a sort of surrender, got none at all. It was during that shaking of hands with the Sheriff, so brief as to be contemptuous, that Andrew caught the likeness between father and daughter, and saw a vision of them as king and princess scheming, alone in this palace on the lonely island, how to bring upon the expulsion of the trespassers, who were protected by God.

He introduced his grieve, Cloud, as ruddy as he himself was pale. It seemed to Andrew that not only must the operation have been wholly successful, but also that the subsequent commotion over the squatters had made for an excellent convalescence. Certainly Cloud, behind his pug nose and small eyes, seemed to have some happy secret, which peeped out in smiles that had no noticeable outward cause: obsequiousness on such a face would have been shiftier.

They waited for the launch to arrive; it could be seen entering the bay. Mr. Vontin bantered Andrew.

"So you are Jason?" he asked.

Andrew glanced at the yacht and then up at the great house.

"A Jason, sir," he replied, "who doesn't know what the Golden Fleece is he has come for."

"I understood, Andrew, it was for the true soul of man."

The amiable sarcasm was chuckled at by the Sheriff; even Nigg smiled, sadly.

"That might be it, sir," said Andrew. "Are we not looking for that all the time?"

"Are we?" repeated Mr. Vontin.

Again the Sheriff chuckled.

"Shall I find it here, sir?" asked Andrew.

"Why not, if you know where to look? The whole island is open to search." He waved his short arm. "One advantage is that there is no dragon with a hundred heads."

"I thought, sir, today the dragon has a million, ten million, heads."

"Do you anticipate having to strike them all off?"

"That," interposed the Sheriff, "does sum up Andrew's ambition very fairly."

The two little men laughed. Andrew saw a gull's wing glint in the sky, and for a moment wished he too had a sword to strike down in the one the arrogance of wealth, and in the other the cynicism of experience. Beside him Marguerite smiled, representing, for all her beauty, the sly and corrosive patience of women.

Then upon the pier clambered the policemen and Quorr. Speer led them. With gentle commands he lined them up.

Accompanied by the Sheriff, Mr. Vontin approached them.

"Welcome to Sollas," he said. "I'm sorry you had to be dragged all this distance from your homes. While you're here you must try to make your visit as enjoyable as possible under the circumstances. My grieve, Mr. Cloud, has got quarters ready for you in his house. It may be irregular, but while you're here I want you to regard yourselves as my guests. Tomorrow I've given permission for some newspaper reporters to come over from Mula; but tonight we'll have the place to ourselves. If there's anything in particular you'd like to do, just mention it. For those of you who are keen on billiards there's a good table up at the house, and I'd be pleased to see you there after you've had a wash-up and a meal."

Speer thanked him on their behalf. Seldom was gratitude so valiantly and tenderly expressed.

Mr. Vontin stared at him. "What happened to your mouth, sergeant?" he asked.

It was the Sheriff who explained, without passion.

Mr. Vontin, also without much passion, was indignant.

"I hope the fool who did it is now in jail," he said.

"I am sure of it," replied the Sheriff. "The authorities on Mula are fully aware that softness at this juncture might well be dangerous."

Then the boatman from Mula sneaked into the circle.

"They are talking about crossing in the dark," he muttered.

They stared at him; cringing, he enjoyed their astonishment and disgust.

"For what purpose?" asked the Sheriff.

"Just to make trouble. They said they should burn down the big house."

That was received with some alarm. Speer, indeed, touched his mouth as if it was a medal won in the first engagement.

Mr. Vontin laughed. "The threats of children," he said. "They would not burn down a rick of straw."

"Their ancestors," said Rollo, touching his helmet in apology for intruding, "once burnt down a church with a hundred and fifty-three people in it. I read that in a book coming up in the train. Maybe it would be as well, sir, if we mounted a guard."

"There was a moon last night," said Mr. Vontin. "There will be one tonight. A reivers' moon? Is that what they called it?"

"Did you see the gannet, father?" asked Marguerite. "Perhaps it was a warning. Do you think it could have been a warning, Andrew?"

"What gannet?" asked her father.

"A cloud shaped like one; enormous. It seemed to be diving upon Sollas."

The policeman nodded; they had seen it from the launch.

"I hope none of you is superstitious," said Mr. Vontin, laughing.

"No, sir."

Bull's was the most emphatic assurance. So far he hadn't managed to catch the eye of this puissant manikin. To Bull that smallness was mystical: this was how it should be, the brains in so tiny and weak a body, the brawn in himself: it was a partnership to run the world. If only, he thought, they would come across that night in their boats and land in the moonlight; in their repulse, who more enterprising than he?

Mr. Vontin was gazing at him.

"You're very young, constable," he said.

"Twenty-two, sir."

Mr. Vontin turned to the sergeant. "Isn't that rather young for a mission like this?"

"Bull—I beg your pardon, sir—Constable Dykes is highly thought of at headquarters."

"Bull?" Mr. Vontin was amused.

"A nickname, sir."

"Yes, I can see that. Very well then, sergeant, if you go with Mr. Cloud he'll see you settled in."

"Very good, sir." Speer saluted. "Right, men." He was about to march them off after Cloud when the latter suddenly stopped, pointed, and stood pointing, like a man hypnotised.

Everyone looked. Coming towards the pier, along the rocky shore, was a small pony, on which sat a long old man with a white beard and bare head; his feet almost touched the ground. Beside the pony walked a girl of about eighteen, with the sun gleaming on her yellow hair. With one hand she held on to the pony's mane, and in the other she carried flowers.

"McInver himself," whispered Mr. Vontin, "and his grand-daughter."

As they waited in silence on the pier the click of the pony's hoofs could be heard, and the piping of some sea-birds that flew over the water. The boatman from Mula, showing his teeth like a dog in a presence it does not understand, retreated behind the policeman and disappeared down the iron ladder back into his boat. On the yacht one of the seamen sank down on his knees, but was hauled up again by a mate lest that disloyal debasement should be seen by their employer.

Cloud, as if in his capacity of overseer on the island, walked a little way to meet the newcomers; but when they reached him, instead of his challenging them as to their intentions, and forbidding them to come any farther, he suddenly lowered his head, in a homage that took most of the onlookers by surprise. Still more astonishing was the action of the old man who, without halting his pony, raised his right hand in what he evidently considered a blessing. The girl smiled shyly. As they passed on Cloud remained where he had been blessed, his head still bowed, his whole body expressing some kind of acquiescence.

Mr. Vontin and the Sheriff stood in the forefront, with Marguerite and Andrew behind them.

The pony halted so close to the Sheriff that he could have put out his hand and parted the shaggy hair from its eyes. Though unsure of animals, he did not flinch or withdraw.

The old man wore the ordinary rough tweeds of a crofter, with a flannel shirt minus a collar. His white hair blew about his face, which was as brown and smooth as seaweed. His long neck was very thin, and his eyes, green and deep, glittered with a strange humour. While he sat there, in meditation or dwam, his granddaughter, dressed in blue and white, with her legs bare, stood smiling. Her yellow hair hung in two long plaits down her back. The flowers in her hand, wild from the machair, blue and yellow and red, had the same

kind of indigenous loveliness as herself. She smiled at everyone, at Mr. Vontin, at Marguerite, at the Sheriff, at the policemen, even at Bull.

Then her grandfather raised his right hand and spoke in a
voice so strong and confident it startled not only his human
listeners but also some gulls which had settled on the pier
during the silence.

"I am here to welcome you," he cried, "in the name of
God and of his faithful servant St. Solla, whose island this is."

The Sheriff glanced aside at Mr. Vontin, who, to his surprise, seemed not only impressed but even overawed. Instead
of denouncing that absurd usurpation, he lowered his head as
his grieve had done. Glancing about him, the Sheriff saw, to
his further astonishment, that two of the policemen had
removed their helmets, apparently in deference to this old
fanatic's misuse of sacred words.

Then the girl stepped forward and handed him the flowers.
He could not avoid taking them and stood with them in his
grasp for a few seconds before turning and handing them to
Andrew who happened to be nearest. Some fell during the
exchange.

Then the Sheriff turned to do his duty. Resolutely he
stared into those green eyes.

"You are Donald McInver?" he asked, in a voice as devoted
as McInver's own.

"Men call me by that name." It was as if he had another,
which powers higher than human used.

"You know who I am?" demanded the Sheriff.

The old man gazed, and then slowly shook his head; at
the same time he seemed to smile.

"I do not know you," he replied. "How can anyone know
you when you wilfully hide yourself from God?"

The Sheriff hesitated and frowned.

"You know very well I am here in my capacity as Sheriff,"
he said, "and as such bear certain powers. Some weeks ago

you and your fellows received court orders to quit this island. You have not obeyed, and so it has fallen to me to come here and see that the law is observed. That I intend to do. No other consideration enters into it. You will return to your fellows and inform them that I shall pay them a visit tomorrow morning, to explain as clearly as I can why I am here. Tomorrow the boat calls to take you and your effects off. Where you go is of course your own affair, but you know that a place has been prepared for you and is still available; the boat will take you there, if that is your desire. However that may be, I must warn you, as the obvious leader and counsellor of these people, that disobedience on their part will inevitably mean enforcement and possible arrest. You will be doing them a service therefore by advising them to make immediate preparations for a departure which must take place."

After he had spoken there was another silence; indeed, while he was speaking it had seemed to himself, as well as to the others, that really he had no more broken the silence than had the cries of gulls or the snorting of the pony. That silence belonged to the old man; only he could break it.

He did not break it. Instead he held out his left hand; in it was an object wrapped in a frond of bracken.

The Sheriff did not want to take it. Obviously he regarded not only the gift itself, but the circumstances of the giving, as foolish and demeaning. His reluctance was plain to everybody. McInver did not coax; he did not even speak; he just kept holding out his hand. It was like a patient adult persevering with a huffy child.

The Sheriff took it, trying to make the acceptance seem like a well-mannered humouring of a dotard, but not succeeding: compulsion was obvious. Unwrapping the bracken, he revealed a piece of stone about the right size for a boy to try how far he could throw into the sea.

It was an ordinary stone, grey with lichen. The Sheriff

passed it from one hand to the other, like a child with a toy whose purpose eludes him. He glanced round at his companions, with a frown that seemed to ask them to forgive him in his bewilderment and betrayal. He showed them the stone as if to demonstrate its ordinariness and so his own folly.

From the offering to the accepting only half a minute passed; yet to all of them, except one, time shone and expanded like the sea.

The exception was Marguerite. She stepped forward, took the stone from the Sheriff, and holding it as if it was as repugnant as a squashed frog, walked to the side of the pier and dropped it into the sea.

It was as if a spell was broken. Her father immediately took the Sheriff by the arm and hurried him away.

Speer marched off his men. As they passed the girl Bull halted for a moment, bent to pick up the few flowers lying on the planks, and handed them to her. Then, his face redder than usual, he hurried after his mates.

Quorr lingered to fondle the pony, and then he, too, with Nigg close behind, left the pier.

Only Andrew and Marguerite remained. She addressed McInver out of whom confidence seemed to have gone with the throwing away of the stone. Now he sat and gazed at her as if, recognising her wickedness, he now lacked force to rebuke it. His mouth worked senilely.

"You have no right to be here," she said. "I don't know whether you understand what the Sheriff said." She turned to the girl. "If he didn't I'm sure you did."

The girl nodded.

"Then you tell the others," said Marguerite. "Though it's likely enough they already know." She turned to Andrew. "They'll be watching. It's a habit they've got. They don't want to live here, they want to haunt the place. Come on."

When he still stood, gazing at the old man, she stepped towards him, pulled the flowers out of his hand, and flung them down.

"I'm going anyway," she said, and went.

He did not immediately follow. He did not even look after her. She halted at the end of the pier to watch what he did.

Here then were the actual people whom hitherto he had seen only as abstractions. Now he could see, hear, and even smell them, for the girl was fragrant with flowers and the old man with peat. He could see a wart at the side of the old man's mouth, a splash of dried cow dung on the girl's leg; he could hear their breathing, the old man's harsh, hers gentle. He could even touch them if he wished. But he could not speak to them. No words would form in his mind. It did not even occur to him to ask what the stone had signified; far less did he think of offering his sympathy.

When he at last left them he felt that that silence must enforce another upon him, as a penance for all his previous prideful verbosity, and this would not be lifted while he remained on this island, and perhaps might never be lifted at all. The Golden Fleece was indeed the true soul of man; but he knew now that though it was to be found within himself, it would take a whole lifetime of searching, with this revelation on Sollas as just one stage. In the end he might still never have found it; he might die with the glory undiscovered.

Ten

AT DINNER that evening only Marguerite was cheerful. She came down to it in a magnificent sea-green gown, armless and low-bosomed. Upon her black hair she wore a head-dress of blacker velvet with pearls resembling tentacles that curled towards her ears and temples. Round her wrists twined bangles like silver eels. Her mouth was the colour of sea anemones, and she had spent much time in intensifying the sub-aqueous darkness of her gaze.

Dinner was served in a large room so sepulchrally lit, in dim red, that eating became for Mr. Nigg at least unavoidably like a ritual; so he confessed to Andrew who sat beside him. He was halfway through his potatoes before he realised they were indeed the humble and innocent vegetables he grew with such pleasure in his garden at home. On the walls, panelled in dark wood, hung paintings in bright yellow frames: they were really imaginative representations of the contortions seen in nature as in the human mind, but were very like, as Quorr had muttered, pages cut out of a medical textbook on the alimentary canal. The table, too, was arrayed like an altar, with snowy cloth, silverware, and red roses. On the floor was a dark-red carpet with designs in gold like fetish emblems. It would have been difficult for Mr. Nigg to enjoy his favourite dish of fried haddock and crisp chips in that room, alone; as it was, feeling himself to be the most menial acolyte, and over-whelmed all the time by the beautiful sea-priestess at the bottom of the table, he ate with tongue numbed, jaws semi-paralysed, and stomach writhing like the red and green submarine growths in the painting immediately in front of his eyes.

The stone which she had flung into the sea had been a fragment from the famous Sanctuary Stone in the north of the island. She had given it to the sea which she was now dressed to honour. As he watched her, Nigg remembered his own wife, Mirren, and her strange command to gather those seashells. Women were like the sea, deep, remorseless, mysterious, and insatiable. He had a fear of drowning. Had not his marriage been a long marooning? He shivered at the thought.

The Sheriff was taciturn. He had not attempted, even to himself, an explanation for his minute of seduction at the pier; nor had anyone asked him.

During the meal it seemed that Marguerite's every smile, every twist of her head, every gesture of her hands, were to remind them all of their collapse into superstition, and of her sole immunity. When she began to speak about it, she did so with sly obliquity.

"Would you think," she asked, "looking at him now, that when Cloud was sent home from hospital he was told he was incurable?"

"Marguerite, please." It was her father who protested.

Hunched at the top of the table in a dark jacket with long white cuffs, he had with difficulty been making conversation without any reference to the business which had brought them to the island. Obvious to everyone was, at the foot of that steep cliff of affability, the deep dark pool of melancholy.

Marguerite laughed. "Don't be alarmed, father," she said. "I'm not going to recite all the grisly details, though Mrs. Cloud has so often boasted to me about them that I could rhyme them off as well as she."

"Boasting is not the right word, surely."

"Yes, it is. Sorrowful boasting, but boasting all the same. I read once that nowadays people are so starved of the love of God that they welcome even His tribulations. Do you agree with that, Andrew?"

"It sounds glib to me," he answered meekly.

"Glib or not," she said, "it was true in Mrs. Cloud's case. She seemed to think her husband was chosen in some curious way just because he'd been stricken with this illness that human skill couldn't cure."

Her father made as if to reprove her for persisting with so unappetising a subject, but seeing that his guests were interested, he kept quiet and tried to smile.

"It's different now," said Marguerite. "She won't talk about it now. Even if one asks she won't."

"I must confess," said the Sheriff, "that Mr. Cloud looked very well to me; in fact, he seemed to have a curious buoyancy."

"Did you notice that?" asked Mr. Vontin.

"Yes, indeed," replied the Sheriff, and the other three guests nodded in agreement.

Mr. Vontin nodded too.

"I have heard," added the Sheriff, "that people under such a sentence frequently show such remarkable contentment. I do not know the reason, but that it happens is perhaps comforting."

There was a short silence. During it Marguerite looked ready to speak.

"Cloud is now cured," she said.

The Sheriff and the others paused in their chewing.

"He now feels better than he has ever done in his life before."

"I believe," said the Sheriff, solemnly, "that is also a symptom of those doomed. Their hopefulness shames all those with better reason to hope."

"That's my belief," said Mr. Vontin eagerly. "It's just an illusion. Poor Cloud will go—just like that!" And he flicked the top of his thumb against the top of his forefinger with hardly force enough to have dislodged a fly.

"But, father, you know you've had him examined yourself."

"Yes, yes. But there could have been a mistake in the original diagnosis."

She took pity on her puzzled guests.

"You see," she said, "Cloud claims he was cured here, on Sollas. How? By prayer on his knees, at the Sanctuary Stone."

"You mean, miraculously?" asked the Sheriff, with driest scepticism.

She nodded.

"I haven't known Cloud for so very long," said her father, "about a year or so, but up to a short time ago I would have said there was no man in the country with a harder head."

"Not to mention a harder heart," murmured Marguerite.

"No," said her father. "Let's be fair to the man. He hadn't any harder a heart than the rest of us. He just thought"— he paused—"that it would be best for everybody if they were cleared out. That was his opinion, and nobody knows the island better than Cloud. He's been living here for ten years."

The Sheriff smiled. "I'm afraid I don't quite understand," he said. "Is the position this: Cloud as grieve here advocated eviction, but in spite of that was shown this peculiar grace?"

Mr. Vontin nodded; he too smiled, but like a man haunted.

Nigg could not keep quiet. He addressed Marguerite.

"Are we to understand, Miss Vontin," he said, in his most piping voice, "that faith, religious faith, was responsible for this cure?"

She leant her elbows on the table in a way Nigg had often been scolded for as a boy fifty years ago. She stretched forward, so that the sinister sea-thing in pearls on her head twinkled, and her bosom could be peeped into, if one looked; and somehow one was compelled to look.

"Cloud thinks so," she said. "So does Donald McInver, of course."

"This was not reported in the newspapers," said Nigg.

"No, it wasn't."

"All I can say is," he said, with a little snigger, "it's extraordinary."

"It is that," said Mr. Vontin. "There's no getting away from it. Three months ago Cloud was ill, ghastly ill. I thought of him as a dead man. I pitied him as such. I had provision made for Mrs. Cloud."

"And is it completely certain he is now cured?" asked the Sheriff.

"I had experts here to examine him. There was no doubt in their minds. Cloud's cured."

"What explanation did they give?"

"They couldn't give any. They said such things had happened before: science doesn't know everything, and that sort of thing. Of course, they were as baffled as we are. They didn't laugh when I suggested it amounted to a miracle. They just said that was as good a name as any. These are men, mind you, at the very peak of their profession. And they said too that praying beside a big rock on the edge of the sea was as good an explanation as any. I may say it made me wonder for a while if I was doing the right thing after all."

"Did this curious . . . coincidence," asked the Sheriff, "have any effect on Mr. Cloud's attitude?"

"Well, in a way it did. I think the poor fellow was terrified that whatever it was that had happened might be revoked. An understandable fear."

"Quite," said the Sheriff.

"But he's never tried to influence me, if that's what you mean. Cloud knows his place too well for that; he's been a grieve for over twenty years, a good part of the time to nobility. But he hasn't needed to say anything. He's just walked about like a man resurrected. For a while it was uncanny to see him. You've hit on the solution of course, Sheriff: coincidence. But all the same it's been very awkward in the circumstances."

"I can appreciate that, Mr. Vontin," said the Sheriff.

There was a pause while each of them appreciated that awkwardness.

"If it ever got into the newspapers, sir," said Quorr, "you'd never get rid of trespassers. They'd come in shoals."

"Yes, we thought of that."

"Looking for cures," added Quorr, laughing. "What about you, Mr. Nigg. You're martyred by rheumatism. Isn't it worth a trial? What would there be to lose?"

"Only one's self-respect," said the Sheriff. "I do not know the explanation of what happened to Mr. Cloud. But I do know it had nothing to do with any magical efficacy attached to any stone." They noticed how his assurance, begun so fiercely, wilted a little as he, and they, remembered how he had been mesmerised by the fragment offered him on the pier. "Religion is mocked by such simplification. For my part," he went on, with pants of horror, "I cannot think of anything more blasphemous than my visiting that stone and kneeling down by it, in the hope of some miraculous deliverance. I should indeed have a revelation: it would be of my own miserable conceit and personal puniness." He glanced sharply at his nephew as if to catch on the latter's face a sneer indicating that such a revelation would in itself make the Sheriff's kneeling worth while. But Andrew wore no such sneer.

"I agree entirely," said Mr. Vontin. "I would not for a million pounds kneel by that stone, even if only the sea-gulls were to see me. In fact, when this business is over, I intend to have it split up and flung into the sea."

Nigg giggled nervously. "I agree too," he said. "But for the sake of argument could not what happened once happen again, even if it was only additional coincidence?"

Marguerite had been enjoying the discussion.

"What do *you* think, Andrew?" she asked.

He shook his head. "I don't know. I suppose it was coincidence."

"I thought you would be far more enthusiastic than that. Perhaps what you came here to find is to be found by the Stone; only you must ask, kneeling."

"Yes, Andrew," said his uncle, with a flash of bitter humour, "perhaps in your case it would be efficacious."

"You mean, sir, because of your revelation?"

"Yes, indeed."

"I had it at the pier. It does not need to be repeated, at any rate not so soon."

Marguerite being contented with that reply, and no one else having anything more to say, there was silence till the end of the meal.

Later that evening she came into the lounge, wearing a white shawl over her shoulders, and invited Andrew to go for a stroll with her. The sun was about to set, she said; she would show him the lily pond, where the lilies were as red as blood; there would be danger only from midges. To coax him she took his hand and pulled him to his feet.

As he went out he noticed Quorr give him a grin of commiseration and warning. Nigg had crept off to bed. Mr. Vontin had excused himself to welcome some of the policemen who had accepted his invitation to play billiards. The Sheriff was engrossed in papers; he gave the impression, as he busily wrote, that that affair of Cloud's must be at once communicated to Authority, so that that giant whom he served might immediately annul it.

Still holding his hand, Marguerite led Andrew between the great pillars, down the steps, across the drive of fine Sollas sea-grit, on to the turf, and so into the maze of tall rhododendrons with their blaze of blooms, where many bees buzzed. Mingled with the scents of the evening, from tangle and many flowers unseen, was that of Marguerite herself. In the house Andrew had noticed it, with the not-so-sweet reflection that a phial of it, not an inch high, would cost as much as would keep a crofter's family for a week. Now in the sunset, amidst other fragrances, he became disturbed by it, almost agitated.

At table, listening to her and watching her closely, he had concluded that her influence, her magic, lay in her consciousness of great wealth. Contemporaneous with the first god, at a time earlier even than Jason, had been this other deity of money. The heir, of every rival's prestige and power, its position in the hierarchy today had become supreme, although it was always careful to appear to be contented with a secondary place. She was its priestess, its Medea, born noble into the cult, and from that circumstance, rather than from any accidental qualities of loveliness or intelligence or courageous ruthlessness, sprang that power to fascinate which had overcome even the Sheriff. But now, under the reddening sky melodious with larksong, he saw her differently, in a way he had never before seen any woman. Morality being absent from that vision, his mind felt strangely naked, and so supersensitive to the beauty of the evening.

As they went through the garden he muttered inarticulate praises, but she kept promising him that the most lovely place in it, indeed in the whole island, was the lily pond, in which crimson, yellow, and orange water-lilies grew, and from which could be had a view of the sea westward, glorious at this time of sunset.

Near the pond they heard voices, and themselves became silent. He asked with a look who these interlopers could be, she replied likewise that she did not know. They smiled at each other, like conspirators, clutched hands still more tightly, and passing some sitka spruces, tall sentinels in their blue and green uniforms, came upon the terrace where the pond was.

Never was a glance briefer; yet during it Andrew saw, in addition to the principals, red water-lilies, two stone fishes green with slime, the sky crimson with sunset, and the sea then most vividly a symbol of cleansing. The principals were the young policeman whom the others called Bull, and one of the maids from the house. It occurred to Andrew that they could not have known each other very long to be so occupied; and at that point morality revived, not so much in him as in the policeman, whose face, like a lesser sun, swelled with astonishment, apology, and penitence.

Then they hurried away, without speaking, no longer holding hands, and yet carrying between them a silence as fragile as a bubble and more binding than a chain of steel.

Eleven

BULL HAD been inveigled.

When he had made up on his colleagues after stopping to pick up the flowers for the girl with yellow hair, he had been shocked by Creepe, who had whispered: "She should be cheap enough, Bull; a poke of sweeties, that's all."

Religion had nothing to do with Bull's being shocked. Unlike Grooner and Dand, who had taken off their helmets, he had not been affected by the old boy's cunning guff about God; but from his first sight of the girl he had been hustled into thoughts of innocence. Fair-haired, sweet-faced, guileless and virginal, with soft swelling bosom and legs as strong as they were graceful, she was the girl he had dreamed about, whose image he had cherished for years, and whom he had described to a bored Grooner on many a midnight beat. Such a girl would be his wife, so that his honour as a husband, and his potency as a begetter, would never be endangered. She would be pure and fertile; and his offspring, with her as their mother, would be handsome, healthy, and above all sane. For this horror, of siring an imbecile, had vexed Bull for a long time. Here then was his guarantee of bliss, pride, and safety.

"You mind your own business, Creepe," he said, with dignity, "and I'll mind mine."

Then he remembered with some indignation that the religious talk on the pier ought to have been Creepe's business. He should now be walking like a man who had had a feed of God. Yet here he was uttering unnecessary filth, and on the pier all the time that Grooner and Dand had had their

helmets in their hands he had kept moaning to them: "Fools!"
It had always been Bull's opinion, sincerely arrived at, after
much pondering and observation, that Creepe was a hypo-
crite. Now it was proved once and for all.

It was proved again in Cloud the grieve's house when they
were seated at table ready to start dinner. Cloud asked if
any of them objected to grace. None did. But Creepe at once
volunteered to say it, and chose one that lasted three minutes.
Long before it was done Bull had his eyes open again, so that
he saw peeping into the room the face of Bridie, a maid
sent over from the big house to help with the serving of the
meal. He had already seen her face, and had diagnosed the
tight expression on it: she was starving, but not for food.
Now here she was winking an appeal at him, in the midst
of Creepe's dreary loud grace.

It was a dinner good enough to satisfy Rollo for quality
and Bull for amount. At a hint from their host the conversation kept off their business on the island. But what was talked
about Bull afterwards couldn't have said, he was too much
taken up with the problem of Bridie.

Not only did her looks become hotter, she kept making
opportunities to nudge against him. Deliberately, causing a
laugh at which she did not blush, though Bull did, she gave
him the biggest steak. His own lust was of course her best
advocate. Though she was about ten years older, and had the
threats of bags under her eyes, she was in every other way
enticing, and had about her a suggestion of amorous enterprise
and vigour. If he had not seen the yellow-haired Sheila, he
would not have hesitated, but would have let her know that
her appeal would be granted, her hunger appeased, the bags
under her eyes kept at bay a little while longer. He had,
however, seen Sheila, and was for the first time in his recollection snagged by scruple.

The others decided to accept Mr. Vontin's offer of billiards;
besides, they were curious to see inside the house. Bull did

not play billiards well; he wielded a cue, so he had been told, as if he was holding it in the crook of his tail. Thus he considered skill at the game a sign of effeminacy, an opinion corroborated by the prowess of Grooner.

He lingered after they were gone, standing outside the door in the lovely scented garden, and listening to their laughter as they walked down the road. It galled him that they were probably laughing at him; before leaving they had twitted him about Bridie; a godsend, Rollo had called her. But Creepe had privately whispered it was a pity she hadn't yellow hair.

Not only was Bridie's hair black, it had even a touch of grey in it. He remembered his bragging in the duty-room that on the island he, too, as well as Rollo would angle, but here it looked as if he himself might be the victim, the fish, hooked by someone else's desire. It was a new experience, and as such attractive; but there was the risk of humiliation; and there was, of course, the shaming of himself in the eyes of Sheila.

Cloud joined him in the garden. Bull was scratching his neck.

"Midges bad?" asked the grieve, smiling.

"Bad enough."

Cloud brought his face close to Bull's.

"You're a young man," he said.

That was true, gloriously true: at that moment Bull felt his youth illimitable; he would never grow old, he would live forever. Against the background of that virile immortality this affair with Bridie was as unimportant as the death of a midge.

"Young enough," he replied, grinning.

"I want to tell you something," said Cloud. "You look as strong as a bull. That's what they call you, isn't it?"

"I let them," said Bull.

"A bull's a magnificent animal," said Cloud. "But that's not what I want to tell you. It's something I don't care to talk to everybody about; but you're young, the future's in your hands."

Bull glanced at those hands; to do it he had to bring one of them down from his ear where it was scratching. He saw the future in them: promotion, a wife like Sheila, children, a house with five rooms, mountains of good food, many brave arrests.

"Three months ago," whispered Cloud, "I was given up for dead."

Bull scowled at that unlucky word, which could shatter even the glory of youth. Cloud was looking up at the sky with the most peculiar conceit Bull had ever seen on a human face; yet it was the face of a man of sixty who had no children and whose wife was small, fat, cross, and past loving.

Then Cloud placed a hand on his own stomach as gently as Bull would have placed his on Sheila's.

"In there," said the grieve, "I had a rat, chewing my guts to bits."

That pride revolted Bull; next to insanity he hated and feared disease.

"I spewed up blood," said Cloud. "I wanted to die quick. My wife thought of getting stuff to put an end to my agony."

"You look all right now," said Bull, with sullen suspicion.

"I never felt better in my life."

"Was it an operation?"

"I had two; no good."

"They've got wonderful drugs nowadays," said Bull.

Cloud shook his head. "Every one of them was tried," he said. "No good. I came back here to die. They would have let me die in the hospital, out of pity, but I came back here. I had a feeling in me like a skylark in a cage: that feeling was just to get back here before I died."

Bull nodded: he himself would have preferred the hospital

where there would have been drugs to deaden the pain at least; but he had once been told by Rollo that in the Antarctic were sea-lions that climbed to a hill to die in loneliness. Without any humour he looked again at Cloud, and saw in those small eyes a resemblance to a sea-lion's: only the whiskers were missing. But Cloud, sea-lion or man, was not dead; his bones were not lying at Bull's feet; he was upright, with that strange conceit still glittering in his eyes.

"I don't get it," said Bull peevishly. "You look all right to me."

"Never felt better."

"You said that. Well, what happened? Did it just get better by itself?"

Cloud gazed at him. As he did so an owl hooted from some trees behind them. Bull shuddered: the owl was the bird of night, he had never yet made love while it was hooting.

"That's right," said Cloud, "it got better by itself."

"Doctors don't know everything," muttered Bull.

As he spoke he caught sight of Bridie at a window upstairs. She had her coat on and was making signs. But he had to hear what Cloud was going to tell him.

"I was over on the north side," said Cloud, "where they are. Of course I shouldn't have been out of my bed; I walked like an old wife with a creel of peats on her back. There was a mist off the sea, too. It was a Sunday. They were in their kirk. That's what they call it, though I've seen better sheds for cattle. I could hear them at their psalms. Do you know what I felt like doing? I felt like rushing up and pulling the place about them. I was dying, I couldn't eat without agony, and there they were, living where they had no right to be, praising God. Now I never was one for religion all my days, but I knew that if there is a Creator, He must create everything, including pain and what causes pain. So I felt that if I had had their God there, I would have taken him by the throat and strangled Him. I felt that so strong I'm sure I did take something by the throat; what it was, I don't know. Then I fell on my knees. I fell, I didn't go down deliberately, one knee after the other, like a cow. I saw then I was beside what's called the Sanctuary Stone. I don't know how long I was there, but when I looked up there was Donald McInver standing beside me. He said nothing, or if he did speak I don't know what he said; he just put out his hand to help me to rise. I took it, though there was a time when I would have put my hand into a fire first. When I was on my feet again I knew right away something had happened. I smelled peat-reek; I thought of a baking of girdle-scones; and I knew I would be able to eat them, and enjoy them, as I had done when I was a boy and my mother handed them to me hot from the pan. When I came to the door here Meg my wife was waiting for me. She thought I was drunk or mad. Since that day I have been as happy here"—again he touched his stomach—"as a baby with its mother's milk."

Choked with scepticism and wonder, Bull could say nothing. He just gaped. Moreover, he was terrified at being dragged into such a secret.

"If you're thinking it was a miracle," whispered Cloud, "what other name is there for it?" Again he came very close. "I want you to tell nobody."

Bull had no desire to tell anybody. His mates might laugh at him: first he was chosen as Bridie's victim, and then as this conceited madman's.

He was given respite by Bridie's arrival. She had her rain-coat on. Bull noticed it without the usual pride in his acumen: she would be thinking it'd come in useful if there was dew on the grass. She did not know that, because of Cloud's sinister story, the dew would be like holy water, and the grass would not be ordinary grass. Even a beetle or ant crawling through it would be fearful. Now the entire island was charged with baleful mystery. Every stone on the beach, pink in this evening light, would look as if it had been newly dropped. Someone had just passed along; who, he dared not try to guess.

As they walked away Bridie playfully teased him about his apprehensive glances from side to side.

"Are you scared the sergeant will see you?" she asked.

"Speer? I'm not scared of Speer." Yet was not Speer's mouth swollen from one of those pebbles?

"Is it me you're scared of, big fellow?"

He tried to give her one of his potent subduing smiles; it did not succeed. He became aware she had led him into cover.

"It's about high time I had some fun," she said. "Don't you get smitten?"

"Smitten?" Was there indeed a plague? He was so alarmed he grabbed her.

"Patience," she said.

"Smitten with what?"

"Misery. For months everybody on this island's been going about with a face as long as a horse's leg. Except Miss Marguerite; she's always as cold in the heart as a mermaid. And of course old Donald."

"You mean, their preacher?"

She laughed. "Aye, their preacher. You could call him other names."

"Such as fraud?"

"I think so," she said. "I can tell you this: once, when Mary and Jean—they're with me at the big house—and I were bathing on the shore, in a place we thought was private, who did we catch watching us but old Donald, white beard and all; and his eyes weren't preaching. I should know, for I had nothing on at the time but a smile."

Then she stopped and rising on her toes ruthlessly kissed him. He had to respond, otherwise his manhood would be subjugated; but he was handicapped by that picture of the white-haired old holy man peeping from among the rocks at the naked woman.

She took him by the hand again.

"We'll go to the lily-pond," she whispered. "We'll go round by the back of the house through the trees."

As he went, he found that this element of senile lechery had by no means annulled the eeriness of everything; on the contrary, it had intensified it.

"Are there fish in this pond?" he asked.

"Wee fish, all colours."

He remembered Rollo's joke about the sea-trout in the lochs here, how eating of their flesh cured a man, or woman, of lust.

"You hear them plopping as they jump for the flies," she said.

"You'll get sea-trout, fresh sea-trout, to eat at the big house?" he asked.

"Often. Why?"

"Nothing. It's just that one of my mates is keen on fishing."

"This is the place for it. Fish this size." She giggled as she indicated how big those fish were.

Bull was serious. "Don't they poach it?" he asked.

"Who?"

"McInver and his folk."

"Likely they do. They'd be even bigger fools than they are if they didn't."

Had the charm worked on Sheila? Was *she* purged of lust? In his confusion Bull could not say then whether a wife without lust would be a blessing or a bane; and his doubt worried him.

"Why in God's name ought we to live like nuns just because they've to be put off?" asked Bridie indignantly.

"Who's living like nuns?"

"Me. And Mrs. Cloud. Did you notice her?"

"She's old."

"Nuns can be old, can't they?"

He had always thought of them, those steadfast feeders on charmed sea-trout, as eternally young.

"He's had nothing to do with her, in that way, for months," whispered Bridie.

Passing a cluster of yellow flowers, he had a vision of Sheila clothed only in her long silk hair. Bees buzzed in the flower-bells, and he was reminded of the business in Cloud's guts.

"This fellow Cloud," he muttered, "what's he like?"

She was wary, as if she suspected jealousy in the question. "What d'you mean?"

"He was ill."

She waited.

Bull was afraid to speak; there was no knowing what might happen in this haunted place if he were to break that promise he had given Cloud. Disease had flown from Cloud's belly; perhaps it needed some other nest now, to keep it fat and cosy, with food for its sharp beak; his own belly, for instance. He felt almost too weak to walk; sweat poured down his brow. Those who were playing billiards were lucky.

"This is the place," she said.

He looked at it, and saw proof of that malevolent transformation: the lilies were red, there were fish turned to stone, the bank on which she was pulling him down was greener than grass should ever be.

An owl hooted.

She kissed him as a witch might have, on the eyes, the throat, the nose, even the ears.

"Is it worrying you?" she whispered.

"What?" He had to push her back a little to get space for speaking.

"What you've to do tomorrow. Put them off. They might not go peaceable. Will you use force?"

"Sure. We'll drag them out by the hair."

"Good. That's what I wanted you to say."

Then she began to make it impossible for him not to co-operate, if his manhood was not to be shamed. It was shortly after this that they were interrupted.

Twelve

LUCKILY the morning was beneficent.

It was important that the purpose of the mission should be apparent in the way the missionaries arrived. They must not come aggressively or arrogantly or triumphantly; neither must they come sorrowfully, for in their keeping was the honour of the Law, whose decisions were just and should cause sorrow only to the wrongdoers; but they must nevertheless come with sympathy and humanity. Eagerness to persuade must be in their every initial glance and gesture, and must give way to enforcement only when that eagerness began to be taken of as weakness. Thus the Sheriff instructed the policemen before setting out. His voice was quiet; he held his hat in his hand; he made sympathetic gestures; so that when one of the newspaper reporters, who had come over from Mula by motor-boat, remarked to his colleagues that the affair had almost a religious atmosphere, he found them all agreeing. It did not make as exciting an assignment, said one, as in the old days, when the evicting policeman had been armed with cans of paraffin and lighted torches, to set fire to thatches and burn the folk out; but it did prove that, in spite of what pessimists and agitators said, civilisation kept making progress. That observation also was approved; it would set the tone for their reports.

The party from Sollas House, Mr. Vontin, Marguerite, and Andrew Doig, watched from among trees. They were going on horseback, across the machair and sands of the west. Mr. Vontin had been requested by the Sheriff to attend, so that he might be able to confirm what the Sheriff himself might tell the people about the homes ready for them on the mainland. It was Marguerite who had suggested going on horseback: the distance by road there and back was nearly five miles; it would tire her father unnecessarily; and besides the ride over the flowery machairs and the shining sands on such a morning would be delightful. When Andrew said he would rather walk, she had changed his mind simply by looking disappointed. Since last night's revelation by the lily-pond he and she were become morally intervolved; only frankness, from which he shrank and for which she seemed to have no desire, could break the spell binding them. Therefore he sat amongst the trees on a quiet pony, while she beside him, in white jumper and tawny jodhpurs, managed with ease what looked to him like one of Pluto's sable chargers by which Proserpina had been carried away.

They saw the officials set off, led by the Sheriff and his two clerks; Mr. Nigg carried his raincoat over his arm. At a respectful distance behind, but not too far in case of trouble, strode the policemen, paced by Speer so that they would not approach too near those in front. Then came the reporters, and a few representatives of religious, humanitarian, and cultural societies, who had been granted permission to come to the island this morning and see for themselves, and for their many members, stern philanthropy in action. As they all walked up the road, seeking with their first steps an appropriate gait, they looked to one of the riders among the trees like mourners going to some funeral where the deceased had been very old and sure of heaven. Gulls screeched above, excited by so much unusual movement on that track by the sea.

"Shall we go?" asked Marguerite.

Her father wore a tweed cap; nevertheless his profile, uplifted, with the long nose and tight mouth, looked particularly Roman and imperial. He did not answer her, but seemed in his mind to be reiterating some form of incantation; on his horse's mane his fingers counted one another, again and again. Thus had he been all morning, so that his guests had silently sympathised: as Nigg had confided to Quorr, sometimes in the peculiar conditions of modern society it required more courage and ruthlessness to persevere in what was for people's good rather than for their harm. Quorr's answer had been typically insensitive: a man who had made as much money as Vontin, he said, had as much scruple left as could be stuffed into one of Nigg's tiny shells.

To Andrew Doig, though he had confided in no one, it seemed that his host's perturbation in the great mansion was reminiscent of Pilate's. It was the kind of cleverness which he would have expounded so eloquently a week ago; now he distrusted his own mind capable of it.

All the same, as they waited among the trees, with the horses fretting to be off, it was not possible to keep that similitude from again occurring to him. Mr. Vontin was rich and had the support of both temporal and spiritual powers; Donald McInver and his followers were poor, and were opposed by all authorities; the mob which watched through their newspapers were interested only in sensation. These were indisputable parallels. Nor could it be denied that the faith of Christ had been born in poverty akin to that of these simple squatters, and it had been nurtured by poor men. Now that far-off poverty was spoken of as hallowed; shrines to honour it had been built and embellished at the cost of vast treasures; and it had thus become so transformed that now it could be praised by archbishop, king, and millionaire, without apparent contradiction or blasphemy. He had noticed on Donald McInver's boots little daubs of hen-dirt. In a way he could not explain they had seemed to him authentically divine; from them could indeed come a power to cure a sick man, silence a conceited one, or jolt a rich one into the fear that wealth, prestige, influence, and acclamation, were in the end barren of joy.

"Well, father?" asked Marguerite again.

He turned towards her with a blink of his eyes so mild that Andrew was astonished and shamed.

"I suppose so, Marguerite," he said.

At first the way led by a high path over moorland down to the shore on the west of the island. Far away on the horizon could be glimpsed the shapes of other islands that lay even farther into the ocean. Great white clouds that soared, turret upon turret, into the blue of the sky, hung over the sea; which, except for a fringe of white movement along the beach, was very still. As they came closer, descending to the green machair, that stillness of the ocean was seen to be illusory; breakers high as a horse's mane kept charging in upon the sands, with roar following roar so closely there never was silence. Yet the roaring soon became a background as tense as silence, so that the buzzing of bees could be heard, the cries of sea-birds, and even, close to the ears, the fluttering of the little blue butterflies which were there in profusion.

Marguerite turned to Andrew.

"I'll race you to the sands," she cried, and off she went, her black horse galloping, while her father shouted after her to be careful.

"Rabbit holes, you know," he said to Andrew. "And the sand's loose on the dunes."

They watched her as she raced across the green sea-meadow and on to the dunes of purple gleaming marram grass. Now she would be out of sight in a hollow, and now gloriously in sight again, her own black hair streaming. Reaching the edge where the bank shelved steeply on to the flat sand of the shore, she did not hesitate but sent her horse plunging down with a recklessness and skill that exhilarated even Andrew following at as canny a trot as he could hold his own pony to.

When he reached the edge he saw her, crouched like a jockey, speed along the sands, close to that mile-long magnificent green-and-blue-and-white cavalry charge of the waves. She was fey. They heard her exulting, and once she rose up in the stirrups and waved her right hand as if it held a sabre. In front of her thousands of gulls, close together in that one spot as if in consultation, seemed to wait till the last safe second before rising like one, so that horse and rider were fleeing under a snowstorm of wailing whirling birds.

Her exultation, Andrew thought, was callous, but in it too were bravery, glee, and confidence: thus she represented the conquering powers that had usurped the heritage of the meek. To those powers she, Mrs. Crail, and his own mother, urged him to belong: to stay out, when invited in, was to them like the huffiness of a small boy skulking in the darkness outside while within the party went on with laughter, paper-hats, and music. Knowing in their blood that he would ultimately come in, they saw neither sense nor value in his resisting, but only loss.

"I will come in," he thought, as he let Mr. Vontin lead him by an easy way down on to the firm sand. "It's hardly likely anything will happen this morning to give me the strength and faith to keep out. What happened yesterday by the pier wasn't enough."

Already Marguerite was far away. The gulls had settled down upon a huge pile of stones in the water, like a shattered stack. The beach was a great shining solitude, yet somehow it seemed to Andrew that they were not alone as they walked their horses slowly along the sand. His companion too kept glancing about, as if to catch sight of that apprehended but invisible third. In the distance a bird screamed; it was like a sound of enchantment, so that Andrew at least could not be sure whether the presence stalking them was good or malignant. Before St. Solla had blessed this island and claimed it for God, many creatures of superstition had haunted it; since these had not yet been driven out of the human mind, why should they not still lurk here, concealed within this beauty and seeming peace?

Suddenly Mr. Vontin spoke. "What else could I do?" he cried. "It's not their trespassing on my privacy I mind so much, it's their smearing it all over with their dreary superstitions. If they'd come here to sing songs of happiness instead of mournful psalms, it would have been different. Surely happiness is the true test of religious faith?"

"Would it not depend on what one called happiness?" asked Andrew.

"Yes, it does, Andrew. Their idea of happiness isn't mine, thank God, and I'm sure it isn't yours either. Happiness for them consists in the gloomy conviction that they alone are sure of salvation, while the rest of us are doomed to everlasting torment. Yes, they're as primitive as that."

So were the originals primitive, thought Andrew.

"Don't you think, sir, that Donald McInver's genuine in his beliefs?"

"Yes, but I fail to see where his beliefs are Christian."

It was hardly likely a millionaire's views on such a subject would coincide with a penniless peasant's.

"He'll get a chance this morning to show whether he's genuine or not," said Vontin, firmly. "All along he's claimed that it was God who sent him here. If that was so, won't God prevent him from being sent away? Surely the Sheriff and a thousand policemen would be as helpless to remove him as those jellyfish, or that dead bird?"

It was a gannet, on the sand before them. It was a large bird, with its long neck and black-tipped wings. There was no blood on it, no sign of injury to account for its death, except that its neck seemed very slack. Gazing down at it, Andrew remembered the cloud of yesterday: there could, of course, in common sense be no connection; but he felt that with every pace of their horses they were moving deeper and deeper into an atmosphere where neither common sense nor wisdom counted much.

"No, Andrew," said his host, "whatever allowances we

make, it's pretty obvious we're dealing here with bigotry, re-action, and ignorance. For our own sakes we can't tolerate it."

"What about Cloud, sir?"

"Cloud?"

"His cure."

"Surely, as your uncle said, coincidence; that's to say, if the poor fellow really is cured. I'm afraid I'm not convinced, and neither is his wife. You don't believe in modern miracles, do you?"

Andrew was about to challenge that qualification "modern"; he decided it would be safer not to.

"No," he replied, with sad reluctance.

"I didn't think you did. Marguerite was telling me you intend to study law. I doubt if I'd care to consult a lawyer who believed in miracles." He laughed at what he considered a joke. "I understand your father's a minister?"

"Yes, sir."

"You know, of course, that I've discussed this issue with Church leaders. I have their support."

"Yes, sir." It was tempting to point out how history proved that those Church leaders in every generation had been ob-stacles in man's hard progress towards compassion. A week ago Andrew would have embraced that temptation, and would have been lavish and impromptu with examples of clerical re-action. Now he said nothing.

"What does your father say?"

Andrew thought of his gentle, ironic father among his prize roses in the manse garden, and heard his quiet voice: "I think, Andrew, you'd better do as your mother says; really she knows best." And he thought too of his pink cheeked and prema-turely white-haired mother, whom he loved, and who, when he had been a boy, had loved him joyously simply for what he was; it was not her fault that now, when he was become a man, about to conquer the world or be conquered by it, she must also love him for what he was to be. Twenty-five years of struggle on a minimum stipend, with an ambitionless husband, had taught her a lesson she was too proud and honest to disown: that though money could corrupt, so could the want of it.

"He didn't commit himself, sir."

"Wise man, to keep out of it."

What his father had done was to go to his book shelves and take down a book containing tales and legends of these western islands. He had read out of it how the Sanctuary Stone had been blessed by St. Solla, washed up beside it after his coracle had been wrecked; how for hundreds of years afterwards men and women had sought refuge here from enemies; and how this right of sanctuary had never been desecrated. When he had finished he had stood with the book open in his hand and his eyes upon the window, outside which the sun was shining; he seemed to have returned to that past which obeyed and honoured God. Andrew, knowing how violent and bloody that past had been, had asked him if he believed that a man on Sollas had always been immune. "No, Andrew," he had replied, with only the mildest reproach in his voice at being asked such a question. Then he had replaced the book.

Marguerite now came galloping back to join them. Pink with swiftness, her face was especially beautiful, and reminded him of his mother's, whose hair too had been black when she was young. Yet in Marguerite's eyes, despite their sparkle and humour and pride in her horsemanship, was that Medean depth, so that, there on the wide sands, with the thousands of gulls again conferring, and with the dead symbolical gannet, he felt not like a modern man at all seeking a buttress for faith, but like the adventurer of fable who needed and obtained the help of the gods in a world where rocks could speak, birds were wise men translated, out of the waves came green monsters to devour, and a beautiful woman was a witch and murderess. And somehow, despite these perils, he yearned after that sunlit magical world so much more appropriate a setting for the battle of good and evil than here in actuality, where a few narrow-minded, gloomy-souled peasants, greedy for a heaven which itself would be narrow and gloomy, were being dispossessed by authorities who did not believe in any heaven at all, and where the God, Who had created the immense and intricate universe, could not now, prisoner of His own inexorable laws, revive a dead gannet or kill disease in a man's belly.

If he were Jason, he would not know what the Fleece was he had to find: not the soul of man, as his host the island-king had said, for that was a quest of despair; but some glorious trophy, gifted by the gods, which could be seen, admired, and honoured by all men, who, having seen it, would partake of its glory for ever.

But he was a Jason without a sword and without the love of the gods.

Thirteen

In the old days there had been a township of about a score of houses scattered on the hillsides above the beach; now six of them had been roughly restored and occupied. Their lichened stone and their pale-blue corrugated iron roofs gave them a strange generic similarity; they looked like huge cattle, standing knee-deep in green nettles and golden ragwort, too sick to browse. So small were the windows that their interiors seemed likely to be as dark and noisome as the insides of beasts. Peat reek rose from improvised tin chimneys.

Everywhere were signs of poverty. Each inhabited house had a few hens scurrying about it, and a cow staked, so that it must nuzzle and nuzzle again, missing not a single edible blade. Those cows were all lean and bony, with shrunken udders, and lowed to one another, lamenting the same harsh hunger. There were no trees in that windy promontory, except for three sycamores, which symbolised the destitution of the settlement. Stunted, their trunks even at the bole were not thicker than a man's arm. The perpetual sea winds had misshapen them so that they reached up to their little height in anguished contortions; their leaves, in the amplitude and splendour of summer, were shrivelled and ringwormed. They were like trees in hell, and under them grazed two goats that looked up at the visitors with faces like forsaken unforgiving men's.

Most of those visitors were appalled by that destitution, some were indignant, but only one rejoiced. Creepe could not help laughing at this confirmation of what he had all along maintained: if God favoured people, He saw to it they prospered. If Creepe had come here, to this corner of this remote island, and seen a luxuriant paradise, he would have been shaken in his belief that these squatters were charlatans, who hindered rather than helped God by bringing Him so unnecessarily into conflict with the authorities. Now that belief was strengthened, so that as he listened to the larks carilloning above he knew that they were the voices of God, praising him.

His colleagues, for different reasons, reached similar conclusions.

"Well," said Dand, "nobody could say God's been good to them; I mean, they're not living in the lap of luxury, are they?"

"You'd wonder," said Grooner, "that people would have to be forced to leave this."

"I doubt if conditions have improved since the days of their saint," said Rollo.

"Putting the clock back a thousand years," said Rickie, "that's what they're doing. No wonder we were sent here."

"As saviours?" asked Rollo.

"Looks like it, Rollo."

Even Rollo appeared to agree.

Therefore the whole procession, the Sheriff and his men, the reporters, and the observers, were suitably solemn as they walked among the houses. Here, it seemed to them, was the graveyard in which was to be buried that old person who had lived long and reverently, but whose wits in the end had decayed. The Sheriff felt an almost mystical sense of rightness in his mission. The reporters knew that, though sensation pleased the public best, their accounts must be restrained, with pity for these unhappy simpletons balancing respect for the humane authorities. As for the others, among whom was the clergyman who counted Sollas within his parish, they expressed the hope to one another that force would not be

necessary, for, although it would be justified, its victims nevertheless would in a pathetic way be innocent.

Had the visitors been greeted by lamentation or even by
abuse, they would have welcomed it: such reaction on the
part of the crofters would have been natural and human,
allowing their own response of protest and firmness to be
natural and human too. Kinship would have been established.
But as they approached the beach over turf bright and short to
where the people were grouped in front of the large stone,
they were received by an outburst of psalm-singing, as
desolating as it was untunable.

They had to stop, the Sheriff in the forefront, swither about
taking off their hats, and wait until that shrill almost exotic
bleating ended. It went on so long that most of them began
to peep up at these bleaters, for whose sake they had come so
far.

Men, women, and children, they sang standing. McInver,
with his back to the stone, led them; but none of them could
follow him either in the vehemence of his singing or the
devoutness on his face. There were seven men amongst
them; some stole shy and anxious glances behind. The women
wore scarves round their heads; they were as sunburnt as the
men, and stauncher; certainly they sang with more assiduity.
The youngest child was in his mother's arms; the oldest was
Sheila of the yellow hair. Seen there, amongst her own folk,
wearing her working frock, she seemed to some of the policemen buxom rather than shapely; and the smile which had
so delighted them with its sweetness at the pier now struck
them as on the soft side, almost indicative of goodhearted
glaikitness.

Even to Andrew Doig, standing beside his horse, they
looked a most unlikely and inadequate company for grace.
What they represented seemed rather forlorn stupidity; indeed, it did seem vexatious that so much money, thought,
argument, and compassion should have been expended on

such unworthy objects. For the first time he appreciated the aggravation of authority, and thus its patience also. He had not expected them to have transfigured lovely faces, but neither had he expected such crassness, such wingless dullness. One man squinted, another was ludicrously bald; a woman seemed toothless, another pregnant, and the children had dirty bare feet and vacuous faces. Even Sheila, whose flowers he had held with reverence at the pier, was now a fat, simpering peasant wench, whose hair, irrelevantly beautiful, looked none too clean.

He was in the process of finding reasons, not only to reject them, but also to condemn them for being the kind of bigots they were, when he remembered, not ethically, but in a way he couldn't describe either then or afterwards, that they were human beings, his neighbours, whom he must love. Often before had he remembered that injunction, but always as an exercise in ethics, accompanied by much irritation, and seldom by the love prescribed. Now he felt that love flowing in and out of him so unaccountably that he glanced round and up seeking an explanation. He did not find it in Mr. Vontin's impassive face, nor even in Marguerite's, although when she saw him looking at her so peculiarly she smiled and nodded, acknowledging that he and she shared a secret. So they did, but it was not this one of his love for these simple, foolish, deluded, unlovely people.

As soon as the singing stopped the Sheriff moved forward swiftly, lest it should start again. He had his hat in his hand, and obviously was determined not to succumb to what he considered the mawkish pseudo-religious atmosphere. He meant to make this great boulder no more significant than any of the thousand others in sight. But suddenly his approach to it was as if to an altar. Donald McInver, with his head bare and his white beard waving, he had meant to treat with courtesy, respect perhaps, sympathy certainly, but by no means with reverence. Yet when the tall old man held up his hand as if in blessing the Sheriff could not have bowed his head more reverently had he been in the presence of an archbishop in mitre and cope.

That moment when McInver raised his hand had its effect not only upon the Sheriff. Everybody there was affected in his own way. Silence fell, in which the singing of the larks, the lowing of the cows, and the breaking of the sea on the shore, were heard as sounds not coming from the old stale world, but from another new, fresh, and merciful. It was like a funeral where, at the open grave, no one disbelieved and no one believed, only vaguely and timidly that the spirit of the dead was risen to join God.

It did not last long. As soon as McInver lowered his hand everybody returned to his own personality, where every path was well worn and every destination known. Those who cared to admit that moment of vision by speaking about it, gave hypnotism as the explanation; in the city theatres professional hypnotists made people say and do and see the most remarkable things. Were not old McInver's green deep eyes uncanny and fierce? Most, however, kept silent, not wishing to admit even to themselves that for that brief space, during which a bird, a stonechat, had alighted on the Sanctuary Stone and flown away again, they had felt themselves to be in an inexplicable presence.

The Sheriff was amongst those who would never admit it. Freed from the spell, or rather rousing himself from his momentary aberration brought on by anxiety and weariness, he addressed the people in front of him. He spoke quietly.

"You all know who I am, and why I am here. It is not necessary for me to enter into the history of the events whose culmination is my presence among you this morning. It has been decided by the courts of this land that you are here in illegal possession. Accordingly orders to quit were served upon you. You did not obey those orders, and so I am come to enforce, if necessary, that obedience."

He had to pause, for not only did his jaws ache, but also what he was saying seemed strangely remote and inconsequential. When he touched his brow with the back of his hand he felt a warm dampness there: it was sweat, though for a moment he had feared it might be blood. It was possible of course he could be taking an illness, a fever or chill caught during the journey to this ill-starred place.

He had to force himself to proceed.

"This duty is distasteful to me, and to all those who have come with me to assist me in it. Nevertheless, we must and shall discharge it. Tomorrow a boat will be here to remove you and your belongings. If you prefer it, you will be returned to your original homes on Mula. But I have Mr. Vontin's authority for reminding you that his offer of new homes on the mainland still stands. He is here himself, and Mr. Cloud his grieve; I am sure they will answer any questions you may like to put to them on that subject. There can be no question, of course, of your staying here. That decision has been made, and it is final."

"Man's decision can never be final. Only God's is final."

It was McInver who spoke, in a voice like a trumpet.

The Sheriff trembled. "No one can deny that," he said, "but it is not relevant here."

"It was by God's command we came here to Sollas," shouted McInver.

The Sheriff kept shaking his head.

"And only at His command shall we leave."

"To be drawn into theological debate," said the Sheriff, trying to find the smile suitable to the occasion, "would be foolish, idle, and altogether useless."

Suddenly McInver laid his hand upon the great stone.

"You cannot even," he cried, in exultation, "take my hand away from here."

The Sheriff, with a reluctance like a shame, glanced at that long, thin, brown, dirty-nailed hand upon the moss of the stone. He could not, perhaps, himself have dragged it off: McInver, despite his age, seemed the stronger man of the two; but surely amongst the policemen there was one who could do it, so easily? To ask anyone to try was of course impossible.

"If you were to take an axe," cried McInver, "and sever my hand from my body it would still stay upon this stone, like a flower."

Everybody gazed at that hand on the vertical stone: they saw it severed; they saw the blood dripping; they saw it still clinging, like a flower.

To go forward, throwing people out of the way, seize the old man, and throw him aside, hand, body, and all, would have been, half an hour ago, glory for Bull. Now he could not move, because he had no wish to move, indeed he had a great wish to stand there in the spot where he was, as if he were a tree which had been growing there for many years.

McInver took his hand away. A few gasped at how easily he did it. Then he raised it again.

"This place is holy," he cried. "Here God is, and has been seen. To live in God's presence is to be alive. You who have come here were dead; now at this minute you are alive. Look up at the blue sky; in your hearts there is the same radiance. Lift a pebble from the beach, and you will feel it warm from the hand of God."

He stood gazing up at the sky himself, in an exaltation almost aggressive. The bones of his brow and cheeks glistened under the strain, and his neck was taut.

Beside him the Sheriff was uncertain, bewildered, and unhappy.

"It's not for me," he murmured, "to doubt the sincerity of your views."

McInver brought his hand down upon the stone, several times, as if it held a sword.

"You have come here to banish God," he cried.

The Sheriff shook his head: it was the feeblest of denials of the mightiest of accusations.

"All over the earth He is being banished," shouted McInver.

The Sheriff could not deny that; in countries anti-Christ prevailed.

"Drive us from here, and God is banished again."

"No," murmured the Sheriff.

"This island will then be accursed," cried McInver, "and those who remain in it. Where God has been, and no longer is, is the true hell."

As he spoke McInver turned to gaze at Mr. Vontin, Marguerite, and Andrew Doig.

"Better to drown in the blue sea," he cried, "than to live in this place when it has been emptied of God."

The Sheriff again took upon himself the burden of rationality; it ought not, he knew, to have been so dreadfully heavy, crippling his soul. What this white-bearded old man was saying represented a form of religion long since discredited. To contradict it, to expose its absurdity, ought to have been the easiest and briefest of intellectual exercises; but somehow he did not find it so.

"Such talk is idle," he said. "What you believe is your own business. Other people have other beliefs, no less sincere. It is our heritage to be free to hold and express our opinions; elsewhere no such freedom exists."

"There is only one freedom," said McInver. "It is to live in the presence of God. Do not expect that presence to bring you wealth or high position or authority over men; it will only bring you freedom. There is only one prison; it is to live where God is not."

"But surely," said the Sheriff, with a smile and simplicity that took him unawares, "in your creed, as in mine, God is everywhere?"

"No!" It was like the sound of a trumpet. "No! God will not persist where He is not wanted."

Then the Sheriff was rescued. One of McInver's disciples, a stout, grey-haired, dour-faced man of about fifty-five, stepped forward. It was obvious that though he revered his leader he was still cool enough in mind to calculate the secular aspect of the business.

"My name is Fergus," he said. "We do not want to leave Sollas. It is where our ancestors lived hundreds of years ago."

Here was an adversary the Sheriff need not fear; here would be no confusing illogicality, caused by faith corrupting in an old man's wits; here were bargaining eyes of cunning, here were large peasant's hands, brown, rough, and cupped in greed.

"I am afraid," said the Sheriff, "that it is only the present that concerns us."

· "We do not want to go," repeated Fergus.

"I am aware of that. But I think I have made it clear that you must go."

"We believe," said Fergus, with a sly grin towards where the owner of the island stood, "that there is good land on Sollas. If it was given to us to cultivate, we could make a good living here."

"That is a matter I cannot discuss."

"The harvests on Sollas were once the best in all the islands. They could be again."

"This is sadly beside the point. My function here is not to negotiate; it is to enforce a decision taken by higher authorities. Obedience is my duty, as it is yours. You must quit this place tomorrow. If to go so soon means inconvenience, let me remind you that you have only yourselves to blame; you were warned months ago that this would happen."

"If we were to be given the machair land on the west——" said Fergus.

The Sheriff felt a liking for this stubborn crofter; his stupidity was of a human kind, and so corrigible, unlike McInver's, who during this conversation had been trying on various expressions of beatitude, each one more distressingly senile than the other.

"I'm sorry there can be no more talk on the matter," said the Sheriff to Fergus. "I am going away again, but I shall return tomorrow, expecting to find you prepared to leave. Every assistance will be given you to transport your belongings to the pier. You seem to be a shrewd fellow, able to see the realities of the case. I beg you to persuade your companions to accept the inevitable. It will be much better for all of you in the long run; and in the short run too."

Fergus shook his head. "We have our peats to cut this afternoon," he said.

The Sheriff was nonplussed. "Peats?" he gasped.

"If Donald says we have not to go," said Fergus, "we will not go."

The Sheriff dared not glance aside at McInver.

"Take care," he said, in a low voice, "take care you do not run the risk of doing Mr. McInver an ill turn. Let him advise you so foolishly, and I am afraid he will incur the charge of inciting you to disregard the law. That is a serious charge, and at his age might well have disastrous consequences."

Fergus then raised his eyes and stared at the Sheriff in an astonishment that, though partly bucolic, was nevertheless impressive. It was evident that he had suddenly realised the Sheriff all along had been thinking he did not look on Donald as genuinely in God's confidence.

"You cannot harm Donald," he said.

"We do not wish to."

"You cannot. Donald has been dead, and alive again."

Before the Sheriff could decide what that nonsense meant, he was addressed by McInver.

"When you come tomorrow," cried the old man, "you will be given God's answer."

"It had better," said the Sheriff wistfully, "be a sensible answer." He prepared to take his leave. "If you are to have an inspiration, let it be the only expedient one possible. Oracles were always shrewd. Do not put your God to shame. To-morrow you must leave this place of your own free will, or else you will be forced out. Many men have found their God standing by. That is not a matter for bitterness, but rather for rejoicing. Then it can be seen that the God believed in was the God created to our own satisfaction, and not the true im-partial God, Who did, I grant you, create this stone, this island, and ourselves who stand here this morning. But what His will is, neither you nor I can know with certainty. Do not, I beseech you, put your God to shame."

Then, amazed by his own words and by the tone in which he had uttered them, he turned and walked past the women and children, past the policemen, and past the reporters and observers. They all stared at him in surprise. He did not know then that he was smiling in a way reminiscent of McInver himself, and carried his hat in front of him as if it was some utensil used in a ceremony for the collecting of truth, and now was to be borne by him to some destination, full to overflowing. That destination he seemed to be sure of, from the lightness and quickness of his step.

In a minute or so he stopped, seemed to waken, looked at his hat in wonder that he was not wearing it, and put it on. With it was put on that intricate and subtle robe which for sixty-three years he had been weaving to cover his soul.

He turned, to find Nigg panting in loyal consternation by his side.

"I really think our mission is incomplete, Mr. Nigg," he said. "We should have brought with us a mental specialist."

"Yes, sir," agreed Nigg, laughing too, although a moment before he had thought that by the missing member of their mission the Sheriff had meant Christ Himself.

Fourteen

THE SHERIFF was remarkably cheerful and friendly. For the first time in their ten years' association he laid his hand on Nigg's shoulder, like a comrade.

"At least you should have a fine afternoon for gathering your shells," he said.

Nigg had been thinking of those shells as warmed, like the pebbles, by the hand of God; now he saw them as cold with the kisses of the sea.

"I hope so, sir," he murmured.

The Sheriff left him and hurried across to where the clergyman from Mula was talking in whispers to two men as white-haired and solemn as himself. One was the Secretary of the Society for the Preservation of Native Culture, and the other represented an Evangelical Mission. Hitherto the Sheriff had not spoken to them; they were on the religious and cultural wings, as it were, of the vast forces supporting him, but they must not there obtrude their support: in the mystical language of the bull-fight, the moment of truth must be his alone. Now he spoke to them cordially.

"I hope you will pardon my taking the liberty of speaking to you, gentlemen," he said. "I should be obliged for your advice. You know these people's mentality so much better than I. I understand, sir, they were your parishioners before they decided to come here?"

The minister was a tall, thin man with a long loose flexible neck round which, snugger than his collar, hung caution.

"That is not quite the case," he replied. "To put it precisely, they lived within the bounds of my parish, but they never worshipped under me. They were sufficient unto themselves."

"Owing to McInver's influence?"

"Precisely."

"Do you mind if I walk back with you, gentlemen?" asked the Sheriff.

They signified that on the contrary they would be honoured.

"Has McInver then always been a self-styled prophet?" he asked.

"More or less," replied the minister. "But he always kept it within bounds until about a year or two ago."

"Is he mad?"

It was a question by no means judicious, in the circumstances; yet having asked it with more than judicial sharpness, he waited for an answer.

None wished to be the first to speak. He had to encourage them.

"I mean," he said, "he evidently labours under a conviction that he is in direct communication with God. Did he not say, in so many words, that he has seen God? Did you not notice his performance with his hand upon the stone? Does not such conviction, such a degree of deludedness, in this day and age, amount to madness?"

The evangelist was plump and benign.

"Our day and age," he said, with a smile, "needs God as much as any in the past."

"Perhaps more," agreed the Sheriff. "And that is why we must beware of charlatans. Is McInver aware he is deceiving these simple people? If he is aware, then his deception is almost criminal; but if he is not aware, then of course he must be mad. Those are the only two ways of looking at it."

"I agree," said the minister at length, with a sigh of reluctance. "It would be a pity, however, if at his age, he were to be removed."

"Do you mean to an institution?"

"Yes. I understood that to be your inference."

"No. I would prefer not to have a say in such a matter; you gentlemen are far more competent judges here."

"I have never heard of such a case before," said the Secretary, pompously mouthing his words. "These people are usually reticent to the point of absurdity about their religion; their relation to God is usually the closest of secrets, most dourly guarded. I have spent a week in the home of a typical crofter of this kind, and everything in it was made mine, with a hospitality stern but admirable, except his religious beliefs, which, by the way, were the very things I wished to investigate and examine; these were locked away in his breast. Of course, I was well acquainted with his superficial austerities, such as his refusing to cycle on Sundays or even to sell milk then; but as for his innermost faith——"

The Sheriff, skilled in the curbing of verbose solicitors, found so slow and elaborate a speaker easy to interrupt; there were so many pauses among the words.

"I see you are indeed expert," he said, smiling. "It is good of you to give me your assistance. You agree, then, the poor fellow is mad?"

"It's the only conclusion," said the Secretary.

"With this qualification, of course," added the evangelist, "that much of what the unhappy old man says is true. I refer," he hastened to say, "to such statements as that where God is not, nothing avails."

The Sheriff nodded.

"What particularly concerns me," went on the evangelist, "is the matter of Mr. Cloud. You know about his wonderful cure?"

"Yes," murmured the Sheriff.

"I have no difficulty at all in believing in that cure," said the evangelist. "The clemency of Our Lord knows no bounds, and is at work always in our midst. For Donald McInver, however, or any mortal man, to claim to be the intermediary, is, to my mind, quite blasphemous."

"To call it senility might be more charitable," suggested the Sheriff. "After all, he is seventy-eight. By the way, what did the other man, Fergus, mean by his remark that Donald had been dead and was now alive? Did he mean physically dead?"

They were silent for a moment.

"It appears so," said the minister. "They found him on the hill unconscious; they thought he was dead. I understand he revived in a somewhat melodramatic fashion."

"He has these poor folk as deluded as himself," said the Sheriff. "Well, I am much obliged to you, gentlemen. We all know what is owed to Caesar, and what to God: that is the crux, surely. McInver lacks that knowledge. He would appropriate all to God."

"To his own God," corrected the minister anxiously.

"Yes, of course. Did he not say that the very pebbles," and here the Sheriff stooped and picked one up, "were warm from the hand of God." He held it out; it was, by chance, as oval as an egg and as smooth as silk; it was white with two blue concentric rings. "It *is* warm," he said, laughing.

"It has been lying in the sun," murmured the minister.

They gazed at it.

"What a magnificent carver is the sea," said the evangelist. "I suppose," he added, bravely, "that in a sense this pebble— may I have it, sir, for a moment?—has indeed lain in the hands of the Creator. Is not the mighty ocean itself part of that creation? Where poor Donald errs, it seems to me, and it is the most grievous error a mortal can make, is to imagine that his hand, when he holds this or any other pebble in it, has become the hand of Our Lord."

"It's this place which affects him in that way," said the Secretary, "so the obvious solution is to get him away as soon as possible. These are issues which haven't been much discussed in the newspapers, but the truth lies within them."

He added that remark, which his companions found rather cryptic, because he had caught sight of the reporters hovering near.

It was obvious they hoped the Sheriff would have a word with them. Nigg had already assured them he wouldn't. But Nigg had under-estimated his master's new affability. A minute or so later the Sheriff came over.

"Good-morning, gentlemen," he said.

"Good-morning, sir," they answered, with much respect.

"I know I have no right whatever," he said, with a frank smile, "to advise you on what you should tell your readers. The freedom of the Press in our country is one of our most shining sanctities. But I am going to be so bold as to ask your indulgence on behalf of Donald McInver. I have been consulting with those gentlemen who represent Church interests about him. They agree with me that publicity of the wrong kind would harm not only Donald but religion itself. It is always distressing to see old age demonstrating its helpless senility; but when that demonstration takes the shape of religious delusion, it seems to me that those of us who still revere our Christian faith must protect it from derision and abuse. Today that faith has many enemies: surely it is not for us to assist them in their scorn and derogation. These are, of course, my personal reflections. You are not in the least obliged to pay them the slightest heed. Indeed, it is courteous of you to have listened to them with so much patience."

One of the reporters had a red face and contentious eyes.

"Don't you think," he demanded, "that there's a chance he's genuine?"

"In what sense?"

"Well, in what he said about this island being holy. Isn't it a matter of history that Sollas was saved here and proclaimed the place a sanctuary? Didn't he also perform some miracles?"

"The miracles are legend," murmured the Sheriff. "Besides, we are a long way from St. Solla."

"So we are. That's just the trouble. His was an age of simple faith. What's ours?"

"Ours is an age of faith too, though not so simple. His was an age of brutality, hunger, disease, cruelty, and suffering. For instance, your journey back to Mula would not then have been so quick, pleasant, and safe; there would have been a strong likelihood that if your coracle did not founder, causing you to be drowned, you would have been attacked by marauders and murdered for no other reason than the joy of murder."

"That's what we've been telling him, sir," said another.

"I admit all that," said the red-faced man," but religion was fresh then; there was a wonder in it. I think old Donald McInver's got some of that wonder. You can't deny that what he said was true about your not being able to remove him if God was not willing."

"What God wills, must be," agreed the Sheriff.

"Joe's expecting a miracle," said a colleague, laughing.

"Why not, Sam? Couldn't we do with one? You can't deny the influence of religion is getting weaker every day. If we're going to get back our faith we need help."

"True," said the Sheriff, smiling. "But we must not expect that help to be given in the form of some trick to mystify children."

The other reporters laughed. Joe himself grinned.

"Of course I'll not say a word about this in my report," he said. "Even if I did, it wouldn't get printed; or if it was, it would be touched up in some way to make it seem silly and vulgar."

"I must leave it to your own discretion, gentlemen," said the Sheriff.

"Do you think they'll go quietly tomorrow, sir?"

"I hope so; I think so, too."

"Now that the old fellow's had his moment, he'll have the sense to give up?"

"You could put it that way," said the Sheriff, laughing. "Well, may I wish you a safe and pleasant voyage, gentlemen?"

They thanked him.

Taking his leave, he set off jauntily across the lawn towards the house. Behind him, raincoat over his arm, trotted Nigg.

In the background Speer stood irresolute with his policemen.

The sergeant hurried after the Sheriff, seeking orders. Rollo laughed as he watched that pursuit.

"You know," he said, "there was a time yonder at the stone when I thought he was going to go down on his knees."

"You mean Speer?" asked Dand.

"No, the Sheriff."

Others nodded.

"It was queer," said Grooner. "Everybody felt it."

"Me?" cried Creepe, pointing to himself.

"You too, Creepe. I noticed you. I noticed you particularly; it was religion, so it was more in your line than ours. You had your mouth wide open."

"Do you know why, Grooner?"

"No, I don't. What I know is, so was mine."

"I'll tell you what astonished me, Grooner. It was their poverty."

"Creepe believes," said Rollo, "that one sure sign God's adopted you is if you look well-off."

Creepe nodded his head vigorously. "I do believe that," he said. "All the people I know who are truly godly are also prosperous. God does not allow his faithful to starve."

"I'm not a religious man," said Rickie, "but that makes sense to me."

"This Solla," said Rollo, "he'd be hungry often enough; he'd live in a hut of mud; he'd eat whelks; he'd wear cloth like sacks; he'd drink water."

"He was a heathen," said Creepe contemptuously.

Bull, who had been listening quietly, suddenly burst out: "Why did they stop me? I would have pulled his hand away like this," and seizing a stalk of bracken he pulled it up out of the ground. "Why did they stop me?"

"Who stopped you, Bull?" asked Rollo.

The others waited curiously for the answer.

Bull, it was clear, was sure he had been stopped, but had not until now considered who had done it.

"I would have crushed his hand to pulp," he said savagely.

"But who stopped you?" asked Grooner.

"Maybe it was you, Grooner."

"Me!" Grooner was astonished.

"Somebody stopped me."

They glanced at one another, recollecting how they, too, when the old man's hand grew like a flower out of the stone, had neither power nor desire to go forward and uproot it.

Speer came panting back.

"All right," he said. "Back to the house for lunch."

"And after lunch?" asked Rollo.

"You'll be told after lunch what's to be done after lunch," replied the sergeant.

"Sergeant," cried Dand suddenly, "what's happened to your mouth?"

"What d'you mean?" Speer in alarm put his hand up to touch, in awe, his lips which no longer felt painful.

"It's nearly better. You'd hardly notice it."

They all gazed at the mouth which, so far as they could remember, had that morning, hardly more than an hour ago, been swollen and cut. Now there was no swelling, and the cut was healed. There was a redness, that was all.

"What about your tooth?" asked Grooner.

Speer, resentful somehow of their stares, far intenser with curiosity than they had been with pity, hesitated a few seconds before opening his mouth. He put his finger up to feel for his missing tooth.

His mates, when they saw the gap, gasped with relief; but he, finding his finger-tip in that space, was disappointed.

"I bathed it last night," he muttered.

"I've never seen a thing heal so quick," said Grooner. "Is it sore?"

Speer shook his head, cannily, lest the pain should return.

"Maybe it's something in the air here?" suggested Rickie.

Rollo laughed. "Maybe it is," he said. "Old Donald thinks it's God. Look out, Bull."

Bull raised his great fists. "I'll strangle anybody that gets in my way," he snarled.

"None of that, Bull," said the sergeant. "The Sheriff wants us to do nothing to offend the people here. If they're off their heads with religion, that's none of our business. We're not here to convert them. All right. Back to the house."

He led the way, still touching the gap in his teeth with his finger-tip.

Fifteen

DURING lunch Mr. Vontin was concerned, indeed almost obsessed, with arranging his guests' entertainment for that afternoon: it was as if he hoped their enjoyment would keep at bay his own melancholy. To oblige him, as much as to divert themselves, the Sheriff, Nigg, and Quorr considered his array of amusements. Only Andrew Doig did not take part; his abstinence, however, seemed for some nobler reason than protest against the selfishness of the others.

"If it's convenient, Mr. Vontin," said Quorr boldly, "I'd like to borrow a horse for an hour or two."

"Of course it's convenient, Mr. Quorr," replied Vontin, smiling at the burly clerk whose eyes, in a face gone red, were blazing like a conquistador's, and whose lips were tight with unashamed callousness. "Do you like riding?"

Quorr's nod had a plumed helmet in it.

Nigg tittered sadly. "Mr. Quorr is an accomplished horseman," he said.

"Indeed?" It was the Sheriff who spoke, amused at finding this odd swashbuckling talent in one who spent so much of the sunlight sitting on an office chair.

"Yes, sir," added Nigg. "He has also a great fondness for horses."

"Let's say I prefer them to most of the human beings I've met," said Quorr. "If it's faith you want, where else would you look for it?"

"Dogs?" suggested Nigg companionably. "Many people consider them the most faithful of creatures."

"I meant *faith*," said Quorr, "not cringing dependence."

Not his words only, but his almost savage utterance of them, brought silence. It was broken by Marguerite, who for the third time tried to banter Andrew out of his vow of aloofness.

"What about us, Andrew?" she asked. "What are we going to do?"

He shook his head. No one knew what he meant; Marguerite was sure he didn't know himself. On the table-cloth his hand lay with what struck her as a characteristic smug calmness. Though he now refused to speak, she remembered his voice speaking to her on the telephone, with such prim capable conceit; and she would remember all her life the look on his face at the lily-pond.

Nigg, well-mannered, was waiting until he was sure the young people were not going to speak; then he spoke himself.

"If there are no objections," he said, "I think I would like to gather my shells, after all. I say 'after all', because I must confess I had some doubt as to the propriety of such an occupation, in the circumstances."

"And that doubt has gone?" asked his host.

"Yes, it has. Indeed, now I can think of no more fitting pastime this afternoon than gathering fragments of loveliness, in peace towards all men."

"And all women, too?" asked Quorr, laughing.

Nigg gazed at his colleague without rancour. Only Quorr knew that those shells were symbols of humiliation, and of a disappointment as wide and profound as the ocean out of which they had come.

"Yes," said Nigg, "in peace towards all women too. I believe that while gathering those tiny shells I shall reap another harvest. Faith reveals itself in many ways."

"If you do not mind, Mr. Nigg," said the Sheriff briskly, "I think I would like to join you in your quest."

"I should be honoured and delighted, sir."

"I envy you both," said Mr. Vontin.

It was a remark that either courtesy, or that degree of flattery which hospitality requires, could have prompted; in which case it could have been adequately answered with a gracious smiling silence. But it was obviously not so prompted at all. The envy Mr. Vontin spoke of did exist.

Nigg was not surprised. He had not forgotten the curse that had been placed on his host that very morning: the withdrawal of God from this island and its owners. Quorr's remark that with a million pounds even a God could be bought, to replace one lost, had been too cynical. Rich men were not barred from heaven, but to find the gate they had to find their way back through a labyrinth as long and complicated as the twistings of an ambitious soul. Therefore even if McInver's threat had been that of a lunatic dotard, as the Sheriff believed, it was still scripturally probable that Mr. Vontin and his lovely daughter were, in the midst of their wealth, doomed to deprivation.

Therefore Nigg felt urgently compassionate.

"Mr. Vontin, sir," he said, "the Sheriff and I would be delighted to have you with us."

"Most assuredly," said the Sheriff.

"I thank you both," said their host meekly. "Yes, I would like to go with you."

"You shall show me," said Nigg, with a chuckle, "the most profitable bays."

Now only Marguerite and Andrew had to be found a pursuit for the afternoon.

"Why not climb Marival?" asked Mr. Vontin. "It's the highest point on the island. It's only nine hundred and eighty feet high, but the view from it is glorious."

"We'll carve your initials on the cairn at the top," said Marguerite. "Mine are there already."

Andrew was not enticed; he shook his head.

"You play golf, Andrew," said his uncle. "Haven't you a small course here, Mr. Vontin?"

"Yes; it's small, but most enjoyable."

"No," said Andrew.

"He's coming swimming with me," said Marguerite, so confidently that the rest thought the swimming all along had been arranged and now was being divulged as a charming secret.

"Very pleasant it should be," said her father.

"Only don't tell us," said Quorr, "that it was warm."

"In some of our sandy bays it *is* quite lukewarm," said Vontin.

Quorr laughed. "Even as a kid I found it freezing my feet," he said.

Nigg was shivering. "As a child," he said, "I always saw the sea as an immense green dragon with many white manes trying to devour me. Now that I am supposed to have put away childish things, I am sorry to say that, even when it is as calm as it appears this afternoon, the sea still inspires me with terror and desolation. That is foolish, I know, but it is so. So much of life is folly, after all."

That humble but desolate confession produced a few murmurs of polite uneasiness and sympathy. These were, it seemed, Andrew Doig's cue.

"I am not going swimming," he said.

"They waited for him to speak again; it was obvious that words were forming in his mind choicer than Nigg's shells, than pearls even.

"I am going to join Donald McInver and his people."

They gazed from him to the table, as if, for a purpose they didn't understand, he had deposited on it, instead of the pearls, little black crabs.

"This afternoon," he went on, "they are cutting peats. I would like to go and help them."

"They will never burn those peats," said his uncle, in a grim by-the-way.

"So this," said Andrew, smiling on the Vontins, "is farewell. I cannot honourably remain here. I am very sorry. You have been most kind." He spoke with dignity.

Nevertheless Marguerite retorted quite rudely: "What do you know about cutting peats?"

"If they are never to be burned," he said, "it will make no difference whether they are well cut or not."

"Have they asked you?" she demanded, knowing they hadn't, for after the meeting at the Stone he had returned with her and her father.

He refrained from answering, but in such a way as to imply that yes, he had been asked, but not by the peat-cutters themselves.

"Even if they do let you help them," she said, "you'll still have to find a place to sleep."

Again he did not answer, and again he implied that hospitality richer than this fine mansion's would be offered him.

"If you think they'll take you into their pig-sties of houses," she said, "you're making a mistake. They know you're a guest here; they saw you today with us; they'll think you're some kind of spy. Don't imagine that because they call themselves godly they aren't suspicious."

"In this case," said the Sheriff, "their suspicions will be wholly justified. Andrew, you must allow me to speak plainly in the presence of these good people. I thought you had learnt a little sense in the short time you have been here; it seems I was wrong. However, I suppose I have some responsibility towards your mother and father. It's hardly likely that these people will offer you violence, but it is highly probable that they will refuse you hospitality on the pardonable ground that you are interested only in prying into their affairs for some inscrutable purpose of your own. They seem to be some kind of moral experiment on your part. If they turn you away, as I think they might, you will have nowhere to go. I am afraid, therefore, that in your parents' name I must forbid you to go."

Andrew's voice was very quiet.

"Do you likewise forbid me to believe that today, at the Sanctuary Stone, God was present?"

"I am not to be bamboozled by such sophistry, Andrew."

"I do believe it, sir: He was present."

"It is your own good father's belief that God is everywhere, at all times. You have been brought up in that belief, along with many millions of others."

"When I said present, sir, I meant actively present."

"To suggest divine sloth, Andrew, would surely be impious?"

Andrew smiled to hint that so blasphemous a gibe ought to be withdrawn. His uncle smiled too.

"You were affected yourself, sir," said Andrew.

"I?"

"Yes. And you still are; you still must be. So with us all."

"We are all somewhat distressed by the sight of simple people being misled to their own hurt, Andrew; and we are furthermore distressed to find you making a conceited mystery out of it."

"Is it not the case, sir, that you, we, all of us, are afraid in our hearts that if we do harm these innocent people, we will never be forgiven?"

"I have said I think the old man is deluded. That you seem to be too, Andrew, does not surprise me. His, however, is an involuntary condition; he deserves some sympathy."

Mr. Vontin laughed nervously. "Let's keep our sense of proportion," he said. "I don't mind your going to visit them, Andrew. Isn't that really what you came here for? Only please don't think this house will be closed to you as a result. We are not vindictive, we want to do what's right. If you find what you hope to find, why not come back and tell us? I for one shall be grateful; and I'm sure so will Marguerite."

Then Andrew and she gazed at each other. It was she who

blushed, who rose suddenly, threw her napkin upon the table, and rushed out of the room. As she went she uttered what sounded like a sob; but Quorr, who had decided she was as healthily hard in the heart as the Sanctuary Stone itself, knew he must be mistaken. It could not have been a sob; more likely a genteel grunt of disgust; which was, in the circumstances, a legitimate noise.

In his room, where he had gone to pack, Andrew was joined by his uncle who, as he entered and closed the door behind him, had the family likeness on his face more marked than ever before; so much so, indeed, that Andrew, like his mother, realised without having to glance again in the mirror, that he must also at that moment be like his uncle, outwardly. Inwardly, since all was changed, or changing, he could not say whom he was like.

The Sheriff accepted a chair. Andrew, excusing himself, went on taking his things out of drawers and putting them with neat humility into his suitcase on the bed. For a minute or so neither spoke. Through the window, wide-open on that Hesperidean afernoon, larks could be heard singing.

"Andrew," said his uncle at last, "I must confess I cannot understand this particular manoeuvre."

"I don't know what you mean, sir?" But was that true? Did he not know very well what his uncle meant? Now casuistry and evasion were not permissible. "Are you referring to my leaving this house to throw in my lot with Donald McInver and his people?"

"No, Andrew, I am not referring to that at all. You are not going to throw in your lot with anybody. You are as sufficient unto yourself as anyone I have known. Let me be frank. If you remember I once pointed out to you how very fortunate you were in having stumbled upon such friends as the Vontins. I admit it exasperated me that you, with your persistent perversity, should have been presented with such a short cut to success."

Andrew waited in submission.

"But I really was very pleased, Andrew. After all, you are my nephew; and I suppose perversity has always been a characteristic of youth."

ʹ Andrew still waited.

"There is no need for me, Andrew, to define success to you."

It was time to speak.

"Why not, sir? Success surely has many definitions."

"You have had your eye upon it ever since you could talk. But I do not blame you for that; nothing was ever achieved without ambition."

"Perhaps before I could talk, sir."

"There is no need to be cynical or flippant."

"Cynicism and flippancy are far from my mind at this moment, sir. I was merely referring to the fact that before I was born success, according to your definition, would be my mother's prayer, as it is almost every mother's prayer. It is true I have dreamt of that success: for instance, I have often imagined myself as an advocate, and later a judge of the High Court; or as the minister of some lucrative and influential church. To outdistance you and my father was my confident ambition. I used to try and convince myself that I wanted that success in order to be able to do good to others. That was humbug."

"It was, Andrew."

"It was, nevertheless, fashionable humbug. I adopted what are called liberal attitudes, partly because they genuinely appealed to me, and partly because for a young man of the twentieth century they represented the best and surest preparation for embracing success. I had noticed that so many of the most successful men of our time had passed through such a novitiate. All had been idealists in their youth; thus it was possible for them to pass from God to Mammon in such a way that they were able to enjoy the advantages of the transference without obloquy."

He closed his eyes and listened to the larks. He also heard his uncles's rather impatient breathing.

"I suppose," Andrew went on, "my sympathy for the evicted people here was part of my campaign. But there was no doubt that I always kept a part of myself detached and uncommitted, the part which in the end says yes, the indestructible ego. I came here at its instigation; like yourself, sir, it saw clearly the value of cultivating the acquaintance of a millionaire; it had my programme worked out for me."

Then he turned to face his uncle, whom he found chewing at his knuckle as if it was a sweet. He spoke cautiously.

"There has been a change of programme," he said.

His uncle chuckled.

Andrew did not heed that chuckle. "I do not yet know what I am to do," he said, "except go to Donald McInver. It may be I am to be instructed by him."

"He is an old man driven daft by religion," observed his uncle.

"No doubt there were many who found Christ Himself daft, sir."

"Don't let us quarrel, Andrew. You have shown with admirable clarity that you and I are on the same side of the argument. There seems, however, to be one little cloud of confusion left in your mind. I shall leave Donald and his friends to dispel it." The Sheriff rose. "I shall say this for you, Andrew: you have one of the most resourceful, slippery minds I have ever encountered. Whatever craziness you are about to embark on now, I think your mother need have no fear. If ever I saw a young man doomed to success, you are he."

By the door he paused. "I understand Miss Vontin wishes to speak to you before you go. I hope, Andrew, that this change of programme as you call it does not involve any discourtesy or hurt to the young lady. Not only is she charming and gracious, but she also seems rather fond of you."

Then he left, with another chuckle, while Andrew caught sight of himself in the mirror. Was this, he wondered, the possessor of a resourceful, slippery mind? Could this be the sweetheart, the husband, of Marguerite Vontin, beautiful daughter of a rich island king? Was this the future frock-coated, black-capped success? Then came the crucial question, which could not be put into words.

Though he had packed his case, when he left the house he was carrying only a small parcel; it contained his pyjamas, tooth-brush, and shaving-kit. To take more, he had decided, would stultify his pilgrimage.

Marguerite was seated in a deck-chair on the lawn, smoking and reading a book. She called to him and sat up, laughing.

He walked over with what he wished to be a friendly farewell smile; but her laughter strained his loving-kindness far more than his uncle's sarcasms had.

She was dressed in blue linen slacks, so fine as to be surely, against sunlight, transparent, and in a white blouse unbuttoned so low at the neck that as he stood over her he saw more of her bosom than he ought, before his gaze, swift and austere as a gull, skimmed seaward.

She stared up at him through her dark glasses.

"So you're not going through with it?" she asked.

"If you mean that I am not going to the peats, you are mistaken."

"Where's your luggage? I thought you went up to pack."

"I have packed. With your permission, I shall leave my suitcase till later."

"So you expect to be back?"

"For my case."

"Is this what you're taking with you?" She lifted a foot and neatly kicked his parcel. Taken unawares, he let it drop. She was first down and snatched it up. He held out his hand for it, but she would not give it to him. She dandled it.

"So you're really going?" she asked.

"Yes."

"You'll not be much help at the peats in those clothes."

He had on his blazer and well-ironed flannels.

"Do you know what I think, Andrew?" she asked coyly.

Not only did he not know, but he was suddenly anxious not to know. There was no doubt the temptation was strong to abandon his journey to those symbolical peats, drop down here upon the grass at her side, and, with his head against her chair or her legs, fence her with witty taunts. In such a pastime would not his resourceful, slippery mind shine? He almost smiled.

"I think it's not old Donald at all you're going to visit," she said.

"No?" Nor was it Donald really, but rather that presence which Donald seemed able to suggest, to conjure up, to turn from a faint-hearted wish to a passionate hope.

"No. I think it's Sheila, his grand-daughter."

He could not join in her laughter, which was, indeed, increased by his inability.

"She's got the reputation of being very bonny. I noticed she seemed to fascinate you at the pier yesterday, with her pretty flowers and her golden hair. Isn't she a bit pudgy, though? They say, too, he's got her as soft in the head as himself. And I wonder how often she takes a bath."

"There is no need to be vulgar," he said.

That silenced her. While she gaped, he added: "I mean, at the expense of a girl who hasn't your advantages."

"Vulgar!" she repeated.

He realised the word had been too severe; but before he could find a way of moderating it, without taking away its truthfulness, she jumped to her feet and flung his parcel into the air.

"You've got a damned cheek," she cried. Her own were pink; it did not appear that her indignation was feigned.

"There is no need for us to lose our tempers," he said.

Perhaps that reproof, if it had been hotly made, might have been more effective; coolly, and indeed meekly uttered, it incensed her more.

"It's about high time I lost my temper with you," she cried. "You're a prig and a prude and a sneak and a fool and a fraud, all cold-blooded. You can hardly walk or talk for conceit." She took two or three paces in what he considered a hyperbolical imitation of his gait. "Shall I tell you how much sympathy you really have for those people? Listen to the grasshopper." They both listened and heard the insect clearly. "It's got as much as you have. That's true, Andrew. You're a humbug." And then she added, with a giggle, "A handsome humbug."

It was not the first time he had been insulted in those terms by a woman, but it was the first time he deigned to defend himself.

"Be fair, Marguerite," he said earnestly. "Surely a humbug's chief object is to further his own interests."

"Heaven knows what yours are," she said, laughing.

He insisted on staring straight into her eyes.

"I may tell you, Marguerite," he said, his voice trembling a little, "that I have never regretted anything more in my life than having to leave here. I shall always regret it. You called me cold-blooded; it may be I am, but I am not a fish without feelings. You called me a prude: so be it, but weren't you and I hand-in-hand at the lily-pond last night? Yes, I'm a sneak and a fool and a fraud; but I want you to believe this, that being with you here, in this paradise, has meant more to me than I can realise now. In a sense I shall be with you here for the rest of my life. You accused me of wanting to go to see Sheila, Donald McInver's grand-daughter. I know you were being humorous, for surely you must be aware that after having seen you, not even I could find that girl, or any girl, lovelier. It so happens, Marguerite, I prefer black hair. I had better say no more. This must be good-bye, but I do not want it to be good-bye. Tomorrow I shall leave Sollas. I believe it is my duty to go, but it is certainly not my pleasure. Good-bye."

With that last word he smiled and put out his hand, took hers which was somewhat nervously offered, shook it, and then walked, all conceit shed, to where his parcel lay on the lawn. Picking it up and tucking it under his arm, he set off northwards.

It seemed to him then that many grasshoppers and innumerable larks and the one mighty sea all joined in a diapason of regret and sorrow. Amidst it came a shriek. It was Marguerite. He turned. She was waving, in annoyance it seemed, and yet in sorrow too. He waved back, and then continued on his way, resolute as Christian, or Quixote.

She came running and soon overtook him. Panting, she seized his arm.

"I'm sorry, Andrew," she cried. "Really, I am."

He saw that there was still laughter in her eyes, but it was neither hostile nor contemptuous. He could not tell what kind of laughter it was.

"You'll come back?" she pleaded.

"Only to pick up my case."

"Don't be silly. Stay for a month. What's to prevent you? I want you to, and so does my father; and so do you. Didn't you say so? Go and help them with their silly peats, if they'll let you. Spend the night with them if you want to. But come back tomorrow, and not just for your case. Please, Andrew. You and I could have a lot of fun here."

He was sure they could. Looking away from her, towards the sky, he saw two ways, as in the old ballad: the braid braid road that lay across the lily leven, and the narrow road thick beset with thorns and briers. How well his resourceful and slippery mind could devise good reasons, reasons to satisfy every authority on earth, for taking that first road which led so pleasantly to where God would never be found. But that other bitter hard road, at the end of which God welcomed and refreshed, was the one he must take; and at this moment it led away from this great mansion and this lovely, pleading girl, across the barren moors to the hovels in the north of the island where a few simple folk, in a test of faith, were cutting black peats from the earth. It was not just Marguerite who held him by the arm, urging him not to go; it was his own mother, whose voice the sweet larks imitated; it was even his father, that gentle succumber; it was his uncle, his professors, Mrs. Crail, the fat policeman and the lustful maid at the lily-pond; it was the whole world of urgent, joyous, sinful mankind. What made his resistance too all the more difficult was that he could never be sure that the other tugging, which drew him towards the bleaker north, was really done by God; it could very well be his own conceit, as Marguerite had said, which was enticing him. To give up what one wanted most might not always be true renunciation; for that very giving up could be looked on by pride as its ultimate triumph.

He did not speak, after that long minute of reflection; instead, he took her hand which clutched his arm, pressed it, and gently took it away. Then he set off again.

She gazed after him, shaking her head, and laughing.

Sixteen

AFTER lunch Mr. Nigg did not feel well: it could not be a physical indisposition, he thought, but rather his native melancholy coming to full flower in the sunshine of this sad holy isle. Nevertheless, he was glad to creep off to his bedroom and lie down on the bed for half an hour or so, beforé venturing on his quest for shells. As he lay, in his lemon-coloured drawers, he tried to see the events of that morning and yesterday simply and clearly; but always this mist of desolation, shot with strange colours and inexplicable sudden brightnesses, hung over his thoughts and recollections. Voices from mouths he could not see sounded in his ears, saying things he could not understand: they seemed mostly to be calling, as were the larks outside the shrouded window, but he could not be sure what their summons was or whether it was really for him.

As he dozed human faces drifted through his semiconsciousness: Donald McInver's, white-bearded and terrible; young Andrew Doig's intense and selfish; the Sheriff's, strangely puerile; Quorr's red and fierce and compassionate; Miss Vontin's beautiful but arrogant; and Mirren, his wife's, wonderfully patient and forbearing, nakedly affectionate, with her lips moving as if she was trying to tell him something which all their married life had been withheld, because of her pride and his own sterile humanity.

Suddenly he sat up. He heard again Quorr's voice roar down to him from the back of a black horse as high as a tree: "I wish you luck with your shells, Niggie. Pick them up in handfuls, as Cortes did jewels in the palace of Montezuma." Then there was the thundering of hooves as Quorr galloped away.

As Nigg shook his head, to get rid of that ridiculous vision and noise, he heard what seemed to be a knock at the door. Listening hard, he heard it again, and smiled: this then had been the thundering of the hooves.

"Yes?" he cried.

It was the Sheriff who answered.

"Mr. Vontin and I will be ready in about twenty minutes," he said. "Will that suit you?"

"That will suit me admirably, thank you, sir."

"It is for us to thank you, Mr. Nigg. Downstairs then, in twenty minutes?"

"I shall be punctual, sir."

"As always, Mr. Nigg, as always." The Sheriff was obviously chuckling as he walked away.

Nigg sank down again upon the bed. The silliest of regrets came into his mind. For ten years he had worked under the Sheriff, who had never once called him by his Christian name, Hector. Surely efficiency did not preclude friendliness? What was the good of reputation and honour if one's face grew like a fox's?

For at least two minutes Nigg tried to remember whose face it was that had grown like a fox's. He saw that face everywhere, but could not say whose it was; just as recognition was about to come into his mind, it slunk away again, like a fox itself.

At last he struggled up into a sitting position again, and pressed his head with his hands.

"What is the matter?" he kept murmuring. "I must get up. I have to meet the Sheriff and Mr. Vontin in twenty minutes."

Then he realised that at least half of those twenty minutes were gone. In a panic he squirmed off the bed, and found himself staggering about the floor; his legs felt and looked as unsubstantial as sunbeams. It must be the heat, he thought, or that glass of wine, or perhaps yesterday's sea-nausea delayed. Whatever it was, it seemed to pass, and soon he was able to pull on his trousers which he had providently removed before lying down. All his life, even as a boy at school, he had been tidy with his clothes: the habit had at first delighted Mirren, but latterly had seemed to exasperate her, surely beyond proportion.

He was not late. Indeed, he had time for a short conversation with Miss Vontin on the lawn. When he appeared ouside the door, she hailed him.

"All set for the big shell hunt?" she asked cheerfully.

"Yes, Miss Vontin." Why, he wondered, had he in that strange dream seen her as arrogant? To him she had always been as gracious and friendly as she was being now.

He took out of his pocket and showed her, with a pathos of which he was himself humorously aware, the striped bag and the thimble, which were his equipment.

"I put them in here," he said, holding out the bag. "The thimble's for measurement: each shell must sit in snugly."

Out of more than politeness she took the thimble from him and admired it as if it was more beautiful in itself than any shell could be.

"And they're to make a necklace for Mrs. Nigg?" she asked.

He nodded. "She says it can be done. She read about it in a magazine. It would seem to me the shells might be too fragile to stand up to the boring of holes in them. But I promised to bring them."

"Do you know what I think, Mr. Nigg?" she said. "I think that this is the most charming thing ever to be done on this island, in its whole history." She spoke as if she meant it, with St. Solla included; and all the time her eyes kept devouring the thimble, as if it were a gem from Montezuma's coffers.

Indeed, with her gleaming black hair and tanned face, she looked not unlike an Aztec princess.

"Thank you, Miss Vontin," he said.

"Some day," she cried impulsively, "you must come back here for a holiday, and bring Mrs. Nigg with you."

He trembled, without quite knowing why, and was glad to rest his hand on the back of her chair.

"Thank you," he said again.

"I mean it," she said. "I should love to see Mrs. Nigg wear her necklace."

He became aware that though she was speaking about him and Mirren she was thinking about herself and Andrew Doig.

"Has Mr. Doig gone?" he asked.

"Yes," she replied, with great eagerness, and stared in the direction where Andrew had disappeared.

"Do you think, Mr. Nigg," she asked, "he was wise to go?"

Nigg was silent. That mist, those voices, were again confusing him. Again there was a summons. He knew all the time it was foolishness. Yet if he had not been holding on to her chair he might have floated up over the trees, out to sea.

"I'm sorry," she was saying. "I shouldn't have asked you that."

"Why not, Miss Vontin? I like the young man and respect him."

That certainly was Nigg himself speaking, he was sure of that; but someone else said: "It is a good thing for a young man to suspect authority." He couldn't understand how that someone else could still be himself.

"I'm afraid I don't quite understand Andrew," she said.

He had a moment of extreme lucidity. "How long have you known him, Miss Vontin?" he asked.

She laughed. "Not very long, true enough," she admitted.

"People can live in close association for almost thirty years and still not understand each other," he said. "Love does not make for understanding; no, it does not; it makes for acceptance."

She was surprised, but just smiled.

"Mr. Doig is very young," said Nigg. "He is also very clever. He is in good health. He is handsome. He has been lucky in his parentage. The world, as they say, is his oyster. Why should he be content so soon with the shabby substitute for happiness that suffices the rest of us? There are many discoveries still to be made in the world; and surely the greatest will be made in the human heart?"

She was looking at him with astonishment, concern, and friendly amusement.

"Are you feeling all right, Mr. Nigg?" she asked.

He, too, smiled. "Why? Am I talking with incoherence?"

"The very opposite," she said. "You were talking very wisely. But I thought I saw you shiver."

"Perhaps you did. What is it the superstitious say? An angel walking over my grave. No, Miss Vontin, I feel perfectly well. Sometimes bright sunshine confuses my dark city mind; and here it is very bright indeed. This island is indeed a paradise."

"Now it is," she admitted, laughing. "In the winter time I believe it's pretty grim."

Intending to agree with her, for cold and rain aggravated his rheumatism, he looked round to imagine this serene warm landscape in its winter bleakness, and saw instead that it was indeed transformed, but in a way he had not anticipated and could never have described: it was as if a background to the fulfilment of hope and the banishment of fear had been provided.

He stood laughing.

Laughing herself, Marguerite had to tug him and point to where her father and the Sheriff had come out of the house. As he thanked her and hurried to join his companions, he was laughing in a way that made her sit up and even stand, to stare after him, and make sure it was really laughter and not a kind of weeping. When she saw him being greeted by her father cheerfully, she felt relieved, and sat down again, not to read, but to gaze towards the green hill Marival, beyond which somewhere Andrew might be having his flannels sullied by peat, or his soul saddened by dour and godly snubs.

So benign was the weather, even the Sheriff went bare-headed. Mr. Vontin wore a tan linen suit. Nigg, who had brought his hat out with him, was persuaded by the Sheriff to leave it. As he set off without it, he reminded them slyly of the earl in the old ballad who, surprised by a night attack, had rushed out of his tent without his helmet, so that in the fight he had been slain by a sword slash on the head.

"We have our swordsmen here too," said Mr. Vontin, laughing. "The black-capped terns. If you wander out on to the promontories, where their nests are, they will make diving attacks upon you."

"Aren't terns small birds?" asked the Sheriff.

"Yes. But in any case they only pretend to strike. I've never heard of any actually doing so. It's only solitary people they go for; so we're quite safe. They'll probably whizz above our heads, screeching."

"Do you often walk alone, Mr. Vontin?" asked Nigg.

"Quite often, Mr. Nigg."

"It is a lovely place for solitude."

"This machair," said Vontin, glancing about it, "is the pleasantest, most consoling place on earth; or so I used to think." He spoke with a sigh, as if he would like the subject to be changed.

The Sheriff briskly changed it.

"Have you brought your thimble, Mr. Nigg?" he asked.

Nigg took it out.

"They must all," explained the Sheriff to Vontin, "fit in neatly."

Vontin smiled.

"It seems to me," chuckled the Sheriff, "that it will take hundreds of such exiguity to make up a necklace."

"Especially as Mrs. Nigg's neck," murmured Nigg, "is on the plump side."

"Now, Mr. Nigg, you know I intended no such innuendo."

"I am aware of that, sir. I was joking. I suppose there are plenty of shells lying about the beach."

"Multitudes," said Vontin.

"Do I just have to stoop and snatch up handfuls, as Cortes did gems in the palace of Montezuma?"

They were startled by the allusion.

"The remark is not original," said Nigg. "That was how Mr. Quorr wished me luck with my gathering, before he galloped away."

"I hope he is careful," said the Sheriff.

"He will not be, sir, but neither will any harm come to him. How many risks did Cortes take, and yet emerge safe?"

"Mr. Quorr is hardly a conquistador."

"He thinks he is, sir; or rather he thinks he should be."

Then they were interrupted by something they saw upon the ground: a heap of white bones amidst blackened sea-wrack; eyeless, and horned, a skull grinned.

"A sheep," said the Sheriff.

Grimacing, the Sheriff prodded the horror with his polished toe-cap. Fat blue flies fizzed in and out of the eye-sockets, and one zoomed boisterously up to alight on Nigg's mouth. He struck at it in disgust, and dragging from his pocket his bottle of insect repellent, uncorked it, and waved it ritualistically in front of him. Up buzzed more and more flies.

"It seems to be a fraud," he said, as they hurried away.

They walked a little way across the smooth turf, parallel to the shore. Above them larks sang; among rocks red-billed, orange-legged oyster-catchers screamed. The sea shimmered.

"It must be easier for the Dyak headhunter," said the Sheriff suddenly.

His companions looked at him in surprise.

"His wife too sends him forth to collect material for a necklace," he said.

Now they understood, but were still surprised.

"In their case," he added, "human skulls, shrunken, are the beads."

He did not apologise for so bizarre and repulsive an observation, but he did not enlarge upon it. Indeed, as if in atonement, he began to collect specimens of the many wild flowers growing all round, until in his hand was a bunch, fragrant and many-coloured, recalling that which McInver's grand-daughter had brought yesterday to the pier as an offering.

Vontin named them. "Heartsease, blood-red crane's bill, selfheal, eyebright, ladies' bedstraw."

"They are very beautiful," said Nigg. "Indeed, we are walking in a garden."

Then the Sheriff threw the flowers away, not one by one, in a kind of Persephonean rite, but all together, with a gesture of completion, like a collier with a crumpled fish-poke.

"Here is the bay I spoke of," said Vontin.

They looked at the tawny crescent of sand, the white water, the blue sea, and the bluer sky. At their feet were irises, with their sword-like leaves gleaming like silver. The yellow flowers reminded Nigg again of Montezuma, rich in gold as well as gems. He thought that these handsome upright flowers would have suited his wife far more than the small-stalked unassuming ones of the machair: it was not a contemptuous or disloyal thought: these irises seemed to him, because of this association with his tall 'straight wife, precious, so that he tried not to step on any as he walked past them.

The Sheriff plucked a leaf to ply it like a cutlass against the flies which were numerous there.

"They'll not be so bad nearer the water," said Vontin.

They stood at last in the midst of that vast crescent.

"A fine harvest of shells here, Mr. Nigg," said the Sheriff.

"So I see, sir."

"Take care, as you gather them, you are not afflicted by the sea-madness."

"What is that, sir?"

"The legends of these islands are full of it. Is that not so, Mr. Vontin?"

Their host nodded, with a smile.

"Usually there is a temptress," said the Sheriff, "in the form of a selchie, or seal-woman."

Close to the sea stood a dappled rock. Might it not, thought Nigg, turn into a selchie, in this uncanny atmosphere? Here seemed to be the edge of eternity; there was no knowing what a sudden turn of the head might reveal.

"But do not be alarmed, Mr. Nigg," said the Sheriff, laughing. "Selchies are creatures of the gloaming."

Two or three yards away lay a jelly-fish. It had been troubling Nigg. Now he walked over to it boldly.

"Dead," called the Sheriff, "dead as Montezuma."

"Yes, of course, sir. But isn't it huge?"

"I believe," said Vontin, "that that sort can sting rather badly."

Nigg looked at the sea still more apprehensively.

"You are really quite safe here, Mr. Nigg," said the Sheriff.

"I was wondering, sir, if I might be able to bathe my feet."

"But I thought it was always for you a great green monster, with many white manes?"

"So it is, sir. But must we not slay our monsters, one by one?"

"Ah, yes. I see now. You wish to place your foot upon its slaughtered neck, as St. George does with his dragon in the children's story-books."

"Something like that, sir. At the same time, I've been told that bathing in sea-water alleviates rheumatism."

"Do you suffer from it, Mr. Nigg?" asked Vontin, sympathetically.

Nigg smiled. "Every winter is a campaign," he said. "I am encased in such armour as flannel steeped in liniment, or cotton wool impregnated with camphorated oil. People sniff as I limp past."

The others joined him in laughing.

"Well," said the Sheriff, "I am sure neither Mr. Vontin nor I have any objection to your paddling your feet. Indeed, we hope fervently you do find it beneficial."

Mr. Vontin agreed.

"So, if you do not mind, Mr. Nigg," said the Sheriff, "we shall leave you here for a little while to your paddling and gathering. We shall go a bit farther, as far as the promontory yonder. Mr. Vontin tells me seals are often to be found basking there; real seals, of course. Will that be all right?"

"Of course, sir."

"You'll manage by yourself?" The Sheriff looked at his little clerk with humorous indulgence.

"Surely."

"After all, there is only one thimble."

"That is so, sir."

They all laughed.

"We won't be any longer than half an hour. Happy hunting."

"Thank you, sir."

Then the Sheriff and Vontin began to stroll along the sands towards the distant rocks.

For a minute or so Nigg gazed not so much after them as at the footmarks they left on the sand. He pretended that the makers of those marks no longer existed; it was somehow an easy pretence, and he felt a loneliness more profound than any he had ever felt before. It was as if these faint marks were now his only contact with humankind, and in a very short while they too would have vanished. He had a sensation of crushing regret for opportunities of love and service neglected and now lost for good.

He decided, despite the dead jelly-fish, to remove his shoes and socks as he gathered his shells. When he had them off, and saw them there forlorn on that vast beach, he saw himself similarly isolated on the far vaster foreshore of time. The sight somehow did not sadden him, so that he was smiling as he went forward to where shells lay in profusion.

He had picked up the first one, and was admiring its tiny but perfect loveliness as it lay nestled in the thimble, when it seemed that the whole sky became black and loud with myriads of swift-winged terns, all diving at his solitary un-helmeted head. Their beaks struck him one concentrated blow. He staggered, but on the sand there was no prop, all the furniture seemed to have been removed, the house was empty, no one would ever be at home again. He was murmuring Mirren's name as he fell to the sand.

Meanwhile the Sheriff and Mr. Vontin had begun an important conversation; it was the Sheriff who introduced it. As he spoke he swung gently a long stalk of seaweed, like a cow's tail, which he had picked up from the sand, with the witticism that he appeared to have the propensities of a beach-comber.

In his talk, what he wished to salvage was his nephew's chance of a quick, smooth, and successful temporal career.

"I must confess," he said, "there are times when I find Andrew's quixotry somewhat trying. Of course we all agree it is a good thing for a young man to test for himself the basis of society, but only if he keeps in mind the distinction between testing and undermining."

Mr. Vontin smiled amiably. "It might be," he said, "that he thinks he has found that basis not as sound as he would like."

"I have no doubt he is guilty of that quite stupendous impertinence."

"Does it not depend upon his criterion? If he judges by strictly Christian principles, then it is little wonder he finds much amiss."

"Only one person in history, Mr. Vontin, was entitled to judge by strictly Christian principles."

Vontin nodded, and then paused to admire the skimming and dipping of some sand-pipers. "I like Andrew," he said.

"His University record has been brilliant," said the Sheriff. "He's a prize-winner in Greek. I'm afraid, however, he has let himself get mixed up in a number of particularly obtuse undergraduate activities."

"I hope you're not referring to his Argonauts' Society?"

The Sheriff had to remember he was talking to a man who had called his yacht *Argo*.

"No," he said suavely. "There is much beauty and wisdom in those ancient Greek legends."

"Don't leave out the mystery," added Vontin. He halted again and looked about him. "You could easily imagine Jason or Odysseus or Perseus landing here."

The Sheriff too looked; it was not easy for him to imagine any of those legendary heroes come striding, with wings borrowed from the gods on his ankles, through the surf up on to the sand beside them.

"I have made a lot of money," said Vontin," but I would give away most of it to be still in the state of search that Andrew is, or even Mr. Nigg."

Both turned, smiling, and stared back along the sand to

where, a quarter of a mile away, Nigg was kneeling, so as to be near to his hoard of shells.

"What is his Christian name?" asked Vontin.

The Sheriff at first could not remember. He tried one or two ordinary ones, but they did not sound right. Then he hit upon it.

"Hector!" he cried. "Yes, that's it, Hector."

Vontin was delighted. "Hector!" he repeated. "Hector, of the glancing helm, champion of Troy."

The Sheriff nodded; he too had been a prizewinner in Greek.

They strolled on again.

"I wonder what he'll bring back with him?" mused Vontin.

The Sheriff wasn't sure whom he meant; at first he thought it must be Nigg, or even that other Hector.

"Andrew," murmured Vontin.

"Disillusionment."

"More than that, I hope. I don't care much for disillusioned young people. I've met a lot of them."

The Sheriff did not say that surely Miss Vontin had few illusions; it was for that reason, indeed, that he had approved of her.

"Green is the colour of credulity," said Vontin. "It is also, in my view, the colour of life."

The Sheriff now regretted having entered upon that conversation; he would have served Andrew better by saying nothing. As it was, it appeared he had been trying zealously to wrench up what he considered weeds of naïveté and youthful conceit, only to discover just in time that to this sad and sated millionaire they were, for some obscure reason, beautiful and vital growths.

Then they both thought they heard Nigg calling them. When they turned they saw he was still kneeling in the same spot. It could not have been he who had called; it must have been one of the seagulls near him.

A thought occurred to both of them at the same time: surely those gulls were very near him, too near.

They looked at each other.

"Do you think he's all right?" asked Vontin.

The Sheriff dropped his stalk of seaweed and, cupping his hands round his mouth, halloo'd.

There was no response; not even the gulls replied, or moved.

"I think we had better go back," said Vontin.

The Sheriff agreed.

By this time they were not sure that he was really kneeling. Certainly he did not seem to be gathering shells. It might be that he had collapsed on to his face.

Vontin set off at a pace too quick for the Sheriff's shorter legs, which had to trot to keep up.

Somehow the sand seemed softer; it hindered them far more; at every step a fist seemed to grip their feet. The whole scene had become much less benign: there was menace in the sea's crash, desolation in the sea-birds' cries, aloofness in the few high clouds.

They could not hurry all the way; they walked, and had breath for shouting. Still there was no response.

"I thought he looked a bit off colour after lunch," panted Vontin.

"I'm afraid I didn't notice."

"Perhaps the heat's been too much for him?"

"Perhaps," gasped the Sheriff, "but I was just thinking that this sea-breeze will always keep the island temperate, even on the hottest day."

Now they were near enough to scare off the dozen or so of gulls which had been standing near Nigg, as if discussing the reason for his immobility. Beside him lay his shoes and socks; his feet were bare, and the soles were showing because of his position. He was on his knees right enough, but had slumped forward so that his arms and head rested on the sand. Near him was the dead jelly-fish.

Vontin reached him first, and went down on one knee in order to be able to touch him and talk to him with the necessary urgent intimacy.

"Mr. Nigg," he said, "Mr. Nigg, what's wrong?"

He touched him in his solicitude, gently but still too roughly for that delicate and lucky balance to be maintained. Slowly, Nigg leaned to one side and rolled on to the sand. His face was revealed. There was sand on it, especially on the blue lips and in the eyes, which were open.

They saw, as quickly as the gulls had, that he was dead; but they could not take so calmly such a swift slipping away from them into eternity, behind their backs. They crouched and stared at each other. There were many signs all round them of the omnipotence under which they still lived, and Nigg lay dead: the very thimble tumbled among the shells, the waving irises, the incessant sea, even the hopping of tiny sand-fleas.

For a full minute they did not speak.

Then they made their dead companion more comfortable, placing him properly on his back, removing a pebble from under his head, and straightening his legs and arms. Then they confirmed what was certain: they felt his heart, and held a watch-glass over his mouth; there were no beats, no mist of breath.

"It must have been his heart," whispered Vontin.

"I never heard," said the Sheriff, his voice equally low, "that it was weak."

Vontin took his handkerchief and laid it over the dead man's face.

"I'll stay here with him," he said, "if you'd like to run up to the house for help."

The Sheriff hesitated.

"Or if you wish," added Vontin, "you stay here and I'll go."

"I should like to stay," said the Sheriff.

"Very well. I'll send for a doctor. The nearest one's on Mula. You'll be all right?"

The Sheriff nodded, and stood watching his host hasten up the bank of sand, through the irises, on to the machair, and so eventually out of sight. Then he took up his other vigil, though what he was now to watch over he could not clearly have said. Soon he thought it better to try and find refuge in considering the practical consequences of this so unexpected death: how Mrs. Nigg, for instance, could be most quickly and humanely informed, how her wishes must be discovered and respected in the matter of the body's disposal, and how tomorrow's business must surely go on.

Seventeen

AFTER being so curiously dammed at the Sanctuary Stone, Bull's spirit now roared in prodigious spate; both his mates' jocular remonstrances and his sergeant's reproofs were swept aside in his outbursts. Every now and then, like a man possessed by a mad joy, he would turn to Rollo, seeking him out if he wasn't in sight, seize him by the arm or hand or tunic, and assure him that if God was on the island, as Rollo had said, then He would have to keep out of the way if He didn't want to get hurt.

They were all present in the grieve's sitting-room on the last of these occasions. It was after lunch and they were all ready to go out.

Rollo's arm still ached from Bull's last grip; this time he was quite vicious in his annoyance; but he could not, despite his angry effort, pull away the great fist that clutched his tunic at the chest.

"What's got into you, Bull?" he asked. "You're giving nobody any peace. All right, we've all heard you: if you meet God, you're going to strangle Him, kick Him to death, toss Him into the sea. All right, go out and meet Him, and do what you like; only don't bother us."

"Sure I'm going out, Rollo, and Grooner's coming with me to see what happens to this God of yours if He tries to get in my way."

"He's not mine, Bull."

"Is He yours, Creepe?"

Creepe was not provoked; indeed, he was the only one who was enjoying this foolish blasphemy of Bull's.

"My God, Bull," he said, "could pull you limb from limb, just as easily as you could a daddy-longlegs."

It was clear that Bull, when envisaging God, saw Him as Christ was portrayed on children's Sunday school prize cards: thin, pale, effeminate.

"Let Him try, Creepe," he roared, laughing. "Just let Him try."

"Or He could," added Creepe, with quiet relish, "make you that if a woman, the most beautiful in the world, was to walk up and down in front of you, naked, you would be as innocent, and as helpless, as a new-born babe."

Bull, as well as the others, was startled by that illustration of omnipotence.

"Do you think so, Creepe?" he roared.

"Quiet, Bull," said one of the others. "We're in another man's house, remember."

"Do you think so, Creepe?" repeated Bull, just as loudly.

Creepe smiled as if he was actually seeing that exhibition of marvellous impotence.

"I do," he said calmly.

Speer, who felt that his authority ought to have been enhanced by the strange quick healing of his mouth, tried again to assert it.

"I'm ordering you all to stop that sort of talk," he said. "It'll just cause trouble. You know what the Sheriff said; religion's not to be discussed. I'm surprised at you, Creepe."

"Am I not to defend the God I believe in, sergeant?"

"Just keep religion out of it, that's all," said Speer.

"It wasn't me mentioned it first, sergeant," said Bull. "Rollo did. He threatened me. You all heard him."

"I thought you could take a joke, Bull," said Rollo.

"Isn't that what I'm doing, Rollo? I'm the only one that's laughing. You think God's a dog, Rollo; you were going to set Him on me. It's the same word spelled backward, see. But if He comes at me, He'll get my boot in his teeth. That's the joke. Why aren't the rest of you bastards laughing? Go on, Grooner, show them how to laugh."

He rushed at Grooner and, seizing him by the shoulders, shook him violently, all the time roaring to him to laugh.

"For Christ's sake, Bull," protested Grooner.

"Now you're at it, Grooner. Now you're threatening me."

"Have you taken leave of your senses?"

"So you're calling me mad now?"

Dand and Rickie, helped by the sergeant, forced Bull back from Grooner, who had to sit down, his face pale and greenish.

"Nobody's going to call me mad and get away with it," yelled Bull.

"Nobody did," panted Dand, "but by God everybody's going to if you keep this up."

Rickie was furious; one of Bull's boots had crashed against his ankle.

"If you've not gone off your head, Bull," he said, "you're acting like it."

"You'll be breaking the furniture," complained Speer.

Bull suddenly went peaceful in the chair into which they had forced him.

"I'm fine," he said. "I'm in the best of health. I'm not like Grooner there, with rotted guts; or like Rollo, that's never had a woman in his life. It's not Rollo's guts that are rotted. So you're going fishing this afternoon, Rollo? You'll catch nothing."

Rollo grinned at that infantile jeer.

"And what about you, Creepe?" asked Bull.

"What about me, Bull?"

"You're going fishing with Rollo?"

"Yes, I am."

"I'm going too, as a matter of fact," said Speer, but nobody heeded him.

Bull leant forward towards Creepe, with a wink.

"Just to show you there's no hard feelings, Creepe," he said, "I'm going to tell you where you'll catch the kind of fish that'll do you the most good. Along at the big house. Her name's Bridie. She'll take you to the lily-pond, Creepe. There are fish in that pond, Creepe, wee fish, all colours. She's the fish for you, Creepe."

Creepe took a step forward.

"Are you trying to pass off your spent whore on to me?" he asked. He seemed insulted beyond what the others thought was reasonable, considering Bull's humour.

"She's not spent, Creepe. She's far from being spent. You'd find her a change from that lump of ice, in the black flannel nightgown, that you have to sleep with every night."

Then Speer, Dand, and Rickie had to hold back Creepe from Bull, who relaxed in his chair, laughing.

"For God's sake, Grooner," whispered Speer, "take him out."

Grooner was sullen and indignant. "Me? Didn't he try to go for me?"

"He's your mate, all the same. I can tell you this, Grooner, if he wasn't here you wouldn't be here. At headquarters they look on you as his mate."

"We're a long way from headquarters, sergeant."

"I know that. Don't think I'm not taking notice. There'll be a report; don't worry about that. But take him out, Grooner. If we get him away from Rollo and Creepe he'll be all right. In a way it's really Rollo's fault." The sergeant began to speak out passionately. "What did the Superintendent say? That the eyes of the country would be on us. And what are we doing? Squabbling among ourselves. We're here to uphold the law. Didn't the Sheriff say that civilisation's in our charge; yes, civilisation. This is no way to behave therefore."

Bull got to his feet calmly. He waved his hand as if to soothe and absolve them all.

"I'm going to give myself a wash," he said. "You're right, sergeant. When I'm clean again, I'll go out, and look for God." He added the last four words quickly, as if to take all his listeners by surprise.

As he went out, laughing, he made a playful lunge at Rollo.

At last he was gone. In the silence they heard the clock in the corner, and the larks in the sky.

"Thank Christ for that," gasped Dand, sitting down. "I think he's gone off his head."

"No." It was Rollo who spoke.

They looked at him.

"It was that girl," he said.

"Bridie?" asked Grooner.

"No, no, the other one, the young one: McInver's granddaughter."

"But she's fat and glaikit," said Rickie.

"That's it," said Rollo. "Did you see Bull at the pier? Did you see him pick up her flowers for her? And did you see the way he looked at her as he handed them to her? I'll never forget it. He must have thought she was an angel."

"God forgive me," said Grooner, "I liked him for it. I thought it was about the decentest thing he's ever done."

"So it was, Grooner. Didn't he nearly go for you, Creepe, because you joked about her?"

"He did."

"He must have thought she was his ideal."

"Well," admitted Grooner, "he's always said he'd marry a girl with golden hair."

"And a big soft bust," said Dand.

"And with no will to say no," sneered Creepe.

Rollo grinned at these corroborations.

"That's right," he said. "I watched him closely. I saw what was going on in his mind. Then this morning at the Stone he saw what we all saw; that she's a half-wit."

"And not too clean," said Grooner.

"True, Grooner; and we all know what a fetish he makes of cleanliness."

"I've never understood that," remarked Dand.

"You're no psychologist, Dand," said Rollo, with a grin. "Isn't he trying unconsciously to wash the filth out of his soul?"

"All the water in the ocean couldn't do that," snarled Creepe.

"But all the same," said Rollo, "I'm right. Why's he taken such a grudge against God? He couldn't tell you himself, but I can tell you: because he blames God for a disappointment that's shaken him to the depths of his soul."

"You'll be making us sorry for him," said Rickie, rubbing his ankle.

"You're exaggerating, Rollo," said Grooner. "I've got no love for him at this moment, but I still remember he's only twenty-two."

"I'm not exaggerating, Grooner. Age has nothing to do with it. We can be disappointed at our mother's breast. They say most of us were."

There was a pause.

"Well, if that's the reason," said Grooner reluctantly, "it's a pity. It's a pity for the girl, if not for him."

"It was no excuse for him behaving like a madman," grumbled Rickie, still fondling his ankle; he had looked at it and found it skinned and purple.

"They say none of us is truly sane, and for the same reason."

"Who say?" asked Dand.

"Those that know."

"Where did you get all this information, Rollo?"

"From you, Rickie. From Grooner. From Dand. From Creepe and the sergeant. From Bull."

"And what about yourself, Rollo?"

"From myself, Grooner, most of all. We are all huffed, as Bull is; and we all blame God, as Bull does; only we've got the sense not to challenge Him openly."

"I thought, Rollo," said Creepe, "you didn't believe in God."

"Didn't you know, Creepe? I believe in God all right, my own God: just like those poor fools we've to put out to-morrow."

That was Speer's cue. During the clever talk he had as usual kept silent, for fear of making a fool of himself in Rollo's eyes.

"I'm glad you mentioned that, Rollo," he said. "That's what we all seem too liable to forget. We're here to do a job. We're picked men. We ought to be proud. We should stick together. There's no knowing what might happen to-morrow. Bringing Bull here was a mistake; we all see that now. It'll go into my report, if that's any satisfaction to you. But in the meantime let's get our minds on what's our proper business. I don't object to a little relaxation this afternoon; I think it's a good thing; but we mustn't forget, at any time, why we're here."

Just as he finished there came a knock at the door. It was Cloud, ready to take them fishing.

Before he went Speer drew Dand, Rickie, and Grooner together.

"You're going down to the beach, aren't you?" he asked.

They nodded, suspicious.

"Wherever you go," he said, "for God's sake keep him well back from those folk. And humour him."

"I feel like humouring him with my boot," said Rickie.

"Remember he's young, Rickie. He'll be all right once he's in the open air. Get him to gallop his steam off along the sands. Exhaust him."

"It seems Bridie couldn't do that."

The sergeant grew wise. "Don't be so sure of that, Dand," he said. "Rollo thinks he's the only one that studies psychology, but my belief is that in some way that bitch Bridie upset Bull. He's sensitive, you know."

"I know," said Rickie, "as sensitive as a rhinoceros."

"No, Rickie, you're wrong. He is sensitive, where women are concerned, especially if they're older-fashioned than he is."

"Are there any such women?"

Grooner nodded. "It's true enough, Rickie," he said. "In some ways he's a simpleton with women."

"Do you think," asked Dand, grinning, "that Bridie took him out last night just to watch the sunset?"

"It might well have been something like that," said Speer solemnly. "You know there are women like that."

"Right enough," said Grooner, "he said nothing when he came in last night; usually he brags."

Speer now wore the smug look of the superior who has proved his compassionate insight into the mind of his underling.

"He's just a boy, when all's said and done," he said. "Didn't Mr. Vontin say he was surprised to see him with us? Well, it's up to us to look after him."

"It seems to be up to us," grumbled Rickie, pointing to his two friends and himself.

"You know I promised Mr. Cloud to go fishing," said the sergeant reasonably. "He wanted me to go." He dropped his voice. "To tell you the truth, boys, I don't think he feels comfortable with Rollo."

"Not to mention Creepe," chuckled Dand. "Off you go, sergeant. We don't envy you your fishing."

"Thanks, Dand. I don't suppose I'll do much fishing. Just to sit in the boat will be a rest. I feel I've been through a lot in the last day or two."

Then Bull appeared at the door; his hair was brushed and perfumed; his face shone with cleanliness; but it was obvious he hadn't washed his ill-temper away.

"Are you coming?" he snarled.

"We're coming," said Grooner, resignedly.

"Have a nice walk, Bull," said Speer.

"You go to hell," muttered Bull. Then he went out, followed most apprehensively by his bodyguard of three.

If they thought that the sweetness of the sea-breeze over the spacious machair would mellow him, they were mistaken. When he heard Grooner praising the beauty and profusion of the flowers, and saying how overjoyed his two children would have been to be there to pick some and play among the rest, he savagely trod on as many as he could. Out of the grass they peeped at him, yellow and blue and pink, ineffably cool, meek, and content, as well as lovely. He rushed aside to murder with his large boots any cluster whose inviolability seemed to him particularly provoking. None was murdered: as soon as his boot was lifted, there they peeped again, cool, perfect, indestructible. Even when he snatched up handfuls and flung them over Grooner, their meekness defeated him.

Then on the green sea-meadow they saw a herd of cattle belonging to Mr. Vontin; there was a bull with a ring through its nose. It bellowed, as if to warn them not to come too close. Grooner, Dand, and Rickie didn't need the warning; they hurried for the protection of the old herdsman, who assured them that the bull, for all his bellowing, was really quite docile. This was soon proved by Bull who, without having heard that reassurance, made his way through the harem of cows to their ringed and horned sultan, whose steaming back he patted, and from whose mild eyes he chased some flies.

He stood talking to the animal for two or three minutes.

Then he came over to join his colleagues beside the herdsman.

"Who's his favourite?" he asked.

The herdsman was an elderly man; obsequiousness seemed to make him deaf; he kept touching his cap every twenty seconds.

Bull was surprisingly lenient with him at first.

"A bull's got to manage them all," he shouted. "I know that. But there's always one that's a favourite at the time. It stands to reason. It's what I would do myself. Who's the favourite just now?"

Still the old man didn't understand; but luckily the bull itself gave the information by nuzzling up to a small, bony, reddish cow with frizzy hair that obscured her eyes. Bull was dismayed by such a chance; to him she seemed the least lovable in the herd.

When he moved on again he burst into a mood of fierce destructive glee. Coming upon a fence-post he tore it out of the ground and heaved it through the air. He pursued rabbits to their burrows, and knelt at the entrances, barking like a dog, to spread terror within. Then, when he rose, he began to shoot larks out of the sky, with his fingers as guns. Little blue butterflies flew about in great numbers, and these too he pursued, trying to catch them in flight. Two he saw linked together, to his exuberant joy; these he chased, with his handkerchief ready to imprison them. They alighted upon a flower, and his dropping of his handkerchief was successful. On his knees, he waved and shouted to the others to come and admire his catch.

They came slowly, grumbling among themselves at his spoiling of their walk. Dand, however, could see a funny side to the situation.

"Some folks' strength goes to their brains," he chuckled, "like the Sheriff's. Where would you say Bull's went?"

"All the time," said Rickie, "he's showing off. He could stop it like that," and he snapped his fingers.

Grooner shook his head. "He's frightened," he said.

"Frightened?" asked Dand. "You don't mean——?" And with the discreetest of gestures he indicated upwards.

"Why not?" said Grooner.

As he spoke he saw at his feet a lark on her nest. She flew away, startling him; he looked after her, in apology. Then he bent down and, pulling aside the screen of grass with gentle fingers, he uncovered five dark-green eggs. He smiled as he wished his children were there to share this marvel with him. He could hear their claps of joy as clearly as he could the lark's troubled song and Bull's impatient bawlings; how they would have loved and cherished these eggs.

Dand and Rickie looked too. Dand was about to lift one of the eggs when Grooner stopped him.

"No, don't touch them," he said. "It'll worry the mother bird. That's her singing up there."

Amused by this sentimentality, Dand gazed up at the sky; it was too bright for him to see the bird, but he thought he could make out her song from that of the others.

"If there's one kind of cruelty that angers me more than anything else," said Grooner, as he carefully covered the nest again, "it's the harrying of a bird's nest. I mean, what could be more innocent and harmless than a bird, especially a skylark?"

"You'd better not let Bull know it's there," said Rickie. "He'd smash it just for the fun of annoying you."

Grooner frowned: he felt that if Bull, or anyone else, was to smash those eggs, he would in a way be smashing his own children Jean and Bob; that he would never allow.

"We'll tell him nothing," he said.

Bull was roaring to them to hurry. As they approached, he lifted an edge of his handkerchief, and out flew one of the butterflies. Angry at its escape, he grabbed at it, but missed. His handkerchief was knocked aside, releasing the other. Both twinkled away into the sunshine.

Bull's fury was astounding. He rushed up to Grooner.

"It was your fault," he shouted. "You kept me waiting. You did it for spite."

"Don't be a fool," cried Dand. "My God, they're only butterflies."

Bull turned on him, with fist lifted. "Don't say that word to me," he howled.

Dand was mystified. "What word? Butterflies?"

"You know the word all right, Dand. I wouldn't let Rollo get away with it, and I'm not letting you."

Dand understood. "I meant nothing by it," he said.

"You'd better not say it to me again," warned Bull. "You're all at it, laughing at me behind my back. Do you know why? Because I'm more of a man than any of you. You're afraid of what's on this island. I'm not. I'm afraid of nothing. Do you hear that? I'm afraid of nothing."

"They'll hear you at the big house," said Rickie, crossly. "We're not like that old fellow with the cows; we're not deaf."

"Leave the cows out of it, Rickie."

"Have we to ask you what we've to talk about, Bull?"

Bull ignored Rickie, and turned on Grooner. He was smiling.

"What was it you had over there, Grooner? What was it the three of you were so interested in?"

Grooner looked at them and shook his head as faintly as he could. "Just some flowers, Bull."

"Liar. It wasn't flowers. What was it?"

"Keep your hands off, Bull."

"If you don't tell me, Grooner, I'll burst your rotten guts for you."

"No, you'll not," said Dand, stepping forward with determination. "There are three of us, Bull."

He and Rickie pushed him back from Grooner.

Bull glared at them.

"What's come over you, Bull?" asked Grooner, with as friendly a smile as he could manage. "We've done you no harm."

"I don't like people to tell me lies."

"For Christ's sake, tell him," whispered Dand, to Grooner. "Anything to humour him."

"No," said Grooner dourly.

"Listen, Grooner." Dand took his friend aside. "I'll not stand by and watch the big bastard bully you. But I'm not going to get into a fight with him over a lark's nest. What's a lark here? There are thousands of them."

"No," said Grooner, "never."

But Bull had overheard. "So that's what it was?" he cried. "A lark's nest. Do you think I didn't know? I saw you looking up at the sky. Why didn't you tell me what it was, Grooner? I'm an expert. When I was a boy there was nothing I liked better than to go hunting for nests. Do you know what I did with them when I found them, Grooner?"

"I've a good idea," muttered Grooner.

"That's right, Grooner; that's right. I liked to feel my fingers sticky with the insides of their eggs. I licked my fingers, like this." He began to lick his fingers.

"Bull," said Rickie, "you're acting like a man that's gone daft."

Bull merely laughed and banged his head with his fist. "You don't worry me by saying that, Rickie," he cried. "I know I'm not daft. There's nothing daft about me. Nothing could ever make me go daft. How many eggs, Grooner?"

"Eggs?"

"Is it you that's daft, Grooner? In your nest, how many eggs?"

Grooner refused to answer, but Dand contemptuously said five.

Instantly Bull thrust out his right hand with the fingers wide apart.

"One for each finger," he cried. "That's what I used to do; I used to wear them on my finger like thimbles. What colour are they? No, wait. I'll tell you. If they're skylarks', they'll be dark green; and just the right size to fit on to my fingers. Lead me to it, Grooner."

"I'd see you dead first," said Grooner.

Bull was greatly amused. He turned to Dand and Rickie.

"What about you, Dand, and you, Rickie? Please, will you lead me to the nest?"

Dand grinned. "Find it, Bull," he said. "Get down on your knees and sniff it out."

Rickie was bitter. "I came out to go down to the beach," he said, "because I wanted some peace and quiet. And that's where I'm going. Do you think I'm going to hang about here, while you squabble like a shower of kids over a nest? If you forget what we came here to do, I don't. I never was happy about it, and I'm still not happy. I want to lie on the sand somewhere and watch the sea." He could not express what it was he really wanted. "This is no good to me here. What about you, Dand? Are you coming with me?"

But Dand wanted to stay and see what happened.

"In a minute, Bill," he said.

Rickie immediately walked away towards the sea.

"I'll be with you in a couple of minutes, Rickie," shouted Bull after him. "Just as soon as I've attended to Grooner's nest."

He marched past Grooner to where the nest had been found.

Grooner and Dand slowly followed him.

"If he destroys it," muttered Grooner, "I'll——" and he clenched his fist.

"Don't be as daft as he is," advised Dand. "He's a big, bloody-minded halfwit at the best of times. We all know that. But he's far too strong for you, Grooner, even if larks' eggs were worth fighting for, which they certainly are not."

"Those eggs," said Grooner, "belong to my two kids." It sounded a silly statement, as he made it; and he wasn't surprised when Dand gave him an odd look. "What I mean is, Dand, when I saw those eggs at first, I thought what a lot of pleasure, innocent pleasure, my kids would get out of seeing them there, especially with the mother-bird singing above. So would your kids, Dand."

"D'you think so?" grinned Dand. "Well, Polly might,

she's seven; but I'm thinking that Gordon, who's three, would treat them pretty much as Bull will."

"There's an excuse for a child of three," said Grooner, but it was apparent he was discouraged by this reminder that cruelty exists in innocence.

Bull was crawling about on his hands and knees. He parted the grass as tenderly as a mother her child's hair to tend a wound.

"I'll find it," he cried, looking up to catch hope on Grooner's face. "Even if I've to stay here looking till the moon comes out, I'll find it."

Again by accident Grooner saw the nest. He stepped over it as casually as he could.

"Rickie's the only sensible one amongst us," he said. "I think I'll go after him."

"Ugh, no," said Bull. "Wait till I find your nest, Grooner. You'll want to see what I do to it."

"Why should I?" But Grooner still waited especially as Bull, delicate as a bear, was pawing in the grass near the nest.

With a howl of triumph Bull found it. "I got it, I got it, I got it."

Grooner came over, pale and pleading.

"All right, Bull," he said. "You've found it. Now I'm asking you to leave it alone."

"Are you just asking me, Grooner?"

"That's right."

"You're not telling me?"

"No, I'm asking you. I'm asking you just to look at them, and then come away with us to the beach. That's the mother-bird up there, Bull. Listen to her. You can hear how worried she is."

"What's she worried about?"

"Because it's her family. She can't help it, Bull. It's a law of nature for birds and beasts and human beings to worry

about their families. You know that as well as I do, Bull.
When you've got one of your own you'll worry about it."

"Did you say human beings too, Grooner?"

"Of course."

"What about the folk on this island? Look what they're
doing to their kids."

"They think they're doing it for the kids' good. They're
wrong, but that's what they think."

"Are women included in this, Grooner?"

Grooner thought of his wife Nell, and smiled in love.

"Especially women, Bull: mothers."

Bull sat on his hunkers. He seemed to be willing to consider
the matter reasonably.

"But, Grooner, I've seen a woman that put a red-hot poker
to her own kid's leg. She got twelve months for it."

"She should have had it put to her own leg."

"That's what I say too, Grooner. I'd have done it myself,
without pay. But she's not the only one. You read about
such cases every day. The courts are full of them."

"Christ knows there are exceptions."

"You're forgetting, Grooner."

"Forgetting?"

"You've not to use that word, not today, Grooner."

"I'm sorry, Bull. I meant nothing by it."

"Then don't say it."

"You're right, Bull, we shouldn't say it."

"Be consistent, Grooner. That's a good rule, be consistent."

"Sometimes it's hard to keep that rule, Bull."

"Sure it is, Grooner. You're the one that should know.
You eat eggs, don't you? I've seen you eat them by the
dozen. They're good for your guts, aren't they? Now, doesn't
a hen like its eggs just as much as a skylark does? Doesn't she
get worried?"

"There's a difference, Bull."

"There's always a difference when it suits us."

"That's true, Bull; and you're right to remind me. But I want you to leave this nest alone: not for my sake, Bull, but for Jean and Bob. You know them, you know how they'd be delighted with that nest. That's how I see it, Bull: if you smash the eggs, you smash them."

Bull appealed to Dand who stood by impartial but interested.

"Did you hear that, Dand?" he asked. "Who's being daft now. If I smash the eggs, I smash his kids. Did you ever hear anything dafter?"

Dand grinned as though he hadn't.

Bull turned back to Grooner. "So you want me to leave it alone, for your kids' sakes?"

Grooner nodded. "As a favour, Bull."

"I give no favours, Grooner; you know that. But I'll make a bargain with you: give me a quid, and I'll leave it alone. Now surely it's worth a quid to save your kids from being smashed? You can afford it out of the bonus you're getting for this job on the island. Just a quid, Grooner. I could make it five, one for every egg; but I'm letting you off cheap, because you're a mate." He held his fist clenched over the nest. "They say a man would rush into a burning house to save his kids. All you've to do is to throw a quid on to the grass."

Grooner's thin face worked in anger. "This is blackmail," he said.

"No, it's just a bargain between friends. Isn't it, Dand?"

"Keep me out of it," said Dand.

"Isn't it worth a quid," cried Bull to Grooner, "to save your kids from being smashed. You said yourself these eggs were your kids. I didn't know Nell laid eggs."

"Keep my wife's name out of your filthy mouth," cried Grooner.

Bull dropped his pretence of amusement; his lips writhed, and above the nest his fist shook with anger.

"Talk to me like that again, Grooner," he said, "and I'll have your mouth worse than Speer's, only yours'll not heal up so soon." Somehow that seemed the wrong thing for him to say, and he glanced round, with a snarl of apprehension. When he spoke to Grooner again he kept choking with anger. "Your kind's always the same. You've got plenty of talk, but when it comes to parting with the cash, it's a different story."

"Why should I pay you money?" whispered Grooner.

"I've told you why; I've told you fifty times. I'm going to smash these eggs, Grooner, and it'll be you to blame."

He raised his fist until it was as high above the nest as it could go, so that it would come down like a hammer, spurting yolk and shell all over.

"I'm warning you, Bull, if you do it, you'll be sorry."

"Sorry? Who's going to make me sorry? You, Grooner?"

"Not me."

"Dand?"

"I said keep me out of it," cried Dand.

"If it's not you and not Dand that's going to make me sorry, Grooner, who is it?"

"You'll find out."

Bull snorted with contempt, but he also glanced round again. "For the last time, Grooner," he said, "are you going to throw down that quid?"

Grooner did not answer; his hands remained twitching at his sides. He and Dand stared at that big merciless fist above the nest.

"I'll count three," said Bull.

Still Grooner made no move.

"One," said Bull. "Two. Your last chance, Grooner. Three!"

Whatever Bull was to say afterwards, it was clear to Grooner and Dand that he meant to strike, and strike with crazy exultation, when he had counted three. That he could not, that his fist remained suspended, astonished him far more than it did the two watchers. His face turned crimson, as if he was lifting some tremendous weight, and his whole arm shook in a kind of frenzy. He gasped loudly and sorely, and sweat glistened on his brow. Then suddenly he relaxed, with a groan, and rolled over on to his face, where he lay with his two hands weakly clutching the grass.

While Grooner and Dand were gazing at each other in amazement, Bull got up and, holding his right arm with his left, walked away.

Before Grooner and Dand could speak or go after him they heard a shouting in the distance. Far down the machair, running towards them, was Mr. Vontin. He was waving to them so urgently they were sure it was not an ordinary greeting.

"Looks as though there's been trouble after all," said Dand. "You know, I was sure they couldn't be trusted."

"Do you think they've attacked him?"

They were running to find out what was wrong. Bull too had noticed Vontin, and had halted; he seemed not sure what to do. Yet this was the kind of opportunity he lived for: to display his brawn and courage in the service of his masters.

Vontin couldn't speak at first for panting. Sweat poured down his face, trickling off his nose; his white shirt was stained with it.

"Is anything wrong, sir?" asked Dand.

He nodded before he spoke, and tried to convey his news with his eyes. For the sixth time since he had left the Sheriff he put his hand into his pocket for his handkerchief to wipe his face. He had to use his sleeve again.

"Mr. Nigg, the little clerk," he gasped, "he's dead."

"Dead!"

"Yes. I met your colleague, Rickie. I think he said he's gone to join the Sheriff, who's keeping watch. I'm going to the house for help. We'll need a stretcher. Perhaps you'd like to come with me?"

"Certainly, sir."

"Thank you. Well, let's go. I've been telling myself it's useless to hurry, since he's undoubtedly dead, but I seem not able to help it. I suppose it's because it happened so suddenly I still feel he's there, to be helped."

They walked fast beside him.

"How did it happen, sir?" asked Dand.

"God knows, really. Heart failure, I suppose. The Sheriff and I left him gathering shells; he was to take them home to make a necklace for his wife. We happened to look back, and it seemed odd the way he lay on the sand. There were seagulls near him too; they weren't scared. Well, we ran to him, but he was dead. Poor little man. Was that one of your fellows I saw back there, the young stout one?"

"Yes, sir."

"What was the matter with him?"

Dand and Grooner glanced at each other.

"Nothing, sir," replied Dand, "as far as we know."

"I'm sure he saw me before you did. He seemed to be in a trance."

They did not try to explain the reason for Bull's remoteness; later they might hazard an explanation, but not then, so soon after that amazing performance at the lark's nest, and after this news of little Nigg's still more amazing death.

Eighteen

To GO *fishing*, on an island where God preyed, like a pike among trout, had seemed to Rollo an appropriate way of spending the afternoon and evening; but he had meant to go alone. When he had mentioned his desire to Cloud, the grieve had not only acceded to it at once, as was Mr. Vontin's instruction, but also offered to accompany him and show him the best places on the best loch, which happened to be called Solla's Loch, since the saint was reputed to have fished and meditated there. To have as his companion the victim of a miracle, however spurious, somehow did not appeal to Rollo's sense of irony, as he had thought it would; on the contrary, it displeased him and helped to goad him into his peculiar baiting of Bull. Then, when both Creepe, whose materialistic piety he detested, and Speer, who wore his mouth like a badge, volunteered to join the party, he felt like withdrawing. Alone on Solla's Loch, catching fish, or just expecting to catch fish, he would have been able to create, with many imaginative strokes, an atmosphere suitable for the divine entrance; and that, too, could have been arranged. Indeed, on that lonely loch, blessed long ago by a saint, he might easily have reached that oasis of absolute faithlessness, for which he had been seeking so steadily and subtly for years; it might be that these last two or three days had supplied him with the missing corner of the map. But now that universal annihilation, announced only by the plop of a fish, the shriek of a hawk or the whirr of a blue-winged dragonfly, could not take place. Cloud, so ambiguously and uselessly ransomed from death, Creepe versed in all the asininities of belief, and Speer himself a small striped

187

god, would sterilise imagination and kill all its secret growths. Even the fishing would lose its symbolical mystery, as they sat and scratched cleg-bites and hoped for a catch to brag about and guzzle. Little Nigg, the clerk, who had transformed the whole creation by making fish squeal with pain, would have been a less annulling companion.

As they made their way in single file along the path to the loch, Speer and the clegs were nuisances. The clegs sucked blood from necks, hands, and faces; the sergeant sucked it from their minds. Attention had to be paid to his pompous conscience; it was uneasy because he felt he ought not to be going to enjoy himself that afternoon; he ought to remain near the house on guard. Hadn't the boatman who had brought them over from Mula yesterday mentioned that there were hotheads on that island threatening to invade Sollas and set fire to Mr. Vontin's house as a revenge. It wasn't enough either to say their threats were only words: his mouth disproved that; and once the house was set on fire there could be no depending on a thunderstorm of rain to put it out before too much damage was done. He had, of course, suggested all this to the Sheriff, and to Mr. Vontin too; but they had laughed away his proposal to set a guard. He was still not convinced. After all, if a raid was made, if the big house was burned, who would be blamed? Not the Sheriff, not Mr. Vontin, not Rollo, not Creepe, not any of the policemen; no, none of these: the man to be blamed would be himself. He would lose his rank, and nobody would sympathise.

Thus Speer talked, with a fishing-rod in his hand, like a martyr's staff; his healed mouth, he said with a sad laugh, would not be considered of any consequence in the Chief's office at Headquarters.

No one contradicted him or consoled him; his noises were as meaningless as those of the burn which flowed beside the path. Rollo, indeed, watching the back of the sergeant's head, with its pointed sun-reddened ears, was reminded of the snorting, long-tailed kelpies which in the days of myth, before Solla arrived with his sleeker magic, were said to haunt these burns and lochs.

They rested at the edge of the path. The three policemen sat with their backs against a boulder down which ran streaks of white quartzite. Cloud sat apart.

They had a fine view of the sea. Larks sang above them.

Speer frowned upwards. "They'd get on my nerves," he said, "if I lived here all the time."

"They'll be quiet in winter," said Rollo.

"I know that, Rollo; I'm not ignorant. Ever since I stepped on to this island, whenever I've wanted a bit of silence to think, they were there to spoil it. You wouldn't believe it, but I could even hear them from the W.C."

Rollo couldn't help smiling at this unexpected originality.

"Most people like larksong," he said. "They think it's one of the pleasantest noises on earth. Some prefer it to human voices."

"I know that," said Speer sharply. "I like it myself; but not all the time. It gets monotonous if it goes on all the time; here there's never a rest from it. You get a feeling there's a watch on you. All the time they're up there, singing and watching."

"If they're spies," asked Rollo, "to whom do they report?"

The sergeant gave him a long official scowl.

"I did not say they were spies, Rollo," he said at length. "I didn't mention the word. Did I, Creepe?"

"No," said Creepe.

"You didn't mention it, sergeant," admitted Rollo, "but I thought it was in your mind."

"What's in my mind, Rollo, I'll let you know, if it's in my interest and in your interest to let you know."

"Still, it was an odd thing to say, sergeant, that the larks were keeping a watch on you. I mean, if you were to ask me for anything that stood for innocence and minding its own business, I'd say a skylark singing in the sky."

"Sometimes you say too much, Rollo," grumbled the sergeant. "Why did you keep on at Bull, for instance? There was no need for it. I thought you were a man of more sense."

"I wonder," chuckled Creepe, "how Grooner's getting on with Bull?"

"I felt sorry for Bull," said Speer.

"So did I," remarked Rollo. "It's not every day a man gets his idealism crushed."

Speer was shaking his head. "You were wrong there, Rollo," he said. "It wasn't the girl with the yellow hair upset Bull. It was the other one, Bridie. She humiliated him. Her kind's not so very uncommon. They lead a man on, and then, when he's steamed up, won't oblige. There are names for them."

"I have heard of those names," said Rollo.

"I doubt it, Rollo," chuckled the sergeant, "I doubt it."

Rollo mentioned two; they were authentic.

"I regret to say," said Rollo coldly, "that there's no type of human depravity I have not heard of."

"I think the sergeant's right," said Creepe. "That Bridie one was trying it on with me."

"She had the brazenness to make eyes at me," said Speer, with a laugh. "But not at you, Rollo?"

"No." Rollo's voice was very cold. "I hope I've reached a stage when I'm not a target for a lascivious skivvy."

Then Cloud, who seemed not to be interested in their talk though he must have heard it, arose. As they got up, too, he remarked that the stone against which they had been leaning was called Solla's Rock. "They say that when he was hungry once coming down from the loch he tapped it with his stick, and milk gushed out."

They gazed at it.

"It's easy to understand how such a story arose," said Speer. "From a distance those white marks will look like milk."

"Stupid superstition," sneered Creepe. "This whole island is filthy with it."

"Milk from a stone," said Rollo. "Surely, Creepe, you believe that such things happened once?"

"I believe," said Creepe, with a sly pause, "that milk comes from cows."

Speer was laughing as they went on along the path. "You're not the only one who believes that, Creepe," he said. "Even Rollo believes it: though, mind you, he's such a doubter I wonder he admits it."

Rollo made no reply; but inwardly he said: "I believe, Speer, you're a kelpie full of stupidity and selfishness; and you, Creepe, are a stone from which no milk of kindness will ever flow." What Cloud was, however, he was not prepared to say with similar certainty.

Like the others, he had heard rumours about the big taciturn grieve; the servants in the big house, especially a skelly-eyed one called Jean, had spoken of Cloud in whispers, with giggles of frightened reverence, and a hardening of her oblique gaze that had turned her into an effigy of medieval piety. Rollo had gathered that Cloud had been seriously ill, but had been cured unexpectedly: there was a hint of a miracle. It was enough to make the grieve an object of pity to Rollo. Those who accepted God were bound to believe that disease and pain came from Him; therefore much of their flattering of Him was really to induce Him not to visit them with cancer or gangrene or liver-rot or arthritis or even toothache. A man cured by surgeons was still under the necessity of thanking and propitiating God, in case of a spiteful recurrence; but a man, whose cure was miraculous, or at any rate directly attributable to God, must feel that his recovery was a loan, to be paid for by instalments of piety for the rest of his life: to default would be to risk relapse. If Cloud was a believer, his position here on this island, was especially difficult: he had to take his master's side in the matter of the evictions; and he had at the same time not to appear antagonistic to the folk who were being evicted and through whom, it might be, grace had been shown him. Cloud's refuge was in silence, and Rollo had already tried to draw him out; yet silence could scarcely deceive the Almighty.

It could be of course that Cloud, like Rollo himself, was not a believer; that he attributed his cure, not to luck, which was merely a way of describing the arbitrariness of God's favours, but rather to physical circumstances, obscure now, but later, with the advance of medical science, easily explicable. Only a week ago Rollo had read an article in which a responsible scientist had stated that virgin birth, in human beings, was not only possible, but had happened. Life was wrapped in mystery, but many layers had already been removed, and the rest, in time, would be removed: then, demonstrably, so that even the God-blinded must see and admit, nothingness would be revealed at the centre. Meanwhile, it was possible for those who had intuitively divined that void, the prophets, to see it in a kind of inspiration. So often had Rollo almost seen it; and never had he been nearer than now on this island.

He made another attempt on Cloud.

"You've been here a long time, Mr. Cloud?" he asked.

Cloud nodded.

"How long?"

"Ten years."

"Summer and winter?"

"Yes."

"When I was coming here," said Rollo, "I passed the time reading a history of the island. There was quite a lot about St. Solla and his miracles. I remembered the episode of the stone and milk, as soon as you mentioned it. There was another one about the saint on a windy day being blown over the edge of the cliffs. He'd have been shattered on the rocks if hundreds of seabirds hadn't flown under him like a great white pillow. Did you know about that?"

Cloud nodded.

"I suppose you'll have seen the cliff?"

"Yes."

"It struck me," said Rollo, "that there was really no need for the birds. I mean, couldn't the rocks themselves have been turned soft for the occasion? Still, the pillow of white birds is a pretty picture. I suppose if we started analysing those ancient miracles we'd find ourselves smothered in absurdities."

Cloud just smiled. Had he been an intelligent man Rollo would have appreciated that smile; but Cloud was obviously stupid.

"You've been here ten years, Mr. Cloud," he said boldly. "You've seen all these places. You've had time to think. Do you believe in those tales?"

But they arrived just then at the loch, and Cloud was able to avoid answering by suddenly asking them to stop and step behind a stone. He pointed to where, beyond yellow reeds exotically high, old Donald McInver was pacing up and down on green grass at the loch's edge, about fifty yards away; his head was bare, and his hands were handcuffed in prayer in front of him. They could hear him talking to himself; yet if they had not seen him, they might have thought those cries were being made by some of the birds which would haunt that beautiful water.

Peering round the edge of the large stone Rollo saw, growing on it, as well as the ordinary grey lichen, clusters of white stone-crop, like little stars; immediately in his mind, in a way he could not prevent, the old, agitated, white-haired man, with his hopes in a mythical sky, became confused with the tiny flowers.

"I know what he's up to," said Speer. "This is him asking for guidance. Remember what he said this morning? Whatever else religion may be, and I've got nothing against it—

all my kids were christened—you can't deny it's convenient. What I mean is, all he's got to do is to tell them he's got God's permission to leave. They'll just have to believe him, because there's no way of proving it. So everybody's happy."

Creepe was not happy. For some reason he could not have clearly expressed, this open-air solitary, passionate communion seemed to him not only impious, but indecent. Interceders ought always to be men of authority; they must also be clean, respectably dressed, restrained in voice and gesture; and above all, they must be under a dedicated roof. This sky above the loch, with little white clouds in it like lilies, was a pagan sky; under it rocks spurted milk, and white-bearded old men without collars imagined they talked to God.

"Will he be long?" asked Rollo.

"That's so," said Speer. "We came here to fish."

"Look at him, the mad old beast," hissed Creepe.

McInver had begun to batter his hands against a stone; it looked as if they were indeed handcuffed, and he was trying to free them.

The three policemen expected to hear the ring of iron on stone.

"What's the matter with him?" asked Speer.

"Mad," muttered Creepe.

Speer began to frown; it had occurred to him what this madness might be hatching for tomorrow. Religion that could be so convenient could also be troublesome.

"I hope he's not going to make a martyr out of himself," he said.

"Have you any idea what he's doing, Mr. Cloud?" asked Rollo.

Cloud shook his head.

They waited and watched. Still McInver could not be satisfied; he unclasped his hands to turn them into fists that shook in front of him; he seemed to be weeping.

"I can't say I like this," muttered Speer. "I think we should let him know we're here."

"Spies," said Rollo, pointing up at the larks.

"So you're keeping that up, Rollo?"

Rollo turned to Cloud. "Who looks after him?" he asked. "Whom does he live with?"

"His grand-daughter."

"The fat girl with the yellow hair who came to the pier last night?" asked Speer.

Cloud nodded.

"Just her?" asked Rollo.

"Yes."

"Where are the rest of her people?"

"Her mother is dead."

"What about her father?"

"I don't know."

"Is he alive?"

"I don't know."

"What keeps him?" asked Creepe. "He doesn't work for his living."

Cloud stepped out from behind the rock and began to walk along by the edge of the loch towards the old man.

"Come on," said Speer. "Let's hear what he's got to say."

Creepe followed eagerly enough, but Rollo was reluctant; he couldn't have said why. As he left the rock he plucked off some stone-crop, but he didn't know it was in his hand until they had almost reached McInver, and then he wondered how he came to have it.

Not only the small white starry flowers in his hand were a mystery to Rollo then: the whole scene was uncontrollably strange, and growing stranger with his every breath: the ripples of the loch, the lilies, the tall reeds, the grass, and, above all, this old man from whose eyes streamed tears, and in whose clasped hands was something infinitely precious, although it was clear that when he took them apart nothing would be seen. What mystified Rollo more than anything was how, in the midst of this strangeness that was overwhelming him, Speer and Creepe remained inviolably themselves, the sergeant puffed up with amiable conceit of his stripes, and the policeman tugging at his black moustache in derision of this old man's home-made faith.

"I've brought these gentlemen to the loch to fish," said Cloud; it sounded as if he looked upon McInver as its true owner or custodian, and was seeking permission.

It seemed to Rollo that McInver was looking at him with peculiar significance, whereas he paid no heed to Speer and Creepe.

"The fishing will be good," said McInver.

Cloud was very calm. "I'm not sure about that," he said. "The sun's too bright."

"It will be good," repeated McInver, and again Rollo thought that he in particular was being addressed.

Speer too must have thought so, for he suddenly held out his hand.

"I'm Sergeant Speer," he said, with a grin. "You know what I'm here for, Mr. McInver, but surely there are no hard feelings?"

But McInver would not shake hands. He looked at his own, bleeding at the knuckles, and then purposely withheld it; but not, so it seemed to Rollo, in arrogance or senile huff; rather in humility, as if at that moment he did not think himself worthy of the sergeant's friendliness. His meekness was in contrast to his confidence that morning, when he had laid his hand upon the Sanctuary Stone and defied the world to take it away.

Speer laughed at the rebuff; he even winked at Creepe, at the absurdity of this daft old man's pride.

"I hope, Mr. McInver," he said cheerfully, "that you're going to be sensible tomorrow. You heard the Sheriff this morning. He gave you the Law's point of view, as it was his duty to do. I'd like to give you the point of view of myself and my men. First of all, none of us has any grudge against you; in fact, we've got sympathy. We're men who go to church, you know. Mr. Creepe, here, is never without a Bible. I doubt if there's anybody on the island who reads it oftener than he does. So you can see that we don't want to bring any harm to you folk. We're here simply because it's our duty; but we've got feelings, and I think it's up to you to respect them. I'd even go so far as to say that for our sakes, as well as for your own, you should go without a fuss. Be sensible now, and jump at this chance which you've been offered."

It was, Speer thought, a good speech, more effective even than the Sheriff's. The larks had somehow tried to spoil it, with a din that had got louder and louder, as if deliberately; but he had not let them put him off.

When McInver spoke it was in an old man's quavering voice. At it Speer and Creepe again exchanged winks; in the sergeant's there was pity. But Rollo found that no sound he had ever heard had struck as so forlorn.

"I have lost the trust of the Lord."

He looked at them, but his green eyes that had glowed so hypnotically like emeralds that morning, were now lifeless as pebbles on the beach. All of him was degenerated from his fiery and patriarchal splendour beside the Stone.

Speer was still sympathetic.

"I wouldn't say that," he remarked. "That's never lost. You'll get it back all right once you're away from here. You're just not seeing things clearly, that's all. Those houses you're living in, they won't keep the winter's rain out. I can see why you're worried all right."

McInver was shaking his head. "I shall never leave Sollas," he murmured.

Then, before Speer could stop him, he turned and staggered away, stooping as if he had a creelful of peats on his back.

Creepe's laughter, as he glared after him, grew louder and louder, until it brought a rebuke from Speer.

"The old chap's off his head," said the sergeant. "There's no profit in laughing at him."

Rollo found Cloud gazing at him in a kind of comradeship.

"All the same," said Speer, "it looks as if he's going to cause some trouble tomorrow after all. I'm sorry about that; I really am." And to show his sorrow, and at the same time his determination to do his duty, he spat on the palm of his right hand.

Half an hour later Rollo caught an enormous trout, the biggest and most magnificent, Cloud said, that had ever been caught on the island, to his knowledge.

Nineteen

AFTER leaving Marguerite, Andrew had walked as staunch as Christian, for nearly two hundred yards, without looking back; yet all that distance a connection persisted between himself and her, as fine as a single gossamer thread but with a pull as hard to withstand as a tug-o'-war rope. His heart panged in his breast as if, along that mystical wire, she was still sending him appeals to return. He could not resist that pull; reckless as Orpheus, he stopped, turned and looked back. He was in a grove of yellow azaleas where a colony of bees was harvesting; he would not be seen, but he would see. He did see, but not at all what he had anticipated. She was not standing where he had left her; no, she had returned to her chair, had picked up her book again—he remembered it was a story of lighthearted murder—and was absorbed in it, with a cigarette as an extra indulgence. Here was no Eurydice, snatched from him by inexorable and malignant fate; here was the pampered island-king's daughter, the haughty and baleful princess, who had taken the fragment of St. Solla's Stone and dropped it fastidiously into the sea. Seen from these fragrant azaleas, she appeared to have as little remembrance of his existence as of that small stone's: another sea had closed over him, that of her indifference; and it was much deeper than that other.

When he became aware that amidst the buzz of bees he was talking aloud, ironically, on the theme of her quick dismissal of him, he made an effort to regain control of himself. Deliberately he gazed now with the smirk and sharpness of the success-seeker such as his uncle had accused him of being. It was easy to see himself affianced to Marguerite, and so at home in that great red mansion. Yonder he was, in white flannels and silken shirt, coming from the house with a drink for her. Look how gratefully and fondly she took it, gave without demur or self-consciousness the kiss he looked for in thanks, and invited him to sit upon the grass by her chair, with his head resting against her knees. Then they talked about fabulous voyages in their yacht *Argo*. Joy illimitable and pure was theirs. They had many grateful tenants on their estates, and none happier than those who had been transplanted from this island. But he was not merely a wealthy and philanthropic landowner, he was also a celebrated advocate, with promotion to the judiciary assured.

Closing his eyes, he opened them again, and this time saw with the eyes of simplicity. If ever he became rich, it would not be enough to use his riches to benefit others: not in that way would he achieve peace in his soul, and happiness. Was not Mr. Vontin perplexed and melancholy, in spite of his benefactions? Long ago Solla, in his hut of wattles and clay, with his oatmeal and water, with his robe of roughest cloth, had known that peace and happiness; it was for that reason that this beautiful island belonged to him forever, no matter who bought and sold it.

How, here on his island, to share that peace of Solla? To support the cause of his followers was not enough; it was necessary to support it for the right reason. There must be not only understanding and approval of McInver and his fellows, there must also be love. What he had felt that morning at the Stone had been merely a sample; it had been given him to prove what he was capable of. Love roved in every heart; like a deer, it could not be stalked cunningly and pertinaciously: that way it was wearied and slain. Love and faith had to be surprised.

He had intended descending upon the crofts out of the hills, but he changed his mind and went by the road. He must not do on this occasion as he had done so often before; he must not set the scene himself, compose the dialogue, and act the principal. He must abandon himself to the turn of events.

What he had expected to find when he reached the crofts, he could not have said: the digging of peats as a sacramental task he had never seen before; but he had certainly not expected to find the crofts deserted. Instead of those devoted people wielding peat spades and chanting hymns of Solla's time, he saw no movement at all, and at first heard only the singing of the larks and the more distant cries of seabirds. His immediate feeling was of betrayal: if they had given in, how could they expect him to go on resisting on their behalf? He felt a great glad desire to turn, run all the way back, and hand himself over, body and soul, to Marguerite.

Then he heard a cow lowing, saw some hens, and smelled peat-reek. At once he rebuked himself. How was selfishness to be curbed and obliterated, when at every opportunity he pandered to it? Here was an instance; as soon as he had arrived, whom had he set at the very centre of the scene? Yes, himself. As he stood there, seeing more and more signs of life about the little bleak community, he remembered— incidents of childhood, not so very far-off in time after all, when his playmates had left him because of his insistence on being the foremost. Whatever the game, he had claimed superior prowess. When he had been left alone he had not been unhappy: the best toy of all, which he could manipulate better than any ball or bat or tin cowboy, had been their envy. Now he saw that as a child he must have been obnoxious to other children: it was an admission that his resourceful and slippery mind could neither assimilate nor eject.

The question then to be faced was: had he outgrown that childish obnoxiousness? Not only the larks, and a sour cow answered: a medley of voices, louder than the surf on the shore, assaulted his unresisting ears. He had of course known that, among his fellow students, though he was well known, he was not popular in the usual sense of the word; but hitherto he had attributed the reason to his vow, so valiantly kept, always to tell the truth no matter whose feelings or pride were hurt. What others called their truth had been pelted back at him: he had dismissed it as a contemptible mixture of envy, pique, spite, ignorance, and ill-humour; it could be, however, that some of it at any rate had been justified.

At least he had never, from his cradle days, suffered from that false modesty, shyness: he could not afford to yield to it there. Advancing, therefore, among the crofts he came upon an old woman in a sunny hollow. She was seated on a chair, knitting; near her, roped to a stake, was a bony, reddish cow.

She was so very old that but for her long black skirt he could not have told her sex. She had white whiskers, skin as dark as peat, and hands warty and mottled like frogs. On her head she wore a man's cap. She appeared to have no teeth.

As he approached her, he was outwardly polite and compassionate; but inwardly he was thinking that it might be as profitable to address his remarks to the cow as to this old crone.

Yet her first glance up, whiskered and hermaphroditish, was also perceptive. She was not surprised, intimidated, or impressed.

"Good afternoon," he said, with a smile.

"There's nothing wrong with the afternoon," she agreed. Her voice, though slow, was firm and dry. "Didn't I see you this morning with the master?" she asked.

He noted that word master. Was she too doted to realise, that by her very presence there, she was acknowledging a far greater Master?

Like himself she was not shy. Though she kept on with her knitting she scrutinised him well through her steel-rimmed spectacles.

"You seem to be alone," he said.

"I've got Poppy."

He realised she meant the cow.

"Where are the others?" he asked.

She considered whether she should tell him or not; she kept chuckling, for no reason that he could see.

"They're at the peats," she said at length.

"And where is that?" he asked.

She jabbed with a needle in the direction of the hills behind the houses. "For all the peats they'll dig," she said scornfully. "In my day I have dug and carried tons of peats; but I had the pleasure of burning them."

"You think then these peats they are digging will never be burned?"

"Why should they not be? They'll be good enough peats. There will be folk left to burn them. You're good at the questions, young fellow."

"I beg your pardon."

"It's all right, you're lucky; you see, I'm good at the answering."

She went off into a fit of cackling.

"You weren't with the master at all," she said, suddenly. "I could see that. And I could see you were thankful to get off your horse. You were with the young mistress. They were saying you're the one that's to marry her."

He could not allow this divagation, even though it was delighting her.

"I am here," he began, but could not continue; to put his purpose into intelligible words was extremely difficult.

"You're here to see if we're all ready packed for the flitting," she said.

"No, no."

"Don't be frightened to talk to me," she said. "I'm packed."

"You mean, you wish to go?"

"If they let me die here, they'll have to take me back to Mula to bury me; so they might as well take me back while I'm still alive. I'm easier carried, that way."

"You sound as if you didn't want to come to Sollas in the first place."

She snorted and made her needles jingle angrily.

"I had a rope put round my neck and dragged here, just like Poppy," she said. "I wanted them to leave me. I could have managed fine by myself."

"I thought you all wanted to come here."

"I came, I tell you, because my son brought me."

"Is Donald McInver your son?"

She was so shocked she stopped knitting.

"Have you got eyes?" she demanded. "What age do you think I am?"

Ninety-one would have been his guess, but he did not utter it.

"I'm just exactly three years older than Donald," she said. "I was at school with him."

Andrew became aware of the parcel under his arm, of the cow urinating, of senile vanity; in short, of the obtrusive world.

"Many's the whack I saw him get," she said, with satisfaction, and went off into her cackle again. "This is me saying what I shouldn't. I know that fine. But I've been wanting to say it for weeks to a human body, with two legs and lugs that don't jump. I've said it to Poppy there, often enough."

She took pity on his baffled face.

"I can see you're not like me," she said. "Laughing was aye my trouble. I got my whacks too at school; and it was for laughing. Donald got his for always trying to be smarter than the master even; he was aye contradicting him. That was more than sixty years back. I have learned a drop of sense since. But has he? Has he? There are two answers to that one, young man. The Lord's work has got to be done, that I know; but it's the Lord that's got to do it, nobody else. That's what I think."

Then he saw them coming down the hill.

The old woman had gone back to her knitting in a fury. She kept munching her jaws and once shouted crossly to her cow, which was wandering into a marsh. She did not look now as if from childhood laughter had been her failing: she looked crabbed, wizened, doted, and as incommunicable as her cow; but Andrew knew better. He knew that she had not wanted to come to Sollas; that she was keen to return to Mula; that she had known Donald McInver all his life; and that she considered him a show-off, fraud, and interloper. It was possible she represented that age-old instinctive materialism of women, which regarded sacrifice for the sake of spiritual satisfaction as a luxury, to be afforded only when all the needs of the body were provided; but it was also possible she represented wisdom.

As they approached, with what for them was dignity, he saw among them McInver's grand-daughter, the girl with the long yellow hair, who had presented the flowers to the Sheriff; now she carried a small child, which he supposed was not her own. One of the women, whom from her haggardness he would have taken to be long past child-bearing, was conspicuously pregnant; and one of the men was bearded. Had it been the other way round, Andrew would of course have been shocked and incredulous; but he might also have been roused into uncommon expectancy. As it was, he thought he had seldom seen a more commonplace, more earthy, group of people. He had not naïvely looked for them to be transfigured, but he had looked for some sign of their adoption by God. There was none. The children were perhaps quieter than usual, but they were also dirtier. The dogs slunk and no doubt stank. The men were hang-dog, the women sullen. Without Donald McInver they were indistinguishable from any other folk on any other indigent island.

The man who had called himself Fergus led them. It was he who turned to give them the signal to break into a psalm as they drew near.

It was not often Andrew was embarrassed, at least to such an extent that the acid of reason could not dissolve it. Here

was such an occasion. They sang with awkwardness and
artificiality; their voices were nasal, tuneless, and doleful.
Children at Hallowe'en, invited in to sing for their meed of
nuts and apples, did better. Thus might natives of some
aboriginal tribe be trained to perform for some gullible anthro-
pologist.

Those thoughts, Andrew decided with an effort, were un-
generous; they did not take into consideration the eccentricity
of grace, which in human beings could assume strange shapes.
God sometimes chose to honour those whom their fellow
mortals would never have thought of honouring; just as no
doubt He often found nothing to commend in those who on
earth had been pre-eminent.

They halted, close to him, and finished their psalm, with
their peat-spades over their shoulders as if they had come from
the fields of paradise; but their faces were the faces of peasants
greedy for all that earth could give them. He was the target
of obsequious, calculating glances. They appeared to think,
or hope, that he was there with a message for them from
Mr. Vontin. When they learned that he had come simply to
find out what message they had, they might well goggle and
grimace and scratch heads in bucolic bewilderment.

When they had finished the psalm, the men who had taken
off their caps did not put them on again. They had stepped
from God's presence into that, as they thought, of the emissary
of the owner of the island; their deference manifestly increased.

Fergus was their spokesman. He twirled his cap in his
hands as if it was some lucky wheel of luck.

"We bid you welcome, sir," he grinned.

"Thank you. I ought to tell you at once that I have not come
from Mr. Vontin. I am here entirely on my own behalf."

They nodded eagerly, as if his own authority was good
enough for them. One tall man's grin he particularly disliked:
it revealed gums large, red, and spongy, like a sea-growth.

"We pray for Mr. Vontin day and night," said one.

So feeble a bribe had seldom been offered.

"And for his lovely daughter, too," added Fergus.

The men laughed; the women were content with smiles, grim and restricted.

"We know that a man in Mr. Vontin's position has many troubles and responsibilities," said Fergus. "We do not envy him his wealth. We do not want wealth."

At that, the first utterance of grace, Andrew unaccountably found his suspicion thickening.

"All we want," said Fergus, "is help to rebuild our houses and the use of some of the machair."

The man with the poisoned gums pushed them forward jocularly: "He is a rich man, worth a million pounds. It would be a drop in the ocean to him."

"I'm afraid Mr. Vontin's mind is made up," said Andrew. "He won't change it at this late date."

"Why does he want rid of us?"

It was a woman who cried the question. Andrew answered her respectfully, because in her voice had been none of that servility which dishonoured God whose protection they claimed.

"I can't speak for Mr. Vontin," he said. "But I believe it's his opinion that if you were to be subsidised now to live on Sollas, that subsidy would have to be repeated again and again. You would never be able to become independent."

"He is very rich," grinned the man with the gums.

"And he is also philanthropic," said Andrew. "But he has a right to decide how his money should be spent. He has provided modern houses for you on the main, and employment. You could be independent there."

There was silence.

Fergus turned and looked about him; his hand went out, in the vaguest of gestures.

"This is a holy island," he said, with a grin which he meant to be reverent, but which Andrew interpreted as sly.

"It was, in the past."

"It still is, sir. It will always be. But it ought not to be left only to the larks and the seabirds and the rabbits."

"It will not be, surely. Mr. Vontin and his daughter intend to live here; and there will be estate servants."

"There will be no one to rebuild the church."

"A new one might be built." Andrew had heard Vontin mention that likelihood.

"It would not be the same. And there will be no one to pray beside the Stone." He pointed beyond Andrew to where above the beach stood the Sanctuary Stone.

Andrew for thrawnness would not look round. These people, in their guileless piety, might well be genuine; but they were not the meek who would inherit the earth. Otherwise why should they turn from God, whose interest they claimed, to him, who was more powerless than anyone on the island, including the unborn child?

"Sollas was once an example to all the other islands," said Fergus earnestly, "and to the mainland besides."

"That is true."

"It could be an example again."

"It could be," agreed Andrew, "but not if subsidised by a rich man's bounty. Surely you must see where your help must come from, if it is to come at all? I came to speak to Donald McInver. Where is he?"

They exchanged glances of anxiety and dismay.

"He went to the loch," murmured Fergus.

"What loch?"

"It is called Solla's Loch. It is where Solla went himself."

"I see."

"Donald is an old man, please remember," urged Fergus. "He is very tired. It has been a great strain on him, listening to the word of God."

Andrew frowned. "Tell me," he said, "do you really think he has listened to it? Remember it is an enormous claim."

"Oh yes." They were not dogmatic; indeed, the childish vagueness of their assurance was somehow convincing. "But he is very old, and tired. It is not easy to listen to God, and obey."

"I suppose not." .

"If you were to speak to Donald," said Fergus nervously, "you might not understand. He is very old and tired."

It must be, Andrew thought, that the inspiration, of whatever kind, which had visited McInver was now gone; broken by the strain, the old man was probably wandered in his wits. That morning at the Stone he had been magnificent, but all the time what a short step away from foolish incoherence!

"Has he advised you to leave tomorrow?" he asked.

"No." But they did not seem to be sure.

Andrew made to leave, though where he could go to he did not know. At once Fergus stepped forward and detained him.

The rest had smiles like the leers of animals trained to cringe to masters.

"You are to marry the young mistress," said Fergus. "We know that if she were to speak the word, her father would give us his blessing."

Andrew could not deny that at least.

"If you were to ask her," pleaded Fergus, "she would listen to you."

Andrew smiled; he spoke gently. "You misunderstand my position. I have no influence whatsoever with Miss Vontin; Poppy the cow there has as much. I am not to marry her. I do not know her well. Indeed, I am no longer a guest in their house. You must look elsewhere for help. I hope you find it. Good afternoon."

As he walked away he noticed how peculiarly McInver's grand-daughter was smiling at the child in her arms; either it was simple-mindedness, as Marguerite had hinted, or it was goodness. Never, to his recollection, having seen goodness before, he could not be sure. There could be no doubt about her hair; lit by the sun, it was a glory.

Behind him Poppy lifted up her head and lowed hoarsely. It was a sound that took him unawares, so that when he arrived at the Sanctuary Stone and touched it in passing, he had a feeling that he was not alone, and that his companion, knowing him to the core, and so aware of his every folly, subterfuge, and selfishness, was nevertheless not prepared to condemn or even judge. It was a moment of ineffable relief.

Twenty

THAT relief soon passed. When he arrived on the beach, at that point littered with boulders as if the legendary giants who had possessed the isle long before Solla had been playing marbles half an hour ago, he no longer had that sense of guardianship. Instead, a solitariness descended upon him so burdensome that as he hurried along, with the foolish parcel under his arm, he felt that his own separate existence, viewed against the cosmic panorama of evolutionary progress, was of no more significance than that of any of the limpets clinging so stubbornly to the rocks.

At last when he was far enough away from the crofters, he sat down on a rock, reckless of the green sea-slime soiling his flannels, and considered how best to regain some sense, however meagre, of his own worthiness. It would be easy enough, well within the resources of his slippery mind, to return to the Vontins' house, confess honestly to having been optimistic or even idealistic, endure with civilised humour Marguerite's teasing, handsomely apologise to her father, arrange a realistic compromise with his uncle, express sincere compassion for the crofters, say not a useless word on their behalf, salute them tomorrow at the embarkation, and thereafter, all inhibitions removed, walk with Marguerite by sea, hill, and lily-pond, and prove to her perhaps that he was not so cold-blooded as she had accused. Thus would Jason do, and there were gods who would help him prosper; but would not that prosperity in the end turn to bitterest grief, as had happened to the Argonauts' leader?

The alternative route was not so well charted: all that was

certain about it was that it did not lead back to the house; metaphorically, it led straight to the desert. In plain terms, he could not stay out on the foreshore all night or even in some cave he might find: not the discomfort made that unthinkable, but the absurdity; he had neither the training nor the disposition for an anchorite. But in whose house could he beg shelter? To go to some cottage occupied by one of Mr. Vontin's employees would be merely a cowardly and insulting way of accepting Mr. Vontin's own hospitality; while to go begging to one of the crofters' houses was, after his recent interview, out of the question. A cave would be preferable: there at least his folly would have no witnesses as it chased its own tail.

The longer he sat on that rock the more clearly he saw his own inadequacy: that was something gained, but not really what he wanted or indeed needed. Had he been a seal, or a seagull perched on one leg, at least he would have been in his natural environment, and so would have added to the loveliness of the scene. Where on God's earth would he be so visibly at home as to create beauty simply by his being there? In a courtroom, with the curled white wig and black gown of the advocate, or the red-ermined robe of the judge? In church, with his bands and gown and the colours from the stained glass on his fair hair and beneficent hands? Unfortunately, nothing else was asked of the seal and gull than that they be there; much more was needed of the handsome advocate or minister; and that extra was not merely the gift of gab.

He became aware he was being spied upon. From behind another rock about fifty yards away keeked two small boys. He remembered seeing them with the peat-diggers, but then they had been silent and still, despite their freckled mischievous look. Now they were free of that spell.

It soon became clear that to them he was indeed little more than gull or seal, for each aimed a stick at him as he sat on the rock. They shot at him so often, and no doubt hit him with such accuracy, that they grew displeased with his invulnerability. They left the safety of their boulder to creep out and advance a few yards towards him. There they halted, with their bare feet, in their shirts and braces, and with their hair, fairer than his own, cut straight across the brow like a monk's tonsure. They gazed at him as neutrally as did half a dozen oyster-catchers which glanced as they skimmed by, screaming.

As he gazed back at them he remembered that morning seeing one of the policemen try to hand to one of the children what looked like a bar of chocolate. The little girl, called by her mother, had not taken it; and the policeman had been disappointed. His offer had not been ingratiation; it had just been an act of kindness.

Now Andrew was in a position to do likewise, only he had nothing to offer, except money, which seemed too sordid. It struck him now that the thin, gaunt policeman must have, before setting out for Solla, thought of these children with pity; whereas he, Andrew, had never thought of them at all: they had not entered into his kind of equation.

Never before had the academic nature of his pity been revealed so painfully as there on that shore, under the gaze of those two small boys. To love justice was admirable; to suffer for that love was still more admirable; but if there was no love of the people for whom that justice was sought, then the sacrifice was useless. Martyrdom for the sake of principle alone was barren. When he smiled at the boys Andrew was not surprised that they did not smile back: he smiled because he knew he should, not because he could do no other. Marguerite had accused him of being a cold-blooded prude, prig, and fraud; she had been right; his ego was preserved in the ice of conceit, but with the admission came no thaw.

As he stood up he let his parcel fall, but he did not care that it fell into a pool of water. At once the boys darted back.

He called and waved to them. They only halted when he did; as soon as he moved towards them they retreated. By the time he reached the rock from behind which they had peeped at him, they were well down the beach, heading for the great Sanctuary Stone near the houses. He could go no farther if he did not want to give the impression he was chasing them. Therefore he stopped, and with the sea's long roar grown infinitely melancholy in his ears, watched them pause finally, aim at him for the last time, shoot, kill him to their satisfaction, and then disappear. As they passed the Sanctuary Stone they whacked it with their sticks, not vindictively or revengefully, but as they had already whacked many other stones in their path. To Andrew watching, those blows were very far from withdrawing from the Stone its sacred quality, rather did it seem to confer on all the rest that quality too. For a minute, indeed, after the boys were gone, the whole beach seemed sacred. When the minute passed, and the glory was gone again, he turned and went slowly back to where his parcel lay in the pool. Nothing had happened, except that he had failed to win the friendship of two little boys; but he fel that, in a way he could never have described, his attempt had been noted.

Leaving his parcel where it had fallen—with its pyjamas, toothbrush, and razor, it represented absurdly the life to which he must return—he walked farther round the coast until he was on the high red cliffs that formed the northernmost promontory. He did not know it, but it was there that the miracle of the pillow of seabirds was supposed to have happened. Not many birds were there now, but some were perched upon a great isolated stack almost as high as the cliffs, which the wind and sea had chiselled into a fantastic shape. It looked as though it might collapse at any moment, like a tower of dominoes built by a child; yet it had stood in Solla's time, and long before. It was called the Old Man of Sollas, and from one point a human profile could indeed be made out, with the birds' excrement like white hair. Far below, round the foot of stack and along the cliffs, the sea frolicked like thousands of white puppies. Cliff's and stack were bright with flowers, campion, sea-pink, and gowans. On the cliff top, where Andrew sat, the turf was soft and clean. To westward, if he craned his neck, he could see a great bay of tawny sand. In front of him was the ocean.

It was from the west that Quorr came, astride the black horse. He wore no jacket and his shirt sleeves were rolled up. His face was flushed with sunshine and exertion. Round his neck hung a garland of flowers.

Andrew frowned in astonishment, but Quorr, fingering that strange necklace, showed neither deference nor self-consciousness. He halted his pony with a touch of his hand, and gazed down haughtily.

"Good afternoon," said Andrew.

The salutation was too prosaic for Quorr; instead of returning it, he raised his arm. Then he gazed out to sea.

Andrew rose. He patted the horse.

Suddenly Quorr dragged out of his hip pocket a sea-shell about the size of an apple.

"I picked this up on the sands down there," he said. "It's perfect."

Andrew took it; usually shells of this sort were broken or blemished; as Quorr had said, this one was perfect. It was very beautiful. He said so.

"I'm taking it back," grinned Quorr, "for Mr. Nigg."

Andrew remembered. "Yes, he collects shells, doesn't he?"

"Do you like my flowers, Mr. Doig?"

"I've been admiring them," replied Andrew cautiously.

"When Cortes entered the city of Montezuma," said Quorr, "he was garlanded with flowers."

Andrew stood dumb, seeing no connection.

Quorr pointed to the stack; he did not speak; he seemed to be in a strange land, with fellow conquistadors around him.

Then with a smile he turned back to Andrew.

"Seen anything of the natives?" he asked.

Andrew remembered Quorr had been at the table when he had announced his intention of leaving the house and throwing himself upon the hospitality of the crofters.

"Yes, I've spoken to them," he replied.

"What's it to be? Are they going to go quietly?"

"I believe so."

"Why not? They've done not so badly out of it: humbug pays nowadays; it didn't"—here he patted his horse—"in Cortes' time."

"He seems to be a hero of yours, Mr. Quorr."

"He was a man."

"I can't claim to know his history very well, but wasn't he rather unscrupulous?"

"Unscrupulous, deceitful, cruel, for Christ's sake; courageous, unflinching, faithful, glorious, for Christ's sake."

Andrew became aware that the blasphemous expression was supposed to be taken seriously.

"I fail to see how one can be unscrupulous and cruel for Christ's sake," he said.

"Of course you fail to see it!" cried Quorr. "I didn't expect you to see it. Go, and for Christ's sake, give yourself a surprise."

Then, roaring with derision, he set off. Once he turned and shouted back: "But I doubt you'll never do that: you never surprised yourself in your life; you knew all the answers in your cradle; at least you thought you knew them."

The words were hostile, but they were true.

In everything I have ever done, thought Andrew, I have been as cautious as a cat stepping across water.

Hitherto he had called it awareness, and been proud of it; now he knew that all along it had really been a precaution lest, unexpectedly, he turn a corner and come face to face with himself, not the outward self reflected in a mirror, for that sight could be and always had been prepared for. Was it then his true self he had come to Sollas to seek? Certainly he had already caught glimpses of it, not as a whole, but in fragments; later, as a penance, he might have to fit them together.

Twenty-one

IN THAT northern sky light was reluctant to fade; it only went when a large yellow moon appeared from behind the horizon clouds to take up the vigil. It detected, that moon, Marguerite Vontin at her window in the great house, gazing down at the moonlit lawn. It saw too, inside the house, Mr. Nigg under a white sheet in his bedroom; on the dressing-table, beside his brush and comb, glimmered the shell which Quorr had set down in homage. It saw, in Cloud's house, the trout that Rollo had caught, which had been weighed and found to be forty-three pounds four and a half ounces; lying for display, it too was dead as Nigg, and indeed to marvelling eyes it seemed as big as he. The moon saw, besides, the owl that sat in the trees at the lily-pond, and there, too, on the smooth green bank, Bridie and Bull again; the latter hoped to reassure himself that that inexplicable impotence by the lark's nest was not to be permanent.

The moon had been watching for over an hour before it caught sight of Andrew Doig. After wandering for hours, he had found a little cave and gone in. Finding the floor dry, he had lain down as if to sleep. The night had to be passed; there being nowhere to go, this cave was as good a place as any. But though dry, the floor was hard; water dripped so loudly and steadily that it irritated him like a tap for which no one could be blamed. Darkness crept in at the small entrance, and sat sighing beside him. Outside the sea snored and groaned, as if it too could not get to sleep. He soon grew cold as well as sore and hungry; worse, all the time his purpose in being there grew more and more foolish and irrelevant.

Thinking of his mother's stern pity for him in that predicament, his own pity began to yap and whimper, like a small puppy that had been spoiled. When his bottom was numbed he sat up, with his back against the wall and his hands in his pockets, and gazed at the sky which was now becoming brighter again. At first he thought dawn was breaking, but soon realised it must be the moon: one dead world was looking at another. Most of the people on the island would be in bed. He tried to think of somebody who would be benefited by this sacrifice of his, but he could think of no one.

It occurred to him that Solla must have spent nights alone in this or similar caves, and had prayed on his knees till dawn. With shame, although no one was there to see, he put himself into a kneeling posture, with some awkwardness, for his legs were cramped and his knees particularly sensitive to irregularities on the rocky floor.

He prayed; at least he muttered aloud words couched in the form of a petition on behalf of Donald McInver and the others, and of himself: the words dealing with his own case were more numerous. But it did not matter; this was no prayer; he knew it and the receiver of prayers knew it; it was a muttering as meaningless as any of the soughs of wind in the tunnels above his head. The Old Man of Sollas could pray as well.

That failure was his excuse: if he was so empty, why wait there? He might as well be comfortable in his bed in Sollas House; whatever surrender was necessary had long ago taken place. So, stiffly but with candid relief, he got to his feet, instinctively dusted his trousers, and crawled out on to the beach where every little pool gleamed with moonlight.

Knowing that his moral stature was at that moment no higher than that of any of the tiny crabs asleep under the rocks, he was astonished to find as he emerged how in a curious way he felt gigantic and exalted, so that his head nodded among the stars and his arm stretched far out over the glittering sea. It must be he was light-headed with hunger.

Whatever its source, that exaltation continued. After the damp chilliness of the cave, the air was sweet, fresh, and balmy. As he walked or rather floated in the moonlight down the beach, he was able to decide, so simply, that the wisest course would be for him to look upon this episode of Sollas as closed. The people would leave tomorrow; he would not leave without them, for his only honest attitude now was neutrality. In a day or two he would go, perhaps on the *Argo*. He would never again, however, be so juvenile as to see himself as Jason: that pagan folly was cured. Nor would he be in future so quick to suspect the motives of those who possessed authority and wealth; he had found his own motives not above suspicion. While he would not go so far as to agree to accept the advice which Mrs. Crail so impishly had whispered in his ears, "row wi' the tide," he thought he had learnt the value of drift.

After Sollas, there remained the exciting and the irresoluble doubt of God. There remained too Marguerite Vontin. Though he had forsworn the rôle of Jason for himself, he could not help, with a thrill, thinking of her as Medea: how beautiful she had been in her sea-green dress, with the pearled octopus on her black hair; how mysterious, like a priestess, when she had dropped the sanctified stone into the water; and how enticing that evening on the lawn when she had pleaded with him to come back to her.

Well, here he was now going back to her, faster than was safe even, for twice already had he stumbled over stones which he had thought were shadows. Indeed, as he gazed up at the moon, and as he gazed across the shimmering path of moonshine on the sea, he felt a great desire to scoop up a handful of sand, hold it up to the moon as a witness, and then throw it into the air with symbolical rapture: thus would go his scruples. In their place he would seize a handful of this glorious moonlight, hold it preciously, and carry it back, a gift for Medea.

My Medea! he murmured to the stars, shaking his fist at them. At present those intriguers held her in thrall, but he would rescue her, he would love her despite her wiles, he and she would walk these beaches hand-in-hand, until the devils that perverted them both were exorcised. So exhilarated was he, during that challenge to the stars, that for a moment the sea became the lily-pond, and he saw again, with her hand in his, the young policeman and the housemaid. He laughed at the sight. Love had to be accepted, in all its shapes; to sift and censor it, and leave out all that was neither respectable nor aesthetic, was to destroy it as an adventure.

He was still laughing at that discovery, which could also have been attributed to the light-headedness of hunger, when he came near the Sanctuary Stone.

When he saw it he remembered the two little boys who had whacked it with their sticks; he would whack it in the same way. Rubbing his hands together in glee, he reflected that he too in course of time would have sons, who would solve whatever problems he left unsolved. It would never do, he confided joyfully to a waukrife gull that squawked somewhere, for one generation to expect to leave no moral ascents for the next. The highest terrestrial mountains might be climbed once and for all, and the flags of possession planted; but mountaineers, in the moral sense, would never run out of mountains high enough, precipitous enough, icy enough, to satisfy the boldest and most aspiring.

Beyond the moon soared a tremendous range of clouds, with shining pinnacles and mysterious darknesses: in a way, it was the future, and it was a magnificent challenge. He forgot that he was now for leaving it to others; rather he felt uplifted by his own generous abstinence.

When he reached the Sanctuary Stone, he made straight for it, intending to give it a smack similar to those of the boys,

light-hearted yet reverent, with fearless matter-of-fact acceptance. It would be a kind of farewell, a pat on the back of
eternity.

That pat was never given. When he came close he saw that
someone, with hair that shone eerily in the moonlight, was
kneeling beside the Stone; it was Donald McInver, and surely
he was not kneeling; he seemed to be crouching, with his face
against the hard rock as if it was a pillow. Once Andrew had
seen a man in the city asleep thus, in a public lavatory; he had
been drunk.

But Donald would not be drunk. Perhaps he had been
praying, and in the midst of it had fallen senilely asleep. Had
not his friends insisted he was old and tired? Had the zeal
deserted him?

Among ideas Andrew was reckless, among persons hesitant;
but at last, whispering "Good evening, Mr. McInver," he
stepped forward. There was no response. Andrew then had
to do what he disliked, he had to touch a stranger. Instantly
his hand recoiled, wet: the jacket was sodden. He held his
fingers close to his eyes to see if that wetness was of blood;
but the moonlight revealed no colour. He smelled it and it
seemed salty: was blood salty? Opening and shutting his
hand quickly he felt no stickiness. In any case, what monstrous
blow could have caused so much blood? The Stone had not
moved from its place where it had been deposited millions
of years ago, and crushed him as a man's foot might an
ant.

Then Andrew boldly felt the old man's head; it was wet
too, but it was still white. The wetness must be of water. The
old man must have been in the sea. Was it some kind of
baptismal rite?

As well as wet, the head was cold.

As he stood wondering what he should do, he heard a
sound which at first he took to be some night-bird's wail. It
came nearer, and he recognised it as a voice, a child's or a

woman's. Stepping out from the cover of the Stone, he looked for her.

"Hello," he cried. "Hello. Who's that?"

She had been heading for the Stone, but when she heard him she halted. He could see why; she was McInver's grand-daughter, and she wore what looked like a white nightgown.

"Are you looking for your grandfather?" he called. "He's over here. I'm afraid he's in need of help. I can't get him to waken up. And he's all wet."

As she approached, shimmering in the moonlight, a breeze from landward stroked Andrew's face, with all the fragrance of the machair in it. He remembered, incongruously, Marguerite's jeer about how seldom this girl took a bath.

Her hair was loose and very long. It floated about her. She was an apparition such as Jason might have seen. Then she was beside him and he saw that she was yawning, and had one hand inside her gown scratching her bosom. Her feet were bare.

"I know you," she said.

It was the first time he had heard her speak, and he was dismayed. Apart altogether from the silly childishness of what she said, so thin and high-pitched a voice, almost a whine, didn't consort with those almost beatific smiles he had seen her wear, or with her buxom comeliness. It was the voice of one whose intelligence was not developed. Had not Marguerite hinted of idiocy?

Keeping clear of her—it was necessary, for she seemed to want to stroke him, as if he was a pet calf—he showed her where her grandfather lay. Immediately she flounced down, and with a cheerful lack of delicacy lugged the old man off the Stone, and dropped him down upon his back. Andrew now noticed that McInver's trousers were almost off; his belt or braces seemed to have snapped. He knelt too, in a hurry, ostensibly to examine the old man with her, but really to try discreetly to tug his trousers up a little. He could not; but he found that they too were soaked.

"Why is he so wet?" he whispered. "Has he been in the sea?"

As if at that suggestion she took her grandfather's head between her hands and rocked it back and forward. For a second or two Andrew thought it might be some primitive but effective first-aid method practised here, to revive half-drowned people; but in the case of an old man, whose neck was snappable like his braces, it seemed rash. He had to stop her.

"I wouldn't do that, Miss McInver," he said. "You might do him harm. I think you should run and fetch help."

She preferred to squat and smile at him. She gurgled with some kind of amusement. She seemed to have forgotten her grandfather.

"I know you," she said again, and poked him with no tender finger.

He rose hastily.

"Where's the nearest house?" he asked. "Time may be precious. Your grandfather may be dying."

She had risen too and was nudging him.

"I know where you're staying," she said. "At the big house."

He was now hoarse. "Miss McInver, didn't you hear me? Your grandfather may be dying. You must fetch help."

She giggled. "I saw Miss Marguerite with blue breeks," she said.

Suddenly she lifted up her nightgown to reveal her own plump legs breeked with moonshine.

Since to restrain her would have been to participate, he looked swiftly away; but he groaned and grimaced to the stars.

"Listen to me, please," he said sternly, with his back turned. "Your grandfather's unconscious; if he isn't carried into shelter very soon he may die." Then it occurred to him that surely there was something he could do before help arrived; without thinking, he took off his blazer and laid it across the old man. A moment later he rued it; not because he felt chilly, but because in the presence of a half-witted girl prone to elevate her nightgown, it would have been wiser to remain fully clothed.

Because she was so silent he turned and found her, illumined by the moon, smiling at him, with her arms held out. At her feet lay her nightdress; she was stark naked, and she seemed to be inviting him to take part in some cantrip, a dance on the moonlit sands perhaps, or a plunge into the sea, or worse.

That was a shock, which was to have as many waves in his mind as the sea had upon the beach; but while that first great breaker was crashing, he heard voices, and caught sight of several people approaching with a lantern.

They were upon him before he could even think of putting on his blazer again. Sheila whimpered, and he soon learned why. One of the newcomers was an elderly woman who made straight for her and, without a word, gave her such a slap on the bare buttock that the sound echoed in the moonlight.

The others were three men; Fergus led them.

"Thank God you've come," said Andrew.

They gazed at him with the curious hostile deference of peasants.

"It would seem so," agreed Fergus.

Oddly, in Andrew's ears, the other two quietly sniggered.

"I hope nothing serious has happened to him," said Andrew. "I was just passing when I noticed him lying here. I couldn't make out what was wrong. Then, just when I was going to look for help, Miss McInver came. I'm afraid she behaved rather oddly, as you saw yourselves. But I think you should have a look at Mr. McInver."

Fergus and another knelt to examine the old man. The third, who was the tall owner of the red putrescent gums, remained by Andrew's side, grinning with an almost lewd servility. A stench appropriate to that grin came from his mouth.

Sheila had had her nightdress forcibly put on her. She still whimpered. The woman had a grip of her, cloth and skin.

Fergus looked up.

"He is dead," he murmured, with what seemed some kind of peculiar satisfaction.

Red-gums grinned up at the sky, in a gratitude that seemed more sly than devout.

"God's will be done," he said.

The third man, whose head was bald, now revealed it by taking off his cap.

"We can go now," he said.

Fergus nodded.

There seemed some secret among them, as they stood beside Andrew. Their leader was dead, and they were glad; not only were they now going to submit, but they were going to do it gladly. Had Donald told them that his death was to be the sign they were to look for?

Sheila suddenly became aware of what had happened to her grandfather. In a frenzy she flung herself down upon him and began to kiss his dead face.

The woman and Fergus, seizing her, pulled her away with a ruthlessness and disgust that shocked Andrew. No doubt she was half-witted, but surely grief was sane?

"Take her away, Elspeth," said Fergus.

Elspeth nodded. "What about him?" she asked, meaning Andrew.

"We'll deal with him."

"Make him pay for it," she ordered, and then went off with Sheila, clutching and shoving her like a wardress.

Andrew was puzzled and indignant; yet in the presence of death he had to appear humble and restrained.

"Are you sure he's dead?" he whispered.

"He is dead all right." Fergus still sounded pleased; but

it did not seem to be the pleasure of the devout who believed that the dead man's soul had already ascended.

Andrew shivered; it seemed suddenly cold. "Then I suppose," he muttered, picking up his blazer, "he won't need this now."

"No, indeed." Fergus helped him to put it on.

"Yet this morning he seemed so vigorous."

"God was in him."

Turning to gaze at the sea, Andrew again shivered.

"Why is he wet?" he asked.

"He must surely have been in the sea," suggested Fergus.

"That's what I thought. But why?"

"When God is in a man," said Fergus, with surprising suavity, "he acts in a strange way."

It was not a satisfactory answer, but there seemed no other.

"Wasn't this where St. Solla came ashore after being shipwrecked?" asked Andrew.

"This is the Stone where he knelt and gave thanks to God," said Fergus, laying his hand on it.

That hand at the same time enclosed Andrew; the barrier at the other side was Red-gum's hand.

"What's the matter?" asked Andrew sharply. "Let me go."

"What were you doing here with Sheila?" asked Red-gums, his noisome mouth close to Andrew's.

"I told you," cried Andrew, indignantly. "She must have come out to look for her grandfather."

"But, you see, sir," murmured Fergus, "she kept on talking about you."

"You took the flowers from her at the pier," said Bald-head.

"You and she have the same fair hair," said Fergus.

"What's all this about?" demanded Andrew.

"You were told she walks in the moonlight, as naked as when she was born," said Red-gums.

"You came here this evening earlier," said Bald-head. "We saw you looking at her."

"She is very bonny," whispered Fergus, "even if her wits are like hens in her head."

They nudged him. They cackled softly into his ears.

"Nobody need ever know," they said, "except us, and Elspeth; and Elspeth can be got to keep her mouth closed."

"There was a rumour," whispered Fergus, "that Mr. Vontin, the master here, would give each man fifty pounds if he went without trouble."

"We would be obliged," chuckled Red-gums, "if you would be so kind as to speak to him for us. We are poor men, sir."

"Sheila tempted us all," whispered Bald-head; "even Donald himself."

Then Andrew found his voice; the words it uttered he must have found too, somewhere in his mind.

"You filthy-minded——" he meant to say "swine", but at the last moment, taking himself unawares, he changed it to "bastards".

It was an enormity, there by the Sanctuary Stone, with the old man dead, and the hallowed sands gleaming in the moonlight; but he did not regret it, or wish to withdraw. Rather he felt within him a tremendous lightening; he saw these small-minded, crafty, grasping, lecherous bigots as they really were, but he did not despise them; indeed, he found he could not, for he and they were members of the same species.

So swift a re-orientation was nothing short of miraculous.

He did not beg their pardons, nor did they demand an apology. All four stood smiling at one another, as if they had just been found out.

"It was Donald's wish," said Fergus, after a long silence, "to be buried here on Sollas."

"In the ancient burial ground by the kirk," added Red-gums eagerly.

"I can't answer for Mr. Vontin," said Andrew.

"You could speak to him for us."

"All right. I'll put it to him."

They thanked him.

Suddenly he placed his hand firmly on the great stone, as McInver had done that morning; it was a gesture of farewell.

"Good night," he said, and pushing past them set off towards Sollas House. Whoever arrived there, that night, would at any rate be no prig or prude or fraud, cold-blooded.

When he remembered that he had left his pyjamas, toothbrush, and razor lying in a pool, where crabs and prawns lived, he did not, as he would have done before, stop, frown, and consider returning for those necessaries to civilised living. Instead, he laughed and marched on even more resolutely. He would sleep in his shirt-tail, would use his forefinger to clean his teeth, and would grow a beachcomber's beard. The nails by which he had been fastened to his rigid place in society were drawn; they were lying yonder by the Sanctuary Stone; now he was free to explore the infinities of life.

He could not help laughing at the surprise Marguerite was going to get.